"A book for those seeking t[...] [...]y [...] [...]s anthology is absolutely incredible and bursting with energy and emotion, demanding to be felt."

— Vo, Goodreads review

"This anthology is a powerhouse of an introduction to the work of some very exciting writers. Their dexterity within the genre is admirable, and made this collection an utter pleasure to read. For lovers of the Gothic, it is an absolute delight."

— The Lesbrary

"It's here. It's queer. Its creepiness levels range from minimal to severe. It's *Unspeakable*, the queer Gothic anthology that you didn't know you needed until just now. Plus, it is positively bursting with queer rep of all shapes and sizes!"

— Metaphors and Miscellanea

"Whether you're looking for a heart-warming story of ghostly love or a terrifying tale of murder and betrayal, *Unspeakable* has something for everyone."

— The Gothic Library

"A reassuring reminder of how flexible and future-facing Gothic can be."

— Gingernuts of Horror

"A great, smart and varied selection of supernatural tales – some light, some dark, some tragic and even some hopeful. Strongly recommended."

— Runalong the Shelves

UNSPEAKABLE

A Queer Gothic Anthology

Published by Haunt Publishing
www.hauntpublishing.com
@HauntPublishing

Second Edition. First published by Nyx Publishing in 2020.

ISBN (Paperback): 978-1-915691-00-2
ISBN (ebook): 978-1-915691-01-9

Edited by Celine Frohn

Cover design by Ashley Hankins: ashleydoesartstuff.com

Typeset by Laura Jones: lauraflojo.com

Printed and bound in Great Britain by Clays Ltd, Elcograf S.p.A.

UNSPEAKABLE

A Queer Gothic Anthology

Edited by Celine Frohn

HAUNT
PUBLISHING

CONTENTS

CONTENT NOTES

The publisher has made every effort to accurately reflect the content in this book. Any omissions are accidental and the publisher's own.

CONTENT NOTES A-Z

Birth: Laguna and the Sirena.

Blood, gore: Brideprice; Doctor Barlowe's Mirror; Moonlight; Rodeo; The White Door.

Bloodletting: Brideprice.

Body horror: Leadbitter House.

Child death: Laguna and the Sirena.

Death of parent: Laguna and the Sirena; Rodeo.

Domestic abuse: Rodeo.

Emotional abuse: Lady of Letters; or, the Twenty-First Century Homunculus.

Gaslighting: Lady of Letters; or, the Twenty-First Century Homunculus.

Gun violence: Moonlight.

Hanging: Quicksilver Prometheus.

Homophobia: Rodeo.

Imprisonment: Let Down.

Loss of a loved one: Moonlight; Quicksilver Prometheus.

Murder: Brideprice; Laguna and the Sirena; The Moon in the Glass; Moonlight; Rodeo; The White Door.

Panphobia: Taylor Hall.

Pregnancy: Laguna and the Sirena.

Violence: The White Door.

CONTENT NOTES BY STORY

Let Down: imprisonment; non-consensual sex.

Moonlight: blood; gun violence; loss of a loved one; murder.

I Am The Master Of My Eyelashes: none.

The White Door: blood; murder; violence.

Doctor Barlowe's Mirror: gore.

Laguna and the Sirena: birth; child death; death of parent; murder; pregnancy.

The Moon in the Glass: murder.

Brideprice: blood; bloodletting; murder.

Lure of the Abyss: none.

Hearteater: none.

Quicksilver Prometheus: hanging; loss of a loved one.

Rodeo: blood; death of a parent; domestic abuse; homophobia; murder.

Lady of Letters; or, the Twenty-First Century Homunculus: emotional abuse; gaslighting.

Taylor Hall: panphobia.

The Ruin: none.

The Dream Eater: none.

My Love Lays Split on Either Side: none.

Leadbitter House: body horror.

INTRODUCTION

Welcome, dear reader, to the second edition of *Unspeakable: A Queer Gothic Anthology*! It's a delight to be able look back on the humble beginnings of this short story collection from the vantage point of a new edition, with a refreshed cover, and now published by the fantastic Gothic indie, Haunt Publishing.

This anthology was born with a single thought: where can I find more explicitly Gothic queer contemporary fiction? While this was essentially a selfish question – I simply adore queer Gothic tales of unease and dark delights – queerness is also intricately connected to the historical development of Gothic literature throughout the centuries. You can for example consider Sheridan Le Fanu's *Carmilla*, the titular character of his 1872 novella and an early incarnation of a female vampire pursuing a young woman. Or perhaps Bram Stoker's famous *Dracula* of 1897, with its sexually transgressive characters (Lucy deserved a polycule with her three lovers – you can't change my mind). Classic Gothic fiction grapples with desires that move beyond the boundaries of the heteronormative, and wonders, are these passions monstrous?

Unspeakable takes these kinds of questions to the twenty-first century, bringing together nineteen authors that share their interpretation of 'queer Gothic'. When selecting these stories in 2019, I left it up to the authors to interpret both queerness and the Gothic in their own way, leaving space for a broad constellation of tropes, settings, characters, and forms of storytelling. The term 'queer' can be used as an identity, as an umbrella term for anyone finding themselves outside of heteronormative social structures, but is sometimes also used as a verb to mean a form of deconstruction. In this anthology, you will both find characters who proudly proclaim their identities, as well as stories that gaze beyond the boundaries of our cultural framework. Additionally, all of the stories engage with the Gothic in their own way: we have classic tropes like vampires, haunted houses, and monsters galore, but also stories that feature unease, the uncanny, or the outright creepy.

Over the course of the last couple of years, I've constantly been awed by the generosity of *Unspeakable*'s supporters. Without the success of the initial Kickstarter campaign in 2019, the anthology might not have reached publication at all. I'm immensely grateful for everyone involved in the creation, publication, and support of both *Unspeakable* and it's successor *Unthinkable*. I dedicate this reprint to you.

LET DOWN

Claire Hamilton Russell

"Hoi! Coo-ee! Is there really someone up there?"

It's not the normal call, but close enough. She is already rising from the bed while her rippling locks of hair cascade out of the window like a shimmering ladder of gold. The man is too far below to be anything more than a pale blob of upturned face and leather armour, but she is singing, summoning him, as the hair curls down towards him.

"Won't it hurt you?" the voice calls up to her.

She pauses for a moment. She cannot recall ever being asked this question before. Yes, it does hurt. Every time. Awfully. But it cannot stop her. She resumes her inviting song instead of giving an answer.

The man seems to hesitate for a moment, but soon she feels the telltale tug as he begins to swarm up the rope of her hair towards her window. By the time he reaches it, she is as caught up in the spell of the moment as he is. She sees what he sees as the song spills from her lips – the shimmering beauty of her face with wide green eyes alight with bewitching promise, the lustrous golden locks curling around her, over her cushions and her shoulders and her lap. She opens her arms and her lips to him as he stumbles forward through the amber tresses, drawing him into her embrace for the kiss.

It is brief, with the faint taste of waybread and hazel-twig. Her eyes meet level grey ones, but instead of a surge of passion that drags them both along and downwards, there is a sudden shock of connection like a bucket of cold water. She falls back-wards onto the bed in confusion, looking up at... Him? Her? It is a face with high-cheekbones, a stubborn square chin, and curly brown hair clubbed back into a sensible warrior's queue. Not tall. Broad shoulders and hips. Wide grey eyes made wider still with shock and horror.

She sees herself reflected in them; no longer the inviting vision, but filthy, naked, gaunt, emaciated, covered in stretch marks and thin ridges of scar tissue where the grasping waves of hair have bound her to the bed and scourged her skin for so long.

"How? How now? We haven't even..." Her voice is thin and hoarse, creaking and cracking with despair. It brings tears of shame to her eyes to hear the desperation in it. She normally has at least a brief moment of adoration first, before the horror and humiliation.

She has long since given up on the curse actually being lifted. She hadn't even realised how much she had come to depend on the brief respite of worship and enchantment that arrives with each new visitor. To go through the horror without it to bolster her is more than she can bear – and the shame of that need cuts like a knife. No matter how much she wills herself to hold them in, tears spill down her cheeks.

The person tentatively reaches out and touches her on the arm. "Please don't cry, miss." They awkwardly pat her shoulder, keeping their hand well away from the thick, tangled skeins of hair that hold her to the bed as surely as any rope. "Are you a faery? Have I touched you with cold iron or summat? I didn't mean to..."

The unfamiliar kindness in their voice nearly leaves her bawling like a polled calf. She somehow finds some surviving shred of dignity and swallows the sobs threatening to undo her.

"No. I am the Lady..."

The panic rises again, threatening to overwhelm her as she realises it has been so long since she said it that she cannot recall her name. She wracks her brain, her heart pounding so hard that it nearly suffocates her as the young person stares, still awkwardly patting her shoulder. Then, with a blessed surge of relief, it comes back into her mind.

"…Lady Melisandre of Curthelm. I have been under a curse for… many, many long years for refusing a marriage proposal from the White Prince."

She flinches as the memories stir in her skull: waking to the face of the chillingly nondescript Mage in her bedchamber. Her voice stolen when she tried to cry out, her limbs surrendering control to him as he puppeteered her out of her bed.

The person thinks for a moment and nods. "Lady Melisandre. Aye. I've seen your painting in the Great Hall in Curthelm Keep when I was little. You were as beautiful as you were painted, when you were…"

They cut off and shrug apologetically, then gesture at the hair filling the room and coiling around Melisandre.

"Is that it? The curse, I mean?"

Melisandre somehow keeps her voice from cracking again.

"Part of it. The rest was… what you saw… It draws men to me, calls them, makes them desire me more than anything. Makes them *embrace* me. And then, after…"

She waves her hand as much as the chains of hair will let her to indicate her real appearance, the stench and darkness inside the tower, everything.

"Then they see the reality and they are disgusted. They… leave."

Eventually, anyway. Not all of her scars are from the scourging of the hair.

"None of them will help me. None will release me…"

The young person nods, surveying her and the tower with their level grey eyes. "You might not be telling me the truth, you know," they say eventually, their voice even and thoughtful. "You might be some fey thing bound to stop you from doing harm and trying to trick me into freeing you."

Melisandre manages not to weep once more. "I could be, yes," she admits dully, the leaden weight of her despair returning full force. She can think of nothing she can say to convince the young person otherwise. She bows her head and bites the inside of her cheek.

They look at her for a long time before giving a firm nod. "But even if you are... I can't leave you like this. It'd be wrong."

They stand back and draw a long knife from a boot. "Call me Tom. I'm going to save you."

Melisandre doesn't quite meet their gaze. She has not let herself even consider rescue for a very long time. Not after all of the visitors who had fled, sickened, as soon as the pleasure had ended. Not after all the ones who turned viciously on her when she gave up her pride and begged and pleaded for their help. The curse was stronger than her, and she had given up on other people long since.

Even still, a stubborn flicker of hope flares up in her chest. She sucks in a long, shuddering breath as if to extinguish it.

Tom begins sawing at the ropes of hair, thick as steel chains, around her arms. It is a good knife but it blunts quickly. Tom takes a whetstone from their pocket and sharpens it, then keeps going. The sun moves as they continue patiently sawing and sharpening, sawing and sharpening. Melisandre leans her head against the dank stone, despair bitter in her throat – the single rope is barely halfway through as the sun sets.

She has fallen nearly into a stupor when Tom exclaims, "You damn ninnyhammer!"

She starts awake and sees them slapping their forehead in the moonlight.

"I beg your pardon?"

Tom shakes their head. "Um... not you, miss... I mean, milady. Me. I'm the ninnyhammer. I always was."

They swiftly sharpen the knife on their whetstone and stand up. "Now, you need to hold proper still for me, right?"

They raise the knife.

Even in her exhaustion, Melisandre's heart races. They are going to cut her throat. A vague relief that she is too tired to flinch — that she will keep that dignity at least — washes through her.

Instead, Tom saws — so carefully, so gently — at the first twist of hair at the back of her neck. Not hardened into a rope, these locks are much less resistant. The fibres part under the blade like lute strings snapping.

The rest of the hair senses it almost as she does. The ropes and tendrils shiver, darting through the air. They lash at Tom's eyes and hands and leave hairline cuts on their skin. Beads of crimson stain the storm of blonde locks. Tom wards them off with their hands and keeps sawing. The ropes uncoil down Melisandre's arms and wrap around Tom's hands, coiling up their wrists to restrain them both.

Melisandre's heart nearly freezes in a terrible moment of selfish hope. The hair will catch Tom. She will remain in the tower — caught, cursed, yes, but… not alone. She'll be with someone who knows who she truly is. Someone to *talk* to.

Then she grabs at the ropes and pries them off, ripping them as best as she is able with her bony, claw-nailed fingers. Smouldering satisfaction wells up as the tendrils writhe in her grip. She will not let them claim *all* control of her fate.

"Tom… go! Leave this place!" She doesn't spare the energy to hold back her sobs, mucus running ungracefully from her nose. All claim to elegance or dignity is gone and she finds that she does not care in the slightest. The only thing that matters is that this great-hearted young soul is not pulled into this endless torment with her.

"Go on! Run! It's *my* curse. It does not want you. It will leave you alone if you just go!"

Tom grits their teeth and thrusts away another golden whip, calmly shielding their eyes with their left hand.

"No. I told you. I can't leave you here. It would be wrong."

Melisandre rips, tears, fights frantically in a way that she has not in endless long years. Perhaps as she never has. Blood paints her scarred shape – a white and monstrous thing mottled dark in the moonlight. Blood blinds her eyes. Blood cloys iron on her tongue. Blood pools at her feet. Her struggles don't let her shield her body from their eyes, but shame no longer holds her back.

"*Tom!* For the Gods' sake, listen! You have been... you *are*... the most valiant rescuer I could ever have hoped for. You should not pay for that with... *Please!* Leave me!"

Tom's level grey eyes meet hers, filled with an incredible serenity even as the knife in their steady hand keeps sawing. An electric jolt shoots through her as they raise their free hand and carefully stroke their knuckles along her bruised cheekbone.

"Brave heart," they say softly, still sawing away in their quest to free her.

She chokes as their gentle voice tightens her throat, breathing in a mouthful of blood and snot. Ragged sounds escape through her – coughs, sobs, it no longer matters.

"*Go! You damned fool! Leave me! Just... just go! Don't let it take you, too!*"

Tom doesn't answer, focused only on the rhythmic motion of their knife.

Melisandre lunges forward to bite at the thick rope coiling around Tom's waist. The motion pulls the twist of hair at the back of her neck hard against the knife in Tom's hand, severing the final strands as the rope snakes up towards their face.

Melisandre drops to the filthy stone floor. Tom lands hard on top of her. The ropes and tendrils are suddenly just heavy masses of dull brownish blonde hair, dirty, matted, and greasy, falling all around them like unpleasant pitches of loose straw.

The breath knocked out of her, Melisandre lies under her rescuer, stunned, only managing a wheeze. Tom rolls off her, face crimson. "By the Gods... I'm so sorry, miss – Milady – Melisandre..."

Melisandre raises herself up on her frail, bony elbows and,

without quite meaning to, she throws her arms around Tom and kisses them long and hard.

"Thank you! *Thank you*, Tom. I... Oh, thank you so much!"

She stops, fear piercing through her elation. She waits for the same look of disgust she has seen in the eyes of every man who lay down with the vision and woke up with the scarred and battered and filthy reality. She is no beautiful young girl any more. She must be twice Tom's age.

But Tom, looking back at her and still red as a ripe tomato under all of the blood and filth, has no disgust in their eyes.

It takes the two of them over a day to escape from the tower. Tom constructs a rope and harness from the quiescent matts of hair while Melisandre treats their wounds with hastily-mixed salves, wearing an improvised blanket skirt and Tom's long coat. Tom lowers her down, mindful of her frail limbs, then slides down themselves after her. Their sleepy dun gelding is still grazing quietly, barely blinking up at the two of them as Tom supports Melisandre and helps her mount him.

"I can take you home if you like," Tom offers, looking up at her as they walk alongside the gelding.

Melisandre smiles down at them, eyes crinkled against the brightness of the early sun even under Tom's wide-brimmed hat. "I don't think so. I've been gone so long... My father must be dead by now, and they've got that picture up in the ballroom. I have no particular wish to turn up as the reality. Not after all these years."

"All right." They meet her crooked quirk of a grin with a quiet nod of acceptance. "Where will you go, then?"

"Where are you going, Tom?"

They shrug, grinning. "Somewhere."

"Would... would you mind if I came along?"

The grin deepens as they flush. "It's all I could ever have hoped for," they say softly, shyly, gazing up at her.

Overhead, the sun is rising on a new day, and the birds are beginning to sing.

MOONLIGHT

Ally Kölzow

The house was dying. It ached and groaned through the night, tiredly holding up walls wounded by cracks. Rain teased the windows as it battered hard against the outside, each drop fighting to be the strongest – the one to finally break the dirty glass that offered distorted glimpses into a house that appeared untouched for decades. Only the moonlight was allowed inside, pouring in through the destroyed roof and bathing the crumbling interior in a silver sheen. She sat and watched from the sky like an old friend, illuminating what had once been a grand country home in a futile attempt to restore it to its former glory. But her light could only do so much to protect a mere ruin from the roar of the wind and the tears of the sky. In truth, what she waited for were the two figures who moved through the decaying maze of rooms and corridors as gently as ghosts.

★ ★ ★

A laugh echoed through the hallway, followed by the sounds of footsteps beating against creaking floorboards. It was a strange sight to behold: flashes of a white wedding dress glowing in the dark corridors and pale skin that seemed almost translucent when grazed by the moon's light. Sometimes it appeared as though she were dancing. At other times, running.

For a watchful stranger, it would have been easy to believe the young woman was alone. No other soul seemed to follow her as she darted from passage to passage, even as the footsteps grew louder. The reverberations gleefully bounced off the walls of the house before striking another pair of ears.

She was being watched. Not just by the moon, or by the mice that would scamper across the hallways when they believed nobody was looking, but by another woman with dark hair and dark skin, who wore a shabby tuxedo two sizes too big as though the cloth was swallowing her smaller body. Her gaze clung to the gaps in the walls, straining to catch glimpses of the figure flitting between them while the rain fell through the gash in the roof, splashing into a puddle a metre away from where she sat.

"Adanna, come!"

The house carried the voice through the corridors to the tuxedo-wearing woman.

She didn't move. Only her lips twitched into a smile separated from any real happiness. "Where are you, Nina?" She asked the house to carry her reply in turn, and it obliged.

"Here, of course," the voice called back to her with a giggle.

"What are you doing?" The house had heard these words before. They understood why they seemed so tired.

"I'm playing with them."

"With who?" Adanna called into the darkness, waiting for words she already knew. The silence that followed was always the one that hurt the most.

Tick, tock, tick, tock. There was a clock somewhere. She knew without being told that it was counting down. She shivered as if a clawed hand was dragging one icy finger down her spine. The night-filled halls felt colder with the clock's warning.

An answer floated to her from what felt like far away. "The people in the walls."

Knowing what to expect was never quite the same as hearing it. Even after all this time, she could not allow herself to become used to such a declaration. It was less about what was said and more about what it meant. What was buried underneath it, rotting and festering. To whom she could articulate this, she was unsure. Sometimes, it truly did feel as though she were alone. The house always turned its back on her in the end, too. How many years of this would it take for her to accept it? It was her choice to play this game; she knew that. It was her decision to start it. Yet every time she heard the words and the confirmation it brought, the same feeling unfurled in her stomach, as painful as poison entering her bloodstream.

The clock continued cruelly. Each tick felt like a cut upon her skin. She rose slowly from the dusty floorboards, her gaze passing over the moon staring sympathetically back at her, before she was welcomed by the dark maze of corridors that once hosted much grander spectacles. It had never been clear how long the house had ceased to be a home before their arrival. Time was a fragile thing, after all. With each passing day, it seemed to evade them more. Seconds, minutes, hours had escaped from them. Adanna was grateful for it. She wanted to forget. She wanted to live.

Wind thrashed angrily against the house, ripping away pieces of ivy crawling up the outer walls. Something about the intensifying storm outside worsened the sickness brewing in her stomach. "Nina?" She called tentatively, trying to keep the worry from her voice as she hurried from room to room, fighting her way through a tangle of large chambers and tight passages that quietly alluded to the secrets the house had once kept.

The grandeur of the rooms had been worn away by time, hurt by the emptiness they had been left with. All that remained were small scatterings of abandoned furniture belonging to no one: a broken chaise longue with one leg missing, a wooden piano that had gone out of tune long ago, a dozen gold-framed portraits filled with the faces of strangers. Adanna longed to step into the past and see those faces come to life in a house that she knew had to have once been beautiful. Now it only harboured the ghosts of the past. She could feel them watching her sometimes, their eyes creeping across her skin, waiting. She spared them no glance now, her mind set only on Nina.

Strangest of all were the passages engulfed in darkness, weaving their way between rooms. Candleholders clung to the narrow walls that could transport a person from one side of the house to another, sometimes without even realising it. Adanna had fallen prey to these tricks of the house one time too many, caution taking hold of her as she moved through the dark cramped space connecting the old library to a vacant chamber.

If she did not know better, she would think that the house seemed to grow bigger each day. Another room appearing, another addition to the maze trying to keep her from Nina. If only there was a spell for finding her way.

A door slammed shut across the corridor from her. There was once a time when such a sudden bang would have caused her to jump out of her skin, but now all she did was stare, her neck snapping in the direction of the door. This is a game, she reminded herself. It was her fault she had to play along.

She stalked across the passage to the door, strangling the doorknob before twisting it.

It did not move an inch. Frustration fell over her like a wave as she threw her weight against the wood. The house seemed to be laughing at her – a deep, bitter sound that drifted from the basement to the very top floor. Perhaps this was their punishment for coming here. Uninvited guests enjoy uninvited consequences.

"Please." It was not a word made for her. Too gentle, too obedient. But she spoke it anyway. Time was turning against her, and that, she could not afford.

Begrudgingly, the door gave way to her. It swung forward with a force Adanna had not predicted, thrusting her forward into the empty room. She fell onto the floor before quickly pushing herself back up, her hands chasing away the dirt clinging to her trousers, the wooden floorboards groaning heavily under her feet. The room was fairly large, though the absence of furniture magnified it, the empty space intruded on only by a towering mirror leaning against a wall with cracks running across it, spreading out like veins. The red wallpaper that covered it was peeling away, as if it were trying to escape from the decay.

Black curtains fluttered in the wind and framed a balcony that overlooked the estate, rolling hills looming in the distance beyond the overgrown black gates. The sky outside was swollen with dark clouds, punctured only by the white glow of the moon.

It was strangely beautiful. Somehow enchanting. Powerful enough to make her forget, if only for a second, why she had needed so desperately to open the door. *Nina.* One name that could send her heart beating feverishly inside her chest and turn her blood to ice in the same breath. The sensation was like somebody walking over her grave. All her eyes could see was the emptiness. Devoid of things and devoid of life. There was nobody else inside of the room.

"*Nina!*" This shout did not echo. It felt small inside of the room, even as she summoned all her breath to cry out the name. The house was receding from her, and taking Nina with it. Everything slipping away as the clock ticked louder.

"Boo!" A cry erupted from right behind her. Adanna's heart dropped in shock before it slammed against her chest harder than ever. Someone was breathing on her neck. It was cold, soft as a feather. Her fear righted itself and she spun around to face the very person she had been looking for.

The relief was short-lived. She savoured it nonetheless, drawing Nina into her arms, her fingers brushing against the white dress stained by dirt and dust. "Don't *ever* do that to me again." The warning would not matter in a few hours, but she spoke it nonetheless.

"You worry too much, *mi amor*," Nina laughed. It was quieter than it had been before, breathier, as though the sound demanded more of her than she was able to give.

"I worry just enough." Not enough, Adanna thought to herself.

Hesitantly, they withdrew from each other. Adanna's grip left Nina's back and she caught her hands instead, their fingers intertwining. The sickly paleness of Nina's skin did not go amiss. Adanna could see that it was everywhere – that pallid, translucent colour. Sickness was sweeping over her. It was as if Nina was shrinking right before her eyes: her face gaunter, her hands bonier. What if her fingers were so fragile that they'd snap under her touch like bird's bones, simply by holding them? Tears pricked behind her eyes but she forced them away with a smile. *Does it hurt?* she wanted to ask. She needed to know. But she couldn't and wouldn't let those words pass her lips.

"I am happy," Nina assured. It was as if she understood what was being said in the silence. She spoke softly, so much so that it was easy to underestimate her. To dismiss her words as that of a child's, even with age on her side. What had happened to her had only made it easier to do so. There were many things that she did not know and many things that her mind did not let her know, but this she knew: "I am happy. To be here. To be with you. Are you happy, too?"

"I shall always be happy so long as you are." It was the truth, plain and simple. That which lurked beneath the simplicity need not be mentioned.

"Then that is all we need." The smile that Nina gave her was enough to halt the worry gnawing at her. A delicate kiss dispelled it further, cold lips gently pressed against warm ones, trying to say the things that could not be said. How long it lasted was unknown to them; it felt like a second and a lifetime all at once. All Adanna knew was that when it ended, it still felt too soon. Perhaps that was simply what love was. Always too much and always too little.

Nina broke away then, her attention captured by the grand mirror adorned with a gold frame. "Oh, it's magnificent," she spoke in a whisper, slowly approaching the glass. The beauty of it reminded her of home. Hazy memories of opulence – lavish fabrics and extravagant jewels – began to slowly rise to the surface, but vanished like mist before clarity could strike. She ran a finger along the golden edge, ignoring the dust that gathered on her skin. "Is this for me?"

Nothing was given away in the quiet that followed. No frown appeared on Adanna's face, no sign of confusion. Her face wore only an expression of sorrow and love that Nina would never understand. "Of course." Was it even a lie? "This is all for you."

"I adore it." Nina's gaze strayed from the mirror for a moment as she looked back to Adanna, reaching out a hand for her to take. "Thank you."

Their hands joined together again as they stood side by side before the mirror. Two sets of eyes peered into its depths to meet their reflections. What they saw were themselves, but not the versions that existed today. Adanna could see Nina's head resting on her shoulder in the reflection, could feel the weight of it on her, and yet the Nina staring back at her from the glass was different. The sickliness had been sucked out of her skin; the difference was so stark that it made it seem as if she was almost glowing. Neither of the women on the other side had been aged by fear. Instead, they were happy – truly happy. They were smiling as though it was the happiest day of their lives. Not a speck of dirt tarnished either one of their outfits. The wedding dress was white as snow while the tuxedo was black like the night sky. Adanna's stomach twisted as she stared at her smiling counterpart.

"Look at us." Nina's voice seemed to come from somewhere far away. A muffled, dreamlike sound. "We look beautiful."

Adanna felt her head turning, her gaze escaping from the mirror's trance and the reflection watching her. Nina's palm was on the glass, pressing harder and harder, as though if she tried hard enough, she might be able to break through and step inside of it. She was grinning, just like her reflection, though the smile did not suit her face anymore. Adanna stared at her. One second, two seconds, three seconds. She was distantly aware of the clock calling her.

"This is such a wonderful day." Adanna could see Nina's lips moving. She could hear the words that they formed, but they made no sense to her. She had prepared herself for something else: pain, anger, confusion. Everything that had stained their lives since the tragedy. She had expected tears, falling like the rain. She had been mistaken. To Nina, this was a bright summer's day, entirely separated from the melancholy of the moon above them. *She doesn't remember.* A reminder: quiet and loud, gentle and violent.

Envy had sprouted inside of her like a poisonous plant the first time Adanna had realised this. Nothing about her reaction had been fair. She had hated herself for it, even while keeping it locked behind the closed doors of her mind. No such jealousy corrupted her thoughts any longer. A pervasive sense of loss clouded her mind instead, the one emotion she had never allowed herself to feel otherwise.

And what was there to remember? One trigger pulled, one gunshot ripping through the air with a *bang*, one barely breathing body on the ground. Blood everywhere. Red seeping into the ground. A wedding dress ruined. A marriage ended before it had begun. Claims of a stolen daughter, of righteous vengeance enacted in the name of God, of restored honour. Death.

The day came to Adanna in flashes. It invaded her sleep. It pervaded her thoughts. Guilt, regret, and loss had become so entangled with one another that sometimes she forgot which was what. She wondered if it would have been better if the bullet had hit her, instead.

Sometimes she had conversations with Nina inside her head. A false Nina. One that remembered, one that knew. When she did, she heard Nina chiding her in her head. *We would never be here if it had been you. We would not still be together and I would never be happy again without you.* And though she knew that this is what Nina would say, she could not help but wonder if this cyclical existence was any better. If Nina was even truly happy. If she might have forgotten what happiness was.

She had learned to be glad that Nina did not remember the day itself. What she found herself wishing instead was that Nina could remember the days they had spent since, and what had happened to ensure those days.

A faraway rumble of thunder drew her from her thoughts. It was closing in from beyond the hills, uniting with the howling wind and the crying skies. She refocused her attention on Nina, whose hand still touched the mirror. The happiness had drained from her expression, exhaustion shading her face. She was turning a strange, almost ashen colour. Somewhere in the house, Adanna heard the clock still ticking.

It was then that she saw the blood. Spreading slowly, spreading silently. Blood stretching out across the dirty white dress. Just as it had that day.

"Nina..." Her legs may as well have been frozen, any command she sent to them going unheard. *Move*, she told them. They had forgotten how.

"There are so many people in this room." Nina's voice was quiet, too raspy.

"People?" The room grew colder and the silence grew louder.

"Can't you see them? Oh, there's a little boy over there. Hello, are you lost?" Nina had turned away from the mirror, peering into one of the room's dark corners, beyond the ripple of the curtain in the wind. Adanna apprehensively glanced around the large room, her gaze landing on each corner. It was empty. "I was playing with you earlier, wasn't I? Yes, it was you. Others as well. You must have friends, are these some of them?"

"Nina," Adanna whispered, lowering her voice. "I think we need to go."

"He says... *come with us*." Nina kept staring into the shadows, a wistful look crossing her face. Her left foot slowly lifted from the floorboards, moving forwards.

"No!" Adanna's hand flung out to grab Nina's wrist, pulling her away from the corner. Nina's skin was cold as winter. She shivered, but her grip never faltered. She could not lose her now. Not after everything. "Don't go – don't leave me." The fear in her own voice terrified her; it felt like it was mocking her.

Nina looked at her, leaving behind what had lurked in the corner. Something in her eyes came into focus then, as if she was seeing Adanna for the first time. "I... I would never leave you." She tried to smile, tried to lift her hand to cup Adanna's cheek, but her body felt as if it no longer belonged to her. It could no longer do what she asked of it. Gradually, her head titled downwards, allowing herself to look at the blood blossoming amongst the filthy white of her wedding dress. She rose a shaky hand to it, feeling the sticky substance, gazing at the deep shade of red.

Cracks were starting to appear, faint lines running across Nina's skin like some sort of secret map. Time was catching up with her. Each *tick* of the clock was a violent echo reverberating around the house. Every time her eyes shut it became harder to open them again.

Adanna watched this happen. She fought the urge to take Nina's bloodstained hand from her wound, to take it and hold it in hers instead, to hide from Nina the truth of her body's betrayal. What good would it do now? There was only so much she could hide. Some secrets demanded to be seen.

"Something is wrong." Those words were the last. Nina forced them out, taking a shallow breath between each one, before her eyes rolled behind her lids. Adanna caught her falling body in her arms, holding on tight.

"No, no, no. Not yet. Nina–" Pleading would get her nowhere. What was right and wrong no longer held any meaning. She could argue that it was too soon. That time had been crueller to them than usual. It did not matter. There was nobody there to listen.

Panic crawled up her throat and she shoved it back down. Her hands started to shake but she stilled them. Summoning the strength that she prayed was hiding somewhere inside of her, she half-carried and half-dragged Nina to the balcony, passing through the dark curtains floating like a ghost in the wind. The balcony itself was barely big enough for Adanna to lay down Nina and kneel beside her. The wind struck her face with a loud roar, rain pelting down on them. She remembered how much she used to hate the rain and how Nina had once managed to coax her outside on a dreary day. They had danced beside the river, the rain falling all around them, drenching them to their bones, and it had been one of the happiest days of her life. She had welcomed the rain ever since, carrying the memory with her into each soaked day.

But she abandoned all memories, then. There was no time for nostalgia. What needed doing required every part of her, every inch of her mind and section of her soul. She glanced up at the moon, shielding her face from the rain with her hand. It shone bright and strong, holding her gaze. "Help me," Adanna called, trembling in the cold night.

I will, my child, the moon answered.

The moonlight streaming down around them brightened, as though the house itself was bathed in white. Something stirred, awakening, inside Adanna, the tension in her stomach soothed by a new sense of alertness. The clock's incessant clicking warped, turning muffled as her focus honed in on Nina and the faint beating of her heart. Her own hand hung in the air above the dying body, right over the chest, as every other sound slipped away from her. The howling of the wind was silenced; the rain fell without echoes.

All she could hear was the faded rhythm of Nina's heart as it stopped and started.

Her eyes shut and words poured from her mouth. They were indecipherable; she felt rather than understood what she was saying. Incantations had never been easily committed to her memory, no matter how many times her mother had tried to teach her while stroking her hair. But this one she knew as well as the moon in the sky. She could recite this spell in her sleep, she could summon it forth whenever and wherever she needed it, and needed it she did.

She had used these words dozens of times to bring Nina back to her, to keep her tethered to the living, even while her body pulled her towards the dead. No matter how many times Adanna repeated them, it would never be enough. Death was calling Nina's name and death could only ever be cheated for so long. And yet, she could not let her go.

The heartbeat strengthened. Adanna could hear it – the faintest suggestion of life transformed into something solid. She could trust that it would beat again and again.

Cautiously, she opened her eyes. The words still escaped her lips – a chant with the hope of a prayer. The moon shone brightest of all on Nina's body, its light draining away death, radiating through her dress and filling the gunshot wound that had shot apart the promise of their lives. The blood slowly receded, retreating from the wedding dress back into the wound, leaving behind the white cloth – a reminder of the day that was supposed to have been only the beginning.

Adanna's hands abandoned the air to hold one of Nina's hands between them, instead. The iciness of her skin was gone, banished by the warmth slowly returning to her body. It was like holding her before any of this had happened. The days when their love may not have been simple to the world but it was certainly simple to them.

The moonlight faded and the rainy wind returned. She understood what it meant; it was over, it was safe. Words stopped falling from her lips, trailing off into the night. Nina would come back to her soon.

And, slowly, she did. It began with the trembling of a finger, followed by gentle stirring movements, as though she was preparing to depart from the land of sleep to sail back to consciousness. Adanna found comfort in how it looked like it had been a peaceful sleep.

At last, Nina opened her eyes. She blinked away the raindrops on her face and gazed at the moon, the ghost of a smile on her lips, before landing on Adanna. Her grin came alive then, her eyes bright with life. "You're here."

She would not remember what had happened. She would not remember the number of times it had happened. And maybe Adanna was glad of that, too. Instead, they would smile at one another in the rain and let it wash away their fear.

"I had the strangest dream."

I AM THE MASTER OF
MY EYELASHES

Enmanuel Arjona

Text inspired by personal experiences and the poem 'Soy dueña del universo' by Guadalupe "Pita" Amor.

I like to look at myself, admire myself, to project secret aspirations, brightly sequined desires of the stage onto my high heels. I observe this nudity which, in other worlds, is not permitted to me, but which is now mine, mine from my own body and my desires. I demand affection from those whom I seek, the safety that I suddenly possess in my hips, the steeled steps of my legs; and I want everything, everything and for everyone to see me from the runway, feeling distant and arrogant, despot, secure, divine, absolutist, powerful, and audacious like a bitch.

And I, like Guadalupe Teresa Amor Schmidtlein, am the master of my eyelashes...

Just as I am the master of the anxieties that undress and redress me every night in mist, mirages, and spectacle. I make myself up for Aphrodite, becoming stained glass in my obsessions and in each wardrobe transparence... my freedoms. So I strip off this disguise of a decent man/woman and become a whore. Because for whores, the kingdom of heaven belongs to he who inhales between my legs, this sex that springs forth like a poinsettia.

And I, like Pita, my little Pita, am the master of the universe...

And from the stars and suns that I invent, I am the master of the firmament of lights this evening; ebullient, like at the beginning of time and of men and of religions, of original sin, and undiscovered virtue, of the fallen angel who strokes/stokes my intentions and turns them to fire, my hands of fire, my hair and my eyes, and my blazing lips. I unravel, I do not recognize myself, and I seduce myself; this dressing room mirror that laughs out loud and bewitches me with its cursed reflection.

And I, like Guadalupe, 'Pita' Amor become someone else.

I transform, chimera of my passions, of my lusts, of this vast intelligence of a witch, turning me into the fortune teller for my own destiny, and ahead of my time, in an unspoken pact with my hells, I condemn myself to freedom. Free is my will, free are my nipples and thighs, free are my movements of man/woman/dragon/serpent, free are my private perversions of a jackal, a hyena, a cat. This hunger of man, of triumph, and of furtive glances. This craving for unusual beauty under the protection of the moon, of obscure vanity, and discotheque ambition. This is what I am on my nights of transvestism, of eternal diva drag, and of the most lucid of my truths.

I am the master – just for tonight – of myself.

THE WHITE DOOR

Lindsay King-Miller

I saw the castle before I saw the town. It towered in the sky, its crumbling grey stone in bleak contrast to the cheery red roofs of the houses below. Massive, windowless walls were coated in dying moss. Even in the bright sunlight, it cast a chilly shadow.

I stopped at an inn with a tavern on the first floor, found a room in which to drop my bag, and bought a pint downstairs. "First time in town?" said the woman behind the bar, taking in my travel-worn dress.

"Looking for work," I told her.

"What's your trade?" She looked me up and down and said, "Wish I could offer you a position myself…"

I understood what she meant by that, the codes in which some women speak to each other. I wasn't as provincial as she might think. The bar matron was pretty, stout with thick brown curls and ruddy lips and cheeks. She looked… vigorous. If I didn't have more important things to occupy my mind, I might have accepted the position she so readily offered. Maybe suggested a few myself as well.

For now, though, I shrugged, pretending I'd missed her hint.

"I haven't learned one, but I'm a quick study." I nodded toward the castle, visible in silhouette through the pub's grimy window. "A place like that probably needs plenty of workers, doesn't it?"

"Probably," she agreed, "but I don't recommend it. There's sickness in that house."

"Sickness? What kind?"

"I couldn't tell you exactly, but the young Duchess must have brought it with her, because it all started when she got here."

"Is she still sick?" I asked, interested. I hadn't come all this way to sit by a sickbed, but a Duchess who was too weak to keep an eye on her jewels sounded appealing.

"Oh, the girl died," the barkeep said. "And then whatever she had, some girls who worked in her kitchen caught it, and it spread all over town. Seemed like every other person I knew fell ill, and a handful more passed away. Terrible time. You know the worst part?"

"The worst part?"

"Well, the Duke went out and got married again, and *again* the poor woman took to her bed within days. She held on longer than most of the others who were stricken, but she died too, just a month ago."

"Never sick himself, though?" I asked, curiosity struggling with caution.

"Not that anyone knows, but then we wouldn't know, would we?" She rolled her eyes. "Couldn't say I'd recognise him if he sat down in the seat next to you. Anyway, after the second Duchess died, everyone has avoided the place. I think he's keeping house by himself in there – all the staff quit for fear of the malady."

A mysterious Duke. A nameless illness. A castle full of beautiful things and no one to guard them.

I smiled, and finished the rest of my beer without taking a breath.

★ ★ ★

The castle loomed in the middle of what must have once been a luxurious garden. Now, despite the bright spring sun, it was just a jungle of skeletal trees. Its black door towered above me, more than twice my height. There was no knocker or bell. I turned in a full circle, uncertain of what to do next. Walk around the manor looking for another entrance? Give up and move on to the next town? I didn't want to do that. And I certainly couldn't go back the way I'd come; that seamstress's husband had been dead serious about what he'd do if he saw me again.

The story of the Duke and his dead wives intrigued me more than it should. I was determined to meet him, to satisfy my curiosity, no matter what it took.

So when he opened the door, I stood perfectly still and silent for at least thirty seconds, having not the least idea what to say.

The Duke's face was similarly blank, waiting for me to explain myself. His skin had an unhealthy, sunless look, tinged a greyish-blue shade. His eyes, too, were blue, but only slightly, as though they had been watered down.

Maybe this wasn't the Duke, I thought belatedly. The bar matron had said there was no staff left in the castle, but she had only hearsay for evidence. This man certainly didn't look the part of nobility – or even of an aristocrat's butler. He wore a suit that looked like it must have been luxurious once, but was now faded and worn. I saw loose threads and a stain of some kind on one shoulder.

"Good morning. I'm looking for work," I said.

The words came out like a stack of plates crashing to the ground, heavy and awkward. I flushed red, but the man stepped back, gesturing that I should follow him inside.

"What's your name?" he asked.

"My name is Margaret," I said. Damn. Usually I gave a false name in a new town, lest angry husbands run into each other and compare notes, but somehow I was so off-balance I hadn't thought of one this time.

He nodded. He didn't tell me his name, but I was increasingly confident that my first guess had been correct and this was indeed the Duke. The thickness of the silence around us, untouched and heavy, made it obvious that we were the only two living beings in this entire sepulchral place. All the servants, even the spiders, must have sensed the pestilence and fled.

Of course I should have done the same. It's something mixed up inside me – not bravery, just an instinct that works the wrong way. When anyone else would retreat, I want to go forward.

"Your quarters are this way," he said over his shoulder, already walking away. There had been no discussion of my qualifications, my duties or my salary, but I followed him without quibbling. The floor was stone, cold on my feet even through my shoes.

We walked past an empty kitchen and a dining room where chairs and tables draped in sheets to keep the cobwebs at bay. It was hard to imagine two new brides setting foot in this cavern over the last year; the castle felt as though it had been abandoned for decades.

We came around a sharp bend in the hallway, and there was the Duchess.

I stopped as though I had run into a wall. The portrait hung above an unlit fireplace, her face three times larger than life, cheerful eyes above a solemn line of a mouth. Her hair was black, her eyes golden-brown. She looked like an irrepressible young woman, just past girlhood, trying and failing to convey the dignity of a matriarch.

I liked her instantly. I wanted to see the smile she was hiding, to hear the laugh she was struggling to contain. I almost reached for the portrait, so perfectly lifelike, I could have sworn I smelled her hair.

The yearning that whelmed through my body was stronger than anything I'd felt in years. Her skin cried out to be touched, her mouth to be kissed. It was impossible to conceive that this vibrant, lovely face was simply a memory, the woman who'd posed for it now a corpse.

The Duke took several more steps before realizing I had stopped. He turned and looked at me with impatience.

"I'm sorry," I managed. "The painting startled me."

He nodded, looked up at the portrait. "My wife, Lucy," he said, his voice surprisingly tender. "She's lovely, isn't she?"

Is? Maybe the bar matron had been mistaken. Maybe this woman still lived. Maybe she was in need of a serving-girl – and oh, I was sure I could serve. "Is she here, sir?"

He looked into the painted eyes. She didn't look back. "Only in my heart," he said.

I started to say something, but he turned away abruptly. By the time I realised our conversation was over, he had already turned a corner and disappeared from sight.

* * *

My room must have once been intended as a guest room, not servant's quarters. The bed was vast, the pillows soft, and the tub in the adjoining bathroom was large enough to stretch my legs out straight with room to spare. I lined up my few clothes on one of the closet shelves, then put them back in my suitcase, because they looked silly surrounded by so much empty space.

Although I didn't exactly sleep, I dreamed about the Duchess from the painting. In my dreams, I called her Lucy.

After hiring me with no interview or qualifications, it was perhaps unsurprising that the Duke assigned me no duties. In the morning, I wandered the halls alone, trying to learn my way around the house.

I found my way into a music room. The grand piano, so neglected its coating of dust had congealed into something like skin, beckoned me. When I raised the lid, the keys were pristine, if a bit out of tune.

I hadn't played in years, but I sat down and picked out a tune I vaguely remembered from childhood. It was mournful, something about waiting for a lost love to return. I thought again of the painting of the Duchess, the way I imagined her hair would smell. If I closed my eyes I could almost believe she was sitting next to me.

Her shoulder warm against mine. I sighed and let myself lean against her, just a little.

The bench squeaked. When I opened my eyes, heart pounding so hard it hurt, I was alone in the room. There had been someone beside me, I knew it, but the only footprints on the dusty floor were my own.

I sat very still for a long time, waiting for that sensation of presence to return. Eventually I rose and left the room.

I didn't remember how to get back to my own quarters, but I thought I could follow my tracks on the floor easily enough. Somehow, though, they led me into a part of the castle I hadn't seen yet. Not my footprints, then – perhaps the Duke had very small feet.

Turning a corner, I entered a long, high-ceilinged hallway, a huge white door at its end. Carved all over the door were women: bathing in pools, floating on clouds, strumming harps or mandolins. It was bizarrely ornate, but beautiful – or at least it would have been, if every single figure's face hadn't been twisted in terror.

I didn't want to go in. I knew better than to go in.

I went in.

Inside, the room was warm, warmer than anywhere else I'd been in the castle. A well-tended fire chuckled to itself on the wall opposite the door. There was a strange smell, which it took me a moment to recognise as an absence: for the first time since arriving here, I didn't smell dust. Why was this room so bright and clean and so empty?

No, it wasn't empty. As I turned away from the fire I saw them, lined up to my right along the wall. Three long, shallow boxes, made from the same white wood as the door standing open beside me.

Three coffins.

The first one, directly to my right, was empty except for a pillow of red satin. I could see in my peripheral vision that the other two were occupied. I closed my eyes and took a deep breath before looking at the next one directly.

Here lay a mummy, a vision of decrepitude. She was nearly

skeletal, skin shrivelled up and clinging to bones as though the flesh and blood beneath had simply evaporated. Her cheekbones looked ready to burst through the pale membrane of her face; her fingers were claws with skin. She wore a white gown embroidered with flowers, bridal and still pristine. Her hair was a cloud of dark curls around her withered face.

The Duchess lay in the last coffin, as lovely as her painting – perhaps even lovelier. Her face was not sunken like her neighbour's, but perfectly still and pale. She might almost have been sleeping, except for the handle of a knife that protruded from her chest. She, too, wore a bridal gown, its bodice stiff with what might have been embroidered flowers, all a deep, earthy red.

Of course it was blood.

I choked down a scream and stepped back from the coffin, my head reeling. I reached behind me for the door and yanked it open without looking, turning, half-blinded by panic, to flee.

But it was the wrong door. It opened not onto the hall I'd come from, but onto darkness. Darkness and a horrible smell of rot.

It took me a moment to understand that I had stepped into a closet. A moment longer before my eyes adjusted – there was no light in the little cabinet but what seeped in from the room beyond – and I saw the shapes lying on the floor.

There were three of them. Three more dead women.

These corpses weren't costumed like brides, but in plain dresses, not too different from my own. Any differences they once had in age, shape, or skin colour were erased; they wore the identical uniform of ugly death. Like the bride in the second coffin, they were emaciated, with their skin peeling like old paper from their bones.

Behind me, the closet door slammed shut. I swallowed a scream as I was plunged into blackness.

Groping in the suffocating dark, my hands found the closet door and scrabbled over its surface for a knob or handle. I felt sharp ridges, splinters that gnawed at my fingers. The inside of the door bore scratches and dents, as though it had been clawed and kicked with a desperate, futile strength.

These women had been locked in here while they were still alive.

Finally grasping the handle, I stumbled out of the closet and burst into tears.

It hurt to cry like that. When I sat up, minutes or hours later, my throat felt like I had swallowed fire. I swiped the back of my wrist across my nose and saw a drop of blood. I'd cried so hard it made my nose bleed.

I took a long, shivery breath, and pushed myself to my feet, turning back to the row of coffins. First, I had looked at them from right to left, as I moved away from the door to the hallway. Now I took them in from left to right, like reading a line of text.

Lucy, the first Duchess. Still and cold, but so beautiful. She was so much like herself that I put a hand above her lips to see if she was breathing. She wasn't.

The dark-haired bride had wasted away into something barely human.

Two wives, three coffins.

The third coffin was empty, but now I understood that it wouldn't remain that way.

★ ★ ★

I ran, letting the huge white door slam shut behind me.

What could I do? The bodies of five murdered women lay behind a door I wasn't sure I could find my way back to. I needed to get away, and then – what? Come back with authorities or just keep running? All the Duke knew about me was my name. I could disappear, and he would never find me.

But if I once got out of the shadow of this castle, I would never dare to come back again.

He'd killed Lucy – that beautiful, perfect girl. It was his fault I'd never be able to touch her hair or to feel her voice against my skin. I had come too late to help her.

But I thought of that third coffin, the empty one. The Duke wasn't finished. He would take another bride and take her life. If I stayed, maybe I would have the chance to save her, whoever she turned out to be. And get my revenge on him at the same time.

★ ★ ★

I found a broom and some rags and I started to clean, beginning with all the grimy floors on which my telltale tracks could be seen. I swept right up to the carved white door but didn't open it. I didn't think about the dead women or weep for them or even plan my revenge: all that would have its time. For now, there was a carved white door inside my mind, and I locked it with all my fears and hopes and heartaches inside. For now, I built a fire in the fireplace below Lucy's portrait, and I tended it carefully. The warmth made it easier to keep moving, to find more chores for myself and do them diligently.

Cleaning helped me learn my way around the castle. I discovered the room the Duke slept in, a spacious suite as far as possible from the room where his brides would never wake.

One morning, I rose early and made him a cup of tea. I carried it on a small silver tray to his quarters and knocked on his door.

It flew open with a ferocity that shocked me. I nearly dropped the tray. The Duke stood in the doorway, his face horrible, but when he saw me, he shook himself and calmed.

"What is it, Margaret?" he asked.

"I brought you a cup of tea, sir," I said, holding it out. Some of it had sloshed onto the tray when I flinched from the opening door.

He stared at the cup, then at me. "That's... kind," he said slowly, as though the concept were unfamiliar. "Thank you."

I smiled at him, thinking that once he was used to me bringing him tea in the morning, I'd start slipping poison into it.

Later, dusting the untouched china in the dining room, I began to hum a song – the same one I'd played on the piano on the day I found the white room. My eyes wandered from my work into impossible worlds. I thought of Lucy, spinning an idle fantasy where we lay on soft grass in the sunlight, her body warm and alive all around me.

I was so certain I was alone that when I turned and saw the Duke in the doorway, I didn't recognise him for a moment. His skin hung from his face like his ill-fitting suit hung from his shoulders. The shadows of his eye sockets and cheekbones seemed deep and filthy. He looked ghastly, and I choked on a scream.

He took a step forward into the room, and his features resolved into the face I knew – the familiarity of my enemy almost a comfort. Now he merely looked sad. "That was beautiful," he said. "It sounded like happier times."

I ducked my head. "I'm sorry to have disturbed you, sir." I meant to slip past him out of the room, but he stepped in front of me again.

"Margaret," he said, lingering over the syllables of my name. It sounded dreadful, like the white door creaking open. "You've brought a little music and light back into this sad house. I can't tell you how grateful I am." I started to say something, but he cut me off. "I know we're nearly strangers, but I feel something for you." The grimace on his face suggested he felt mostly indigestion. "The thought of you leaving for another job is a sorrow to me. Would you stay here?" He reached out and took my hand. "Would you be my wife?"

I stared down at my hand as if it were an unfamiliar object, perhaps an empty glove, limp in his grip. I couldn't feel his touch. My ears were ringing.

"Yes." It came out of my mouth before I thought about it, but it was perfect. This was what I had hoped for all this time: his body within the reach of my hands. I thought again of poison, a toast to our marriage. And waking in the morning a widow, mistress of this horrible house, which I would let rot after locking the door behind me.

I would be his third bride, and his last. I met his eyes and smiled.

★ ★ ★

The gown was laid across my bed the night before the ceremony was to occur. It was plain but clearly well-made, the material soft, the fit perfect. Meant for me.

I dressed before dawn, having not slept at all. Everything in the house was old, my dress was new, and for something borrowed I would have the longest knife from the kitchen, honed to a gleaming edge. I buried it in the folds of my gown's modest bustle. The knife handle, occluded by a small sash, would be easy to reach with either of my hands.

Though I watched for him, I didn't see which way he came from. He was just standing in my doorway. Without speaking, he offered me his arm. Without hesitating, I took it.

He escorted me through the castle through unfamiliar passageways. I wondered who our officiant would be, whether they were privy to the Duke's depravities. Would they help me escape?

Surfacing from my thoughts, I realised that I stood in front of the white door.

Of course. There was no officiant; there would be no ceremony. The murder was to be our wedding. As soon as I walked through that door I was doomed.

I tightened my grip on his arm, letting my free hand trail back toward my sash. I would do it now, this moment, before we reached the perverse bridal suite. I would strike him down just as he imagined himself triumphant. The door was only a few steps away.

My fingers closed around the handle of the knife.

The door opened without the Duke touching it.

Lucy stood in front of me, and she was smiling.

★ ★ ★

She was so beautiful, so impossible and present and achingly bright. Her smile was every bit as incandescent as I'd imagined, and her hair smelled like sunshine. My heart leapt at the joy in her face. I wanted to embrace her, to devour her, to touch every part of her body and know she was real.

She was covered in dried blood. Her own blood, from a wound that should have been fatal. I wanted to run away from her.

I didn't move.

Beside me, the Duke was still and silent. The two of us stood just outside the white door, and Lucy just within.

Where did that door lead? What world was I looking into?

I held the knife in front of me, no longer knowing what to do with it. I looked from the Duke to Lucy and back, trying to understand. Lucy followed my gaze.

"You're no longer needed," she said to him, and he, unspeaking, withdrew his arm from mine and took a step back. It was as though he was a candle whose flame had gone out. Though he was still present, he was absent.

At last, and at quite the wrong moment, I found the strength to scream.

Lucy held her hand out. "Please don't," she said quietly. I choked on the end of my scream, felt it still burning in my throat.

She looked me up and down. "He's done well this time," she said, and her voice was so soft and so kind I wanted to cry. "You're brave, sweet Margaret. Trying so hard to avenge my death."

"How did you know?" I asked, barely a whisper.

"I've been watching you," she said. "Even before you stumbled into my little dining room. I don't have much else to do these days, you know." She gestured to her blood-stained gown, to the spot where I had seen the knife buried in her flesh. "Ever since he put that blade through my heart, I've been trapped in this dismal castle. I was meant to travel the world, marrying one rich man after another."

She waited for me to comment, but I couldn't find words. "That's what the women in my family do," she went on. "Marry men and drink their blood and keep their fine things for ourselves. I meant to start with the Duke, but I learned something inconvenient on our wedding night. I have no appetite for men. None whatsoever."

I looked over my shoulder at the Duke, who gave no sign he heard any of this.

"I couldn't stomach him whole, but I took enough of his blood to make him weak," she said. "Agreeable. He does what he's told."

"Why?" I understood, but I wanted her to say it.

"Because I need him to bring me wives," she said.

"Those women. You ate them?"

"Yes."

"And—" my stomach heaved, "and now me?" I found I was still holding the knife. If she came toward me, could I use it? Would it even matter? Was it possible to injure – whatever Lucy was?

We had been standing on opposite sides of the white door this entire time. Finally, Lucy stepped across the threshold. She was so beautiful. Her wedding dress whispered against the stone floor. Her feet were bare. She smelled like flowers and blood.

"Don't," I said, gripping the knife's handle in both my shaking hands.

"No, my Margaret," she whispered. "That isn't what I want from you."

She gestured to the Duke, still motionless behind me. "I've had enough of this half-corpse. I tire of his presence. But I'm too weak to leave this castle. I must feed much more before I can be free again, and I need help. I need a companion." She smiled and took another step toward me. "You make such a beautiful bride."

Lucy was directly in front of me now. The tip of my knife touched her skin, just above the plunging neckline of her down, dimpling her pale skin. Her smile grew larger. Impossibly large. So wide and dark I could have fallen into it headlong.

"I can make you like me," she whispered. "We've never shared our power, because no man was ever worthy. But I could share it with you." She reached out and tenderly brushed a lock of hair back from my shoulder, her fingertips lingering on my bare throat. I shuddered with something that was neither revulsion nor fear, though it should have been.

All at once, I heard a roar of anger. It took me a moment to realise it had come from the Duke. He had been so silent I'd almost forgotten he was alive. Seeming to summon all the strength he had left, he lunged past me and grabbed Lucy by the throat. He flung her against the white door.

"Beast," he snarled. "Monster!" Over his shoulder, to me, he shouted "The knife, quickly!"

Lucy looked more amused than afraid. "Haven't you tired of failing to kill me, husband?"

He spat on the floor. "I'm not your husband, and I won't be your dog any longer. Margaret, give me the knife!"

I had been rehearsing this moment in my mind for weeks. It was easier than I ever imagined. I stepped forward, and with one smooth motion, I cut the Duke's throat.

His eyes fluttered in surprise as his hand went to the wound. He coughed once, sending blood spurting across my white dress. Then he slumped to the floor.

Lucy stepped across his body and into my arms. I tasted blood. I tasted her. We were both of us stained with red.

* * *

"I didn't think I'd see you back here," said the woman behind the bar. "Expected you had moved on to look for work somewhere more likely."

"Not at all," I said. "I went and asked that Duke of yours for a job."

"Caught the plague yet, have you?" she asked, smirking.

"Do I look sick to you?" I replied, spreading my arms and twirling. She took a long look.

"You look the very picture of health," she said finally. "That creaky old castle seems to agree with you."

"Luxury will do that," I said with a wink. "The poor widower stays in his room, and the whole lovely rest of the palace is for me to explore." I let the word "explore" stretch out as it rolls off my tongue, leaving plenty of room for interpretation.

"I've lived here all my life and never been inside the place," she said. Her neck flushed an enticing pink.

"I'd love to give you the tour," I said, leaning closer. "Can you come by tonight?"

DOCTOR BARLOWE'S MIRROR

Avery Kit Malone

Matthias carried the hand lantern down the narrow spiral steps, exited the stairwell, and slowly pushed open the great oak door. The room was spacious, despite Doctor Barlowe's seeming determination to clutter it. It was filled with thick, leather-bound journals of notes, haphazard stacks of books (was he still using that tower of dust-coated tomes by the door? Matthias made a mental note to stow them back on the shelves later) and other errata. The stolid, dark wood walls were lined corner to corner and floor to ceiling with shelves. The doctor often moved like a spider amid them, reading by the watery orange light of a single candle which roiled the shadows in the corners and left the vaulted ceiling above cavernously dark. The doctor was knowledgeable in a vast array of subjects, and his sizable collection reflected his staggeringly wide net of interests, ranging from philosophy to electric systems to natural science to other, stranger things.

Matthias heard the dry scraping of a turning page, and so entered quietly, shuttering his lantern and letting his eyes adjust in the dim light. He found the doctor standing in a corner, brow furrowed at the book in his hand. From the other end of a bookshelf, he observed Doctor Barlowe, loathe to disturb him. Matthias appreciated him like this, when he was focused studiously on some matter. In truth, Matthias appreciated the handsome doctor in a wide variety of contexts.

When Matthias had first grappled with his slow-dawning understanding of his own proclivities in romance – particularly his interest in other men – it had taken him considerable time to accept it. And then, some time after becoming the doctor's assistant, he'd learned that the doctor had a secret of his own. It had nearly thrown his newly stable sense of identity into turmoil once more, before Matthias had realised it didn't matter: both because the doctor was indeed a clever, comely, man – though one prone to inscrutable moods – and because, ultimately, it was all moot, as Doctor Barlowe knew nothing of his idle thoughts and desires.

Matthias roused himself from his thoughts when his stomach quivered, and he cleared his throat. The doctor's grey gaze cut upward in a questioning glance, eyebrow raised. He seemed entirely unsurprised to see Matthias standing behind him.

"I've been sent to fetch you, Doctor. Dinner is served upstairs." Matthias's stomach growled imploringly. "Marie insists she won't wait a minute longer, sir," he added, smiling sheepishly.

"Ah. Very well," the doctor said, snapping his book closed and taking up his cane from where it balanced against a shelf. "And I suppose," he added with a sly smile, "that your hurry has everything to do with our cook's irascible nature."

"Of course," grinned Matthias. His stomach gave a bear's warning. They laughed.

The tap of the doctor's cane as they walked silently side-by-side was a familiar comfort.

★ ★ ★

In the doctor's laboratory, there stood an elaborate machine. The central component was a large rectangular slab less than a meter wide and nearly two in height. It was as black, smooth, and reflective as volcanic glass – and indeed, Matthias, who read often from the library with the doctor's blessing, wondered if that was what it was.

None of the books he had read lent him any indication as to the purpose of the thing, however. The large, glassy pane was affixed to a metal apparatus that led, in a tangle of wires, to two great electrical devices on either side that thrummed and snapped when Doctor Barlowe turned the pull-lever. The ins and outs of the machine, or what it meant, exactly, when the black glass buzzed with electrical force, were beyond Matthias's ken. The doctor, as he often was with regard to his passions, remained enigmatic.

"Mark me well, Matthias," Doctor Barlowe called, fitting a pair of goggles over his face, "when the machine has power, you must never, under any circumstances, touch the glass. No," he lifted a hand, "even I don't know what would happen. And to find out is not a scientific endeavour I care to pursue. Now, let us step back. Goggles, friend."

Matthias lowered his goggles over his eyes and watched through the uncomfortable fish-eyed view. Beside him, the doctor pulled the lever. His latest machine, the product of three years' past work, woke with a wild, piercing buzz. The waking of a caged animal, Matthias thought, or an untamed demon reluctantly meeting the doctor's summons.

Then – to his amazement – the black glass began to fade from the outer edges and smoothly, quickly inward. No, Matthias realised, blinking. The glass had not disappeared. It had become perfectly reflective, as any mirror. He turned, astonished, to find Doctor Barlowe regarding the mirror with his goggles lifted from his face and the distant, satisfied smile that Matthias so rarely saw.

Matthias paced tentatively toward the glass, hesitated, then turned back over his shoulder to the doctor, who gave a nod. With his attention returned to the mirror, he took a few steps forward and found himself centred in it, his reflection returning his wide-eyed stare, the glass humming faintly. The noise, some-how, was much quieter directly in front of the device itself. In its flawless surface, he saw his own worn face. He had not confronted his reflection at length recently, and he noted the lines of his forehead, the creases near the corners of his eyes, and the tinge of grey at his temples.

He turned his back to his reflection and shouted to the doctor, "What is it?"

"Isn't it obvious?" called Doctor Barlowe, a near-madman's grin replacing what remained of his typical sombre affect. "It's a mirror."

★ ★ ★

When they next returned to work on the mirror contraption, Matthias still had little idea as to its ultimate purpose, but the doctor had graced him with a patient, "You'll see."

This time, the doctor sat dictating much of the work, his fist reflexively gripping his cane and tapping it anxiously on the floor. Matthias knew he was under considerable strain. Matthias could only guess at the sort of pain elicited by the garment binding the doctor's chest beneath his shirt and vest, and though he wanted to offer some comfort, he did not dare.

"It's done, I believe," he said, rising from where he had knelt behind the black glass and mopping his brow with his forearm.

"Step back, then, and get your goggles. Let's see."

The machine sang to life, and once again, the obsidian mirror cleared. At first, as Matthias lingered several meters away and warily watched their reflected room, he could not fathom what was different. He approached it slowly, the electrical devices on either side giving off a roaring hum, the strange pylons above them arcing and snapping. Doctor Barlowe had risen from his chair and walked softly to his side, placing a hand congenially on Matthias's shoulder.

"I suppose I wasn't entirely true with you, dear friend," he said, smiling, with a nod toward the glass. "It's less a mirror than a… window. What I've really created is a window."

Matthias looked doubtfully at their reflections. He startled.

His gaze was drawn by the piercing glimmer of his eyes — clear sea-glass eyes that exuded a cool and luminous strength compared to the muddy, dim green of his own. Watching that chiselled face, unblemished and achingly sharp — was that an insolent smile, looming faintly in the upturned corner of his lips? — he ran a hand over his own chin, over his tired skin, the scar on his cheek, the softness near his jaw.

"I won't ask you what you see," came the doctor's voice, sounding distant, and Matthias was surprised to realise he had forgotten Doctor Barlowe was there. "I can tell you how I see myself, but…" he chuckled. "A bit taller, I suppose. And with a fair bit of fur. Hmph."

The doctor scratched his hairless jaw idly, staring deeply at a reflection Matthias could not see. Then, as though waking from a daydream, he came back into himself and clicked his cane decisively on the stone floor of the laboratory.

"But, Doctor, *what* are we seeing?" Matthias asked.

He found himself unsettled, and he could not say whether it was due to the comparison between his lacking body and the reflection that gazed steadily, impudently back, or something else. He peeled his gaze from his reflection-self and noted for the first time that, in his view, the reflection of Doctor Barlowe that stood beside his better self was entirely unchanged from the man who stood beside him in the room.

"A window, as I said. To where, precisely, I cannot say. We think of our world as the only one, but there are many worlds strewn throughout the interstices of the universe and isolated from one another. We are seeing, I believe, one of them now."

"Another world."

"Indeed. I have much to learn about it. Well…" The doctor turned decisively, walking back to the power lever. "Come! Let us retire to the parlour and celebrate our success."

Matthias watched his perfect grin dissipate, fading until he saw only his own, true body faintly reflected in the black pane, his face nearly subsumed by the dark.

★ ★ ★

Matthias, despite his trepidations, found himself compelled to return to the mirror days later. If he could face it once more, on his own, perhaps he could finally put the whole matter to rest. He stole down to the laboratory late in the night, hoping against the odds that his insomniac employer was asleep. He took some small comfort in knowing that nearly no sound in the underground laboratory leaked to the higher floors.

He pulled the lever and approached the mirror, standing face-to-face with the glass before it had even wholly cleared. His reflection stood patiently waiting for him – no, what an odd thought, he decided with a frown. Surely a reflection didn't wait for anything at all. But there was, he noted as he stared himself down, a certain keenness to his perfect version's eyes.

Matthias was no longer sure why he had come down here. To prove to himself, he supposed, that his anxiety was entirely unaccountable – but his heart was starting to pick up its pace. As he watched in astonishment, his reflection's smile sharpened – mocking, he realised: its mocking awareness was what so unsettled him – and turned its head. The doctor entered the mirror at his side.

Matthias wheeled around to face the air beside him. "Doctor Barlowe? Gideon?"

There was no response. He was unequivocally alone in the laboratory. Turning back to the glass, he watched his reflection-self gather the doctor in his arms. The doctor gazed back at his reflection-self with a longing smile.

Matthias's throat constricted.

His reflection-self pulled the doctor closer, leaned in and, slowly and firmly, kissed the other man on the mouth.

Heat rushed Matthias's cheeks. He couldn't bring himself to turn his gaze from the mirror.

His reflection-self turned back to him with a leering, arrogant grin.

Red-faced, fuming, Matthias drew back a fist with a wordless cry and reared to strike the mirror–

"–Matthias!"

He jumped and whirled to face the voice behind him. There the doctor stood, dark-eyed and still dressed in his vest and cravat. He had not slept, after all.

"Doctor!" Matthias's face flushed anew. "There's something on the other side, some... intelligent thing. *We're being watched, too*, doctor."

In his periphery, he saw something dark and amorphous, and he snapped his head to face the glass.

Only his own reflection looked back at him.

"I suppose that's the issue with windows," murmured the doctor, perhaps mostly to himself.

He stepped forward, his heels echoing authoritatively in the room.

"Listen to me, Matthias. I don't yet rightly know what resides in the other world. It may truly be other versions of ourselves – or perhaps it's something else entirely, something that shows us what we would like to see. But I can tell you this..." The doctor wearily took a seat and looked at Matthias with rare earnestness. "I understand the temptation to view the reflection as a better self. Believe me." He fell quiet for a moment. "But *there is no such thing as a perfect self*. I love this body in some ways even as I despise it. What I see reflected in the mirror – whoever that man is, he wouldn't truly be me. Not as you know me, at least. And that presumes that what it shows us isn't just an illusion, some sort of disguise designed to invoke jealousy."

Wouldn't be you, Matthias echoed silently. *Not the man I know and love.* The fierce teeth of envy toward his reflection-self did not fully release themselves from his heart, but they did loosen their grip.

"I'll tell you something else," the doctor added. He produced a kerchief and mopped sweat from his brow. "I believe what's on the other side wants something, too. Call it intuition, I suppose."

"What could they – it – whatever it is, what could it possibly want from us?"

Doctor Barlowe raised his hands in a gesture of helplessness.

"I have no way of knowing. However… as there is no such thing as a perfect self," he repeated. "I conjecture that it's rather jealous, too."

Matthias's spine tingled with what he swore was another glimpse of something shapeless and dark. He spun toward the glass and met only his handsome reflection, gazing innocently back.

The doctor stood. He pulled the lever and the electrical humming ceased at once.

Matthias's reflection dissipated, leaving him with only the impassive black glass.

"We should rest," the doctor said.

Matthias followed the echoes of his footsteps out of the darkened room.

* * *

Matthias spent several days following the late-night incident without placing a foot into the laboratory. He occupied himself with tending to the doctor's study, transcribing the man's cramped and hastily-scrawled notes, and organizing and cleaning the library. Doctor Barlowe, for his part, had not asked Matthias for assistance underground and performed his studies on the machine alone. Matthias, embarrassed as he still was, had not dared ask to join him.

Finally, nearly two weeks later, Doctor Barlowe emerged from the laboratory and called to Matthias from his study.

Matthias found him seated at his desk, his open journal in front of him and a tome from the library in his hands. He adjusted his reading glasses and looked up as Matthias entered.

"I intended to review this passage and walk immediately back down to resume my experiment. However, I can see now that this reading will take me quite some time. Will you please return to the laboratory and simply shut the machine off? It shouldn't be left unattended while powered."

Matthias's throat felt stiff. He nodded.

He could see trepidation growing in the doctor's eyes, and before Doctor Barlowe could change his mind about sending him back alone, he added, "I'll turn off the machine right away, and I'll be back promptly."

Matthias hurried from the room. He took the narrow steps by twos and threes, eager to turn off the machine and be done with it. When he entered the underground laboratory, the machine was indeed thrumming with life. All he needed to do was pull the lever. *Don't look at it. Don't look at it.*

But he could not help one quick glance. Hand poised above the lever, he looked over at the mirror at the back of the room. It was empty. He froze. He should have been able to see himself, distantly, from where he stood. The mirror obediently reflected the room around him, and he could see the wall behind him in its entirety – even the lever just in front of his hand – but it was as though he wasn't there.

His throat closed. Had *it* somehow escaped?

He crept over to the mirror, and no reflection matched his approach. He could still see only the wall behind him.

Then – in a flash of motion – it leaped into view from somewhere off to the left. Matthias jumped back with a shout. His dashingly handsome reflection-self stood before him with a cool smile and gave him an exaggerated wink.

"Why – you – devil," he snarled. "To hell with you! To hell with your perfect world. It can all rot for all I care."

His reflection-self grew deathly serious. Its face morphed,

subtly, and then reflected him accurately – as he would see in any mirror, imperfect and genuine. But it kept changing. He watched in horror as his eyes receded back into his head, dull and soft, and his skin mottled. His nose and lips blackened. His face stretched inward, giving way to pale grey.

Matthias's own face was a mask of revulsion and fury. Some remote corner of his mind recalled that he needed to flip the switch; he needed to turn the thing off. Yet he was transfixed.

All the while, his corpse pushed its loose jaw open and shut, open and shut. Laughing. Mocking. His shrivelled tongue writhed like a worm.

Matthias's shock twisted into adrenaline. This was too much. Whatever place was on the other side of the doctor's window, the world was better off without it. He raised an instinctive fist at the vile sight before him and struck the glass.

And then, for a moment, the ground seemed to fall away below him – as though his fist was magnetised and held to the mirror while everything else faded. He kicked out but couldn't break away from the pull. The thrumming glass vibrated through his body. He screamed, the sensation mounting until the black spots in his vision spread into a dark flood that cut off his sight entirely.

He was distantly aware of his body collapsing. He landed on the floor and lay, breathing heavily, until his vision cleared. He pulled himself upright.

Matthias stood in a dim, cold place. Thick swathes of fog swirled around his shins. The sky above him was a shifting black canopy. Save for his breathing and the very distant warbles and moans of wildlife utterly alien to him, it was quiet. The only light came from a bright rectangle suspended in mid-air in front of him. He circled it, and found that, somehow, he could see nothing of it when he stood on its other side. He stared at it, and realised, with a sickening jolt, that he saw the familiar laboratory's walls and floor through the rectangle.

And here, around him, was nothing and no one.

No such thing as a perfect self. An illusion.

A desperate howl ripped from his chest as he gaped at the vision of the laboratory and something dark and fluid and formless shifted into his view on the other side. As he watched, it sharpened and moulded itself into the shape of him, and smiled.

He lashed out at the mirror with a shout but his fists moved through the vision as if it were empty air. His reflection-self stepped out of sight. A sudden terror of being alone laced icy fingers around his heart. He called frantically, futilely, for help through the glass.

His reflection returned with something in its grip – a heavy length of metal piping, he realised – and he understood that there was worse to fear than simply being alone before the mirror. His reflection-self drew back the metal pipe and struck.

Matthias flinched, his heart skipping a beat even though he felt nothing. Then his view of the laboratory, with its bright familiar lighting, fractured into a kaleidoscope – a hundred splintered reflections of the room with his own leering face centred in all of them.

Too soon, the splintered visions began to fade. The light from the laboratory dimmed into nothing. His strange, hovering window dematerialised in the air, leaving him utterly alone in the true dark.

LAGUNA AND THE SIRENA

Katalina Watt

Laguna had been born in the water. Her mother had been thick in labour pains when she had stumbled out of the hut, across the sand, and into the sea. She cried out, awakening the bushaellas, and Laguna had slid out between her legs, the caul still surrounding her. Waters separated by a thin layer of skin.

Kapati had stood on the shoreline, shielding her eyes from the sun and watching the blood mingle with the waves. She hurried over to her sister and grabbed the floating baby. She forced Laguna's mother on her back, sand freckling her damp and bloodless face. Kapati took the knife from the sheath at her hip and cut through the umbilical cord with an arc of her arm. She carefully pierced the caul, watching the liquid drain out, and she unwrapped the baby like peeling an orange. Laguna breathed in a lungful of salt air as she was lifted from the waves. Her mother was lying still in the water, legs parted gently. Kapati carried Laguna to her mother's breast, the baby smoothly uncaked from her inside world.

* * *

Aunt Kapati's husband had been a fisherman. He tempted the seagods, or bantay tubig, by riding storms. He would slap down a hunk of fish boasting that those who seek adventure reap the largest and rarest catches. He was right to be proud, and kept Kapati in a good home which she readied for children who

53

never lived. He had been taken by a sea creature, some kind of shark, it was said, while fishing far out beyond the shore close to twilight. The incident had been witnessed by another fisherfolk who didn't dare angle as far out as he did. The body never washed ashore, but for months afterwards the villagers diligently scoured the beaches and shallows. Kapati would later bitterly tell Laguna that it was only the gold tooth in his head which interested the villagers.

When Laguna's first blood came, Kapati showed her how to pad her clothing and the knots for tying everything in place. It was then Laguna noticed the rash on her inner thighs, running up to meet the growing curls. Not red like insect bites or plant rashes; it reminded her of the silver webbing which patterned her Aunt's belly from childbirth. As she slept in their bed, she would think about Aunt Kapati's dead babies, unable to tell if the tightening in her chest was grief or the ghosts sitting there.

★ ★ ★

Laguna was wide awake in bed. The crashing waves kept her awake at night. The sea was a cacophony of breaking and shushing sweeping through the house. The brine cloyed in her throat and the sea salt bristled her skin, calling to her. She thought about her uncle's death. She wasn't sorry. But Kapati mourned him, even though he had hurt her again and again.

The unbroken heat of the summer was so unbearable, sweat rolled down her skin in rivulets. She eagerly searched for a cool patch on the bed. Finding no relief, she rose and crept along the cool earthen floor. Easing the door open, she looked at the sand bathed in moonlight. It squished between her toes. The foam nipped at the soles of her feet, tantalisingly refreshing. The waters seduced her with promise. Laguna's mouth dried as she tried not to think about coconut water. Her skin was on fire.

She slid into the sea with unfamiliar focus and gave a gasp of pleasure when the water reached her groin. She bobbed down to wet her hair and encased herself in the coolness. She drifted, observing the coral and seaweed within her grasp, and broke the surface. She floated on her back, enjoying her body enveloped and submerged. With curiosity, she studied her burnished skin, the curves of womanhood so new and strange to her.

She studied the silvery rash in the moonlight, and then the curls like an animal's fur. Her fingers explored inside. She tried to understand what she had briefly glimpsed on other women during washing day swims in the river. She slid her fingers around, amused by the twin reactions in her hands and vagina.

She looked at herself, seeing with both her eyes and hands as they reached deeper. The waves beat calmly against the shore, rhythmically and caressingly pulling her out to sea. Laguna touched the silver rash on her thighs, inspecting the reflective shine, perhaps from the moonlight on the water. She existed in the movements of her fingers and her breath until the pleasure washed over her and she shuddered into the water, diving under.

Something was watching her. The creature glinted in the moonlight, scales on its head rippling in the water. Laguna floundered for a moment and then started frantically treading water. She smelled something raw and bloody. Laguna felt the heaviness of her limbs on the sand when she saw it. She turned to hide her body but kept her gaze fixed on it. The shape disappeared below the waterline and emerged closer, the iridescent whites of two wide eyes reflected back at her.

★ ★ ★

Over the coming weeks, Laguna delighted in her secret self. She began taking indulgent baths and Kapati chastised her for her flagrant use of rainwater; they were moving into the dry season and Laguna was fast diminishing their stockpile. To divert her Aunt's exasperation, Laguna began to swim more. The feeling of lightness in the water became a hunger and she derided her past self for the wasted opportunities when she couldn't bare the dampness on her skin. The young folk of the town basked in the thrill of Laguna's uncovered body. They spoke nonsense on the beach in the prime of a post-learning afternoon, and they noted how her smalls stuck to her skin. Previously Laguna had been solitary, tied to her Aunt and the hut. Now the intrigue of her smile and her verve to befriend them made her prior ghost-like presence melt away. They noticed her, and Laguna grew full on the attention.

As she examined herself more often, Laguna observed the silver webbing unfurl across her thighs until it was the size of her palm on each leg. It wrapped inward, so she needed to use her Aunt's compact mirror to mark its chaotic path.

She took to the waters almost daily, a ceremony of bathing, washing her hair and methodically running her fingers through the strands. One evening, right before the sun was setting over the horizon, Laguna spotted it: a glimmer in the corner of her eye, like the speckled web which fills the periphery after looking at a bright light.

The creature glinted in the sun, its lithe and epicene body rippling, each scale perfectly formed and making her fingertips tingle to trace them. It was closer than Laguna had expected, silently cutting through the waters without breaking the surface. She saw it silhouetted against the sunlight. She stayed as still as she could, not wanting to startle it. It disappeared beneath the water again, and Laguna held her breath. She felt the waters move below her and it emerged from the murky depths, inches from her. It took everything for her not to scream. The instinct caught in her throat as she drank in the creature's striking strangeness. Its eyes were tubular, translucent, and with dark chasms for retinas. She was pulled into that gaze. The creature shone with an unearthly iridescence, its body lithe and epicene. The gills at its neck fluttered a warm jet of air onto her face. She wanted to touch it. It opened its mouth, full of teeth like razor blades.

Laguna reached out before her mind knew what her body was doing, and the creature caught the movement, its body pulling away and its head flailing from side to side. The ridges at the side of its head fluttered and she felt on her fingertips a warm jet of air and water escape the opening. Lit by the last rays of daylight, Laguna listened to the gurgling coming from the creature. Its features melted, squished together in places and slid down its face, and its bulbous eyes swam. A mouth gaped open, full of teeth like razor blades, silently voicing an eternal scream.

★ ★ ★

Laguna had tried to put the strange encounter out of her mind. She had turned back to shore to hear the distant calling of her Aunt Kapati to come in for dinner. The creature had been startled by Kapati and disappeared with a gulp beneath the waves. Laguna swam to the beach, feeling a heavy aching in her limbs which had slowly come to feel like an unnatural burden, as though something were crushing her body on land. Her chest pounded in the night as though her heart would burst, and she couldn't stop touching the silver rash. Her Aunt chastised her for scratching it during dinner, Laguna's leg raised up on the chair, her foot resting on the edge of the seat.

"What is that?" Kapati asked, vexed, as she spooned more rice on to her plate.

"Just a rash," Laguna dismissed, putting down her leg and squeezing her thighs together.

"Are you getting sick?" Kapati asked, meeting her niece's eye and examining her face.

Laguna hated moments like this. Her Aunt's concern reminded Laguna that they were tethered together by tragedy, that they had no one else and so they were forced to love one another. It had been easier when Laguna was younger; she had been a curious hurricane child, absorbing everything Kapati showed her and leaving devastation in her wake. Kapati could see the wild abandon of her sister in the girl, something primal in the way she held herself. Kapati knew that folks were wary of them both, and Laguna had a difficult time making friends. The villagers whispered they were cursed, and Kapati was inclined to believe them. Everyone they loved had died and Kapati had seen an omen, a tigmamanukan, skimming the surface of the water at night. She caught enough fish to keep them alive, but every money-making endeavour turned to ash. She had washed and mended clothes, beat the dust from houses with a walis tambo, and in the early days was a wet nurse for other mothers. Laguna grew painfully and Kapati suspected they both felt trapped by the sea, ever encroaching. She knew Laguna never saw her as anything other than comfort, sustenance, shelter, and home. Laguna had curled her fingers around questions of her parents and uncle. She was morbidly fascinated, an ember Kapati tried and failed to stamp out early. Now Laguna had taken an interest in the sea; Kapati could tell she was bathing more. There was a constant salt damp smell and feel to her. She was spending time with the other young people. A fleeting worry about illness, pregnancy, death, passed over Kapati like a cloud, but then Laguna dipped her head, letting her hair fall in front of her face as she surreptitiously continued to scratch the rash.

★ ★ ★

That night Laguna was sweating and shivering uncontrollably. She felt as though her body was on fire, her bones melting away and crushed beneath the weight of being on land. Her hands wandered, and the air was still with sweat and lust. She released a breath, took in another, trying to steady herself. She was in the eye of the storm, calm descending too rapidly to be permanent. She knew that if she stayed she would cry out and wake Kapati. She crawled out of the hut, the rash a bright pain between her thighs. She looked down, the silver webbing glowing bright like embers inside her skin, the light pouring out from the split of skin. She gasped as she hit the water, sliding into it like a snake, not caring about the sand and shells and coral which tore at her skin like teeth on flesh or how the salt water burned the wounds. She floated, her flesh dancing deadly and aching to be touched.

"Sirena," Laguna whispered, chanting the summoning slowly.

She swam through the kelp forest, the silk wrapping itself around her as she felt the air escape from her mouth and nose. Underwater she could see dark shapes moving around her in the moonlight. The sirena's webbed extremities clutched onto her skin and with the touch came a coolness sweeter than ice on a summer's day, and it took all her strength not to sink beneath the shallows.

Laguna felt transported back to a full-moon night in her childhood where she had desperately wanted to know her parents. She had executed a ceremony to bring them back to her with wild flowers in her hair and lavender on her lips. She had plucked calamansi and squeezed them into a fire, made wombs and yonic symbols out of animal bones and stones, and burned them to dust. She was helpless and could only pray, words halfway between the ritual of church and the older furtive rites passed down from mouth to ear.

Laguna came back into herself, wrapped in the creature's arms, her lungs aching to burst. The silver webbing was dazzling and incandescent as Laguna breathed slowly and heavily, the creature echoing her movements. She tentatively moved her fingers across its body; she would count the glittering scales if it would let her. It was so inhuman and yet there was something behind the bulbous eyes, something tender in the way it held her. They explored one another's strangeness with every part of themselves and Laguna sank into it, not understanding but surrendering to it. A wave barrelled in front of her, rolling in on itself, and a portal opened just for a moment, a glimpse into the landscape beyond. Through the eye of the wave Laguna could see the distant mountains, the coral just below her feet, the arc of the water like a potter's hands moulding clay, spindrift speckling the edges. It curved in on itself, the perfect sphere collapsing. Foam and bubbles whipped round in distinct strokes, like knives in the water, closing Laguna's view.

She gave a garbled cry as the creature grabbed her arm and pulled her through the current to an air-filled cavern, where the dappled moonlight gave glow to the umbra. Laguna spluttered and cried out with the shock of air. The creature remained submerged, cocking its head barely out of the water and moving its body towards a stone ledge nearby, as though presenting it to her. Laguna peered through the murk and the mottled light. She saw the rough ridges of stones, but as she looked harder she saw the distinct jagged sutures of bone. She started back, flailing and submerging herself in the water. The more she struggled, the more bones she disturbed; a butterfly pelvic bone with darkened hollows grinned at her until she kicked up the silt and enveloped herself in the storm. She snorted out air hard and fast as she shot to the surface and the creature moved into the clearing beside her. Laguna was juddering, her throat constricted, as she allowed the creature to bring her towards the graveyard. It stretched out Laguna's arm, as though to pet a dog, and stroked one of the bones, revealing it beneath layers of silt. When Laguna stiffened, the creature held the skull up to Laguna's face. The girl looked at it and let out a howl of demented laughter, mirroring the gold-capped smile.

THE MOON IN THE GLASS

Jude Reid

They found her body on my wedding night.

She was floating face-up, they said, her unbound hair spread around her like flames. I was not there at the time, of course, but when I close my eyes, I see her all the same: the wind stirring the pond and shattering the moon's reflection into shards, the emerald silk of her bridesmaid's gown congealing like pond-weed on the surface of the water. I imagine her white skin, the smooth curve of her lips, still beautiful even in death, like Millais's *Ophelia* among the water lilies.

Ness Suilvain always did have a flair for the dramatic.

It was the groundsman, stepping outside for a midnight pipe, who chanced across her body and raised the cry. When it was clear that any chance of saving her was past, it was he who waded in to lift her from the water. He bore her in his arms back to Suilvain House, the water dripping as thick and heavy as footsteps in his wake. I remember the look on his face as he peered through the bedroom door – that strange mixture of sorrow, dread, and discomfort at the sheer *lèse-majesté* of being sent above stairs as the bearer of bad tidings – and how her brother's face seemed to crumple in on itself, the rawness of his grief more painful to behold than the loss itself. His sister – now my sister-in-law, a description so new and strange that it barely seemed to fit her at all – was gone, drowned in the lily-pond. It was a terrible ending to a day that should have been one of unadulterated joy.

* * *

What you have to understand is that before I came to Suilvain, I had nothing of my own. My parents died in India when I was ten, leaving behind enough of an inheritance to complete my education and little else. At eighteen, I could write in a pretty hand, speak fluently in French and Italian, manage a little German, and converse intelligently on literature, history, and the topics of the day. My skills were perfectly suited to life as a governess or companion – a genteel and respectable life, but one dependent forever on the whims and generosity of my betters.

By contrast, Ness Suilvain was destined for a different life. Born into an ancient family of Scottish aristocracy, she had good breeding, money, and the prospect of life on her own terms. She was not precisely beautiful, but her vivid copper hair and darting green eyes added to a lively, vivacious charm, and from our first meeting we were the closest of friends. When our schooling was complete, I gladly accepted the invitation to return with her to her family home for the summer. She was eager that I should meet her one surviving relative – her brother Angus, a mere three years her senior but already Lord and Master of Suilvain and its sprawling Highland estate. She assured me that he would love me just as much as she did. In that regard, she was entirely correct.

* * *

The minister made no mention of suicide, nor of the long delay between Ness's death and burial in the brief and moving sermon he gave before the burial. The Suilvain family were well-loved in the village, and it seemed that every local had dusted off their threadbare black coats and moth-eaten veils to pay their respects. I looked for signs of accusation in every face as they pressed my hands and told me how they grieved for my loss and, to my surprise, found none. If anything, the mildest of reproaches was aimed not at me, but at Angus, as though they grudged him the happiness of a new bride to bear him company when his sister was cold in the grave. She must have felt her position under threat, I heard them whisper, relegated to the role of the spinster sister now that the house had its new mistress. To me, they apportioned no blame whatsoever.

When the wake was over, the villagers had taken their forelock-tugging leave and we returned to the candlelit silence of the parlour. Angus took my hand and squeezed it gently in his own. I raised my gaze to meet his and found his green eyes brimming with sympathy.

"You must not blame yourself," he said, his voice so soft I had to move my veil to catch every word.

"What do you mean?" A stab of fear sunk into me. What, exactly, did he know?

"I am aware," he continued, his tongue flicking lizard-like across dry lips, "that the friendships of young women can be of an intense nature. I should have seen in what high regard my sister held you; how deeply the loss of you, or her perception of it, would have hurt her. Even as a child, she was prone to an excess of emotion – delighted by the simplest of things, and grieved to the point of desolation by the most trivial of losses. Had I not... Had I not loved you, she might not–" his voice faltered and failed. "The guilt," he concluded in a whisper, "should be mine."

"You are not at fault," I said, and placed my lips softly against his. His wiry ginger moustache prickled against my skin.

"Charlotte–" He frowned. There was a question in his eyes, but I saw no condemnation there. "If you and my sister – that is to say, if there was some intimacy between you that exceeded the bonds of mere friendship – if that were to have been the case, I would not... I would not judge you harshly for it." His gaze slid away, downcast. I laid a finger along his jaw and guided his eyes back to mine, where they met an expression of sincerity of which I was justly proud.

"I loved Ness in the purest and most sisterly way," I told him. "If she felt a different kind of emotion for me, then my only regret is that I could never have returned that love in kind." I allowed a single tear to creep its way down my cheek, and he wiped it away with the gentlest of caresses.

"You are the best of women," he told me, and took me in his arms.

It was then that I first saw it.

He must have felt me stiffen against him; he took a step back, holding my shoulders at arm's length and scrutinising my face.

"What is amiss?" he asked.

I said nothing – in truth, I could not have told him exactly what I had seen, only that something had moved in the crepe-draped mirror over the mantelpiece. It had been without form or substance, little more than a shadow, and yet I felt an unaccountable chill in spite of the fire blazing in the hearth. I took a step closer to the mirror, but saw in its flawless surface only the contents of the room and the reflection of the sky outside. The moon's light stung my tired eyes.

"Nothing," I said. "I saw a shadow pass across the moon, I think, and it startled me."

"You are tired and overwrought," he said. "Come to bed. Tomorrow will be a little easier, and the day after. This grief will pass in time."

I let him guide me to the master bedroom with its wood-panelled walls and feather bed, and I laid down beside him. He stroked my hair and placed a chaste kiss on my forehead, our pillows side by side, but when I closed my eyes, it was her face I saw.

★ ★ ★

I dreamed of her that night. My hands tangled in her fiery hair, the silken curve of her waist, and the exhalation of her breath that carried my name with it like a prayer. Desire crashed over me like a wave, ebbing and surging as it carried us together towards ecstasy – and then the white sheets on which she lay turned to water lilies and her skin took on the chill of alabaster. Her face was turned to the sky, her eyes open, and twin moons reflected in their glassy surfaces.

"Charlotte?" It was Angus, his blunt-ended fingers resting on my shoulder, his face inches from mine. "You cried out – were you dreaming?"

"I don't remember." My nightgown was soaked with sour sweat, the covers tangled around my ankles. "A nightmare, I think. It's nothing."

He nodded and gathered me close to him, asleep almost as soon as his head touched the pillow-slip. I strove for sleep, but each time I closed my eyes that same dreadful image of Ness's drowned face floated into my mind. In the end, all I could do was lie in uneasy wakefulness and wait for daybreak.

The moon in the looking glass was as full as it had been on the night of her death. It was hard to believe that a full month had passed since the night of my wedding, but I supposed it must be so – the peculiar limbo of mourning played tricks on the mind's perception of time. The local Sheriff must have lingered over passing the verdict of death by misadventure even longer than I had thought. Had Ness been a common villager, he might have been satisfied to write the whole matter off in a day or two, but a proper and thorough investigation, mindful at all times of scandal, was as much her birthright as her family name. For the body of a woman of her station to be laid out in the local poorhouse would have been unthinkable, and so she had been taken to the nearest mortuary on the mainland to await the arrival of the medical examiner from Edinburgh. It was only after the lengthy post-mortem that her body had been returned for interment in the family crypt.

In the time between her death and burial, everything had changed. If the moon was full again, then I had been a married woman for four weeks: mistress of my own house, financially secure for the first time in my life. I should have been suffused with contentment. Instead, as the cold white moonlight reflected from the mirror into the room, I felt only a creeping sense of unease, as though I were being watched.

Angus slept as only the innocent can, and I lay beside him, tense and wakeful. I could not have said with any certainty from which direction the presence emanated, only that it was close at hand and filled with a sense of malevolent and patient purpose. In the end, unable to lie still any longer while my heart raced, I rose and crept to the washstand, filling the basin with cold water from the china jug. Angus stirred a little at the noise but did not wake. I splashed my face and felt my thoughts clear, a little of the formless dread departing. I had been foolish, I thought, for allowing a dream to unsettle me so. Ness was dead and gone. What harm could she do me now?

I raised my head and wiped my face dry on a towel that smelled of lavender-water. In the mirror above the washstand, my reflection was colourless in the moonlight, and I saw that my hair had sprung free of its braid. By reflex, I reached back to fix it. Instead, I found my neatly bound hair still lying across my shoulder in defiance of the image before me. My mouth gaped in shock, but my reflection's mouth did not. Staring back at me from the mirror, her corpse-pale features outlined in the vivid corona of her hair, her eyes fixed on mine in an expression of accusation and betrayal, was the unmistakable face of Ness Suilvain.

* * *

Afterwards, when the maid had cleared away the shards of the broken mirror and the doctor had cleaned and bandaged my bleeding hand, I listened through the haze of the brandy and the bedroom door to the soft conversation outside.

"But she will be quite all right?" Angus was saying, a pleading note in his voice.

Quite all right," the doctor echoed. He was an Englishman, as much of a stranger in these northern parts as I, and I took a strange comfort in the familiarity of his accent. "Hysteria isn't so uncommon in a new bride. We see it quite often, you know, and is all the more to be expected if there's been a recent bereavement. In a few weeks or months, I dare say she'll have something else on her mind, and the whole thing will blow over, you wait and see."

I listened to Angus offer his grateful thanks and the doctor issue a solemn promise to return in the morning. His footsteps receded and I heard the great oak front door close. Angus crept back into the bedroom and lowered himself carefully into the bed, assuming I was asleep and taking great care not to wake me. I waited until the monotony of his snores had begun before opening my eyes to fix them on a square of wood panelling opposite the bed, where I could be sure that the moon would cast no light.

★ ★ ★

"I feel so foolish," I said, when the golden morning sun had dispelled all of the prior night's strangeness. "I'm so sorry for all the trouble I caused."

My head hurt from the brandy and whatever sedative the doctor had slipped into my glass, but I felt otherwise clearheaded and more than a little ashamed of my bewildering outburst. I was a rational woman, after all, not a foolish housemaid seeing spooks in every shadow.

"There's nothing to apologise for," Angus said, his tone full of false brightness. "The doctor says it's only to be expected, what with all the changes you've had to deal with of late."

I could see the unease in his eyes — that half-formed worry that these were the first signs of madness in the woman to which he had so recently yoked himself. I did my best to dispel his fears.

"You're quite right, I'm sure." I forced a light laugh from my throat. "Everything is rather strange and new here at Suilvain, but I'm sure it'll feel like home soon enough."

"Exactly!" My words seemed to have done something to reassure him, and when he went on, his voice had regained a little of its usual confidence. "It's such an empty old house, with only us and the staff. But in a few years, once there's some new life to the place, I expect we'll hardly recognise it."

It took me a moment to catch his meaning, but when I did, it came with a dull stab of resignation. At no point in his brief courtship had Angus expressed a desire for children, but I should have known that he would expect, at the very least, an heir to the title and estates. I had no inclination in that direction whatsoever, but to make the attempt was, I supposed, part of the price of my security here. I curved my lips into a smile of delight.

"I can hardly wait," I lied.

★ ★ ★

I was confined to my bed all morning, but after the doctor returned I was permitted to rise and sit in the parlour. Later, when my hysteria showed no signs of re-emerging, I was allowed to take a short constitutional around the grounds. Angus accompanied me, his concern almost a physical presence as he fluttered at my shoulder. Despite his attentions, I was soothed by the cool air and the colours of the turning leaves. Our path led us past the kitchen garden and all of its enticing herbaceous smells, through the little copse with the folly that Angus's father had built as a wedding gift for his wife, and down to the brook that divided the park from the acreage of the Home Farm. We followed it in companionable silence, and I felt my anxieties about the future ease as I saw how quickly my husband had allowed his fears to subside. Perhaps this episode had been a good thing, I reasoned. A little vulnerability on my part would be no bad thing when it came to kindling a sense of manly protectiveness in him.

I had forgotten where the little stream – the burn, I supposed, the family would call it in their lilting Highland accents – led, and the sight of the lily-pond took me by surprise. I managed to hide it well. Angus's hand squeezed mine, and I looked up at him in mute sympathy. We stood at the edge of the water, both lost in our thoughts, although I could read his as clearly as any book in the library. He was thinking of his sister, floating amongst the lilies. My thoughts were of her too, but not as she had been in death.

* * *

On the night of the wedding, every window in Suilvain House had been lit, the golden lamplight spilling across the park and down the torchlit driveway. As I'd stood by the pond, the sounds of celebration, music and laughter echoed from the distance. The taste of champagne lingered on my tongue, and despite the chill of the night air, my face burned as I picked my way across the damp grass towards her. She was lovely in the moonlight, the emerald of her gown complementing the glorious mane of her hair. A lesser woman might have worn it curled in a tight chignon as fashion demanded, but not Ness. Her hair flowed around her shoulders and down her back, a curl on either side spilling forward across the bodice of her gown. From the colour of her cheeks, I could tell she, too, had been drinking.

"I was looking for you," I said. I slid my arm around her waist and kissed her. She tasted of honey and woodsmoke.

"I needed some air," she said. She turned away, her gaze fixed on the moonlit waters before her.

"What's wrong?" I asked.

The silence between us stretched out like a dark forest path.

"I can't do this."

"What do you mean?" I took a step forward so that we were

standing side by side. She had kicked off her shoes and was standing in her stocking soles. Even so, she was a head taller than me. She swayed a little.

"This," she breathed. "I thought I could watch you marry him and not feel..." She shot me a haunted glance, and I saw her eyes were rimmed with red. "Not feel like I do."

Dread squeezed my heart. "I know it's difficult," I said as gently as I could. "For both of us. But it'll be worth it. As Angus's wife, I can stay at Suilvain as I could never have done as merely your friend. We can be together every day and no one can say a thing about it."

"And every night, I get to watch you go to my brother's bed, while I go and sleep on my own." Fat tears left slug-trails down Ness's freckled cheeks.

"Isn't that better?" I took her hand, twining her trembling fingers in mine. "Better than having nothing, at all?"

"It didn't have to be nothing," she said wretchedly. "We could have gone away together, had a proper life, somewhere no one would know us or care what we do—"

"And where did you have in mind?" I pressed. "People see things, and they talk. Here, if anyone were to suspect, we would at least have the protection of the family name."

I tried to hold onto her hand, but she wriggled her fingers out of my grip and snatched them away.

"The family name," she echoed, and then fell silent. I could hear the faint splash of some small living thing making its way through the water. "It's your name now. I wish you all the joy of it, truly I do."

"What do you mean?" An icy finger traced my spine, and the world lurched in a way I couldn't entirely blame on the champagne.

"It's not fair on Angus, me being here. You're *his* wife now. What was I thinking? That it was right to deceive my own brother, to make a lie of his marriage, his whole life? That's not what I want."

I stared at her, open-mouthed. "And what about me? What about what *I* want?"

"You have it," she said. Her voice was thick with self-pity. "What you always wanted. And I was a fool to ever think that it was me."

She turned her tear-stained face to me, her eyes and nose streaming and swollen, her gown muddy and stained to the knee. "I won't go on pretending, Lottie."

It was easy to let my pain turn to disgust, to spin on my heel and leave her standing like her own effigy by the silent water.

★ ★ ★

"She loved to come here when we were little," Angus said. "I suppose it makes sense that she wanted to be here at the end. Where she'd been happiest."

"I hope it brought her some comfort." My eyes prickled with tears that, to my surprise – maybe even my horror – were not entirely feigned.

"I prayed it was an accident," he said, as we walked across the park back towards the house. "That she had lost her footing and fallen in – I know she had drunk too much that night, with that taste for whisky of hers. I saw her leave the party, and now I wish… I wish I had thought to go after her. But I was so happy, everyone was." He swallowed. "And now to know how she must have felt, so desolate as to take her own life…"

"We cannot be sure of that."

"No." He gave me a weak smile. "I suppose we never shall be."

Above us, the colour slowly drained from the sky.

"We could plant a tree," he added, almost as an afterthought. "A willow by the water, perhaps. Something living. She would have liked that better than a granite headstone."

I nodded. At least he hadn't suggested naming our first daughter after her, but I was sure he would express that sentimental notion before long.

Dusk had fallen by the time we returned, and the chill of autumn was in the air. We took a late supper together in the parlour. Once the last plates were cleared away, I felt restored to some semblance of equilibrium.

"I shall hope for a more restful night than the last," I said, permitting myself a smile, which my husband returned with a warmer one of his own.

"It could hardly fail to be more so," he said, and I rewarded him with a laugh.

"They'll be guising in the village tonight," he said, "but they'll not disturb us here. Not with the house in mourning."

Something troubled me about his words. Guising, Ness had told me long ago, was the local custom where the village children would paint their faces with soot or ochre, and go begging for sweets from house to house – but the night for that was All Hallows, and it should have been two weeks past.

"They are a little late for that, are they not?"

"No, it's the night for it, sure enough." The black crepe around the mirror-frame had fallen over the clock and the little brass calendar beside it, and he moved it to one side to show the date. If it was to be believed, only two weeks had passed since Ness's death.

"Surely, the maid has simply failed to turn the day?" I offered.

He shook his head. "I have yesterday's *Herald*, and Thursday's."

I looked up at the mirror and saw the window reflected, with the grounds outside and the moon hanging heavy and silver in the sky.

"But what about the moon?"

Angus's brows furrowed. "What do you mean?"

"The moon in the glass–" I managed. "The full moon – do you not see it?"

His face creased with worry. "Charlotte, listen to me. There is no moon. There is no moon in the glass, nor in the sky. Look."

He turned me from the mirror to the casement and threw the window open to display the majesty of the night sky beyond.

There were Venus and mighty Jupiter, Orion the Hunter and the Seven Sisters, all twinkling in the clear Highland air. But there was no moon. Only a circle of perfect darkness obscured where it hid amongst the stars.

"But there was a full moon the night of the wedding—"

Angus was shaking his head. "Yes, and it has only been two weeks, Charlotte. We were married on the eve of Saint Luke. Remember?"

Two weeks? Two weeks since she had drowned, two weeks that had turned me from a bride to a wife, and yet the moon in the glass was still full. Had it been so every night since the wedding, perceptible to me alone? How had I failed to notice what should have been obvious from the outset?

I ran from the parlour and out into the hall, heedless of the startled maids and Angus's shouts of alarm. The mosaic floor and sweeping staircase were lit with white moonlight that shone, not through the rose window high above my head, but from the vast mirror on the wall. And there, her face as familiar to me as my own, was Ness, twin moons reflecting in her open green eyes.

My shrill scream of panic hardly seemed of this earth. I fumbled blindly at the hall table behind me and felt my fingers close around the narrow neck of a vase. I hurled it at the mirror. With an echoing crash, water, flowers, porcelain and glass flew into the air, each glittering shard glowing with an unearthly pale light. Heavy footsteps heralded Angus's approach behind me, and I fled up the stairs, ignoring his cries. Each mirror I passed, each polished vase and picture frame, reflected the unforgiving moonlight, and in it, the dead face of Ness Suilvain, her eyes always fixed on mine.

There was no moon in the sky, and the light that wrapped around me like a shroud was the light of an older moon – borrowed through time, cast through a mirror, shining from the dead moon's ghost. And I knew that moon: the precise angle that it hung in the sky displayed the lines and craters on its surface – that same silver orb had reflected in the water of the lily-pond and in Ness's dead and staring eyes.

★ ★ ★

As I had walked away from Ness on my wedding night, I heard her weeping in loud, ostentatious sobs that seemed deliberately intended to draw attention towards her. True, the house was a good distance away from the lily-pond, and the music still echoed merrily across the grounds, but what if a drunken guest or a courting couple should stumble across her and find her playing the part of the heartbroken heroine? How would she explain her grief on this happiest of nights? Even the least perceptive of the guests would realise that something was amiss, and rumours would spread – the sort of rumours that would tarnish my reputation as the lady of Suilvain. A few words from her lips could destroy me entirely, and a sudden fear grew in my gut that she would confess all in a spurned, self-destructive fury. Her love now loomed as a greedy, twisted obsession – one that would see me destroyed if her only alternative was to see me in the arms of her brother. Had she not insinuated as much a few moments before? But I had gambled too much to lose everything now. Besides, was she not the one who had reneged on our deal? Who had spurned my own feelings? We had agreed on a course of action, and she had turned against me. The consequences of that decision were hers to bear.

She half-turned as I reached her, her lips parting in confusion. An altogether different sort of surprise seized her face when I shoved her into the water. Her willowy frame toppled with a too-loud splash – I had always been the stronger of the two of us – and she managed only a few feeble kicks while I pushed her head beneath the water and held it there. Slowly, her pathetic struggles ceased, and I found myself standing alone in waist-deep water. I had no cause to fear Ness's words any longer. A little more work and my secret – my future – would be safe forever.

I bundled the ruined gown into the trunk that had once carried my shabby possessions from my old life to Suilvain and dressed myself in a fresh gown, another gift from Angus and quite as lovely as the one I had discarded. I rejoined the party, blaming a spilt glass of red wine for my sudden need to change. Angus was in such a state of merriment by then that my absence – and his sister's – had escaped his notice. I took that as a good omen for my future marriage, and did my best to put the past behind me.

* * *

My headlong dash came to an end in the attic, in a bare-walled little bedchamber that held only a pair of iron bedsteads and a barred and shuttered window. I stood in the centre of the room, sweat dripping from me like from a windblown racehorse, my limbs trembling so vigorously I could barely stand. The skin of my hands was torn and bleeding. Dimly, hazy as a nightmare, I remembered smashing mirror after mirror while I fled through the house, followed always by her reproachful moonlit gaze. There was no looking glass in this room, but still, I could feel her eyes upon me. My hands trailed bloody smears across the walls as I searched for a hidden mirror, for any polished metal or reflective surface, through which she might perceive me. There was nothing, only the maddening pressure of her disembodied gaze.

"Where are you?"

My hands were raised, bracing me against the wall, and I caught a glint of silver light on my wedding ring. It was a plain gold band, polished to a mirror shine, and my stomach lurched. I tried to tear it from my hand, but the fit was tight and my fingers were slippery with blood. There was no weapon in the room, no knife nor shard of glass that I could have used to sever the digit. I stood, helpless, unable to tear my eyes from hers.

The door burst open, and Angus was there, his hair wild and his face crazed with concern.

"Charlotte! What is it? What can be the matter?"

"It's her!"

His mouth was gaping open as he looked from me to the blood-streaked walls and back again. "Who?"

"Ness!" I shrieked, hearing the shuttered window rattle in its frame in sympathy with the sound. "In the mirror, in the glass, in the metal – everywhere – her face! Tell me!" I shouted at the night, "What is it – what is it that you want?"

Though the room was dark, her face reflected in her brother's eyes – so like her own in colour and shape. Her lips formed silent words:

Tell him. Tell him what you did.

"Then will you give me peace? Dear God, Ness – yes, anything, only let me be!" Angus seized me by the shoulders and held me firmly, though his hands trembled against my skin. "Charlotte, for God's sake, you must calm yourself! The doctor is coming, he will help you–"

"No one can help me! She will not stop, she will never leave me unless..." I raised my hand; from the metal of my wedding band, Ness looked back at me in mute accusation. "I killed her! I loved her – and I drowned her for fear she'd tell the world what we were to one another!"

The door hung wide open, and in the passage beyond, the servants were gathering. Their alarm turned to shock and horrified realisation as they absorbed the meaning of my confession.

"There! Are you happy now, Ness? Is it enough? Will you *let me be?*"

Angus let his hands drop from my shoulders. Ness was gone from his eyes.

Reflected in her place was a wide-eyed, wild-haired harpy of a woman I no longer recognised. Her gown was torn, her cheeks streaked with tears and the bloody marks of her own clawing fingers. It was the face of a woman with nothing, a woman fit only to end her days in Bedlam.

BRIDEPRICE

S.T. Gibson

Firstborn

Constanta is what you called me when you found me bleeding out in front of the smithery, holding onto life out of spite.

I heard you first, the creak of leather and clink of mail. Then saw the tattered hem of a cloak and an insignia old as the Carpathians pinned to your throat.

Constanta, you whispered, touching my mangled red hair; *can nothing kill you?*

Did I ever have another name? I had a family at least, before the greed of a king's war swallowed them whole, leaving nothing but a daughter beaten half to death. My bunἴ had whispered stories of a demon who roamed the battlefields after the killing had ended, a night creature so unholy the devil never invited him in for dinner.

I suppose I half expected you.

You knelt in the rainwater and pressed your lips to the pulse quickly going quiet in my wrist.

You will not last long, steel willed though you are. They have broken you. Badly. The drunken singing of the raiders wafted towards us on the breeze as I coughed up bubbles of blood.

This was my land once, Constanta. Your people, my subjects. I am going to do you a twofold kindness, you said, kissing me softly on the mouth. *I will raise you out of the dirt and into queenship.*

I felt the pain of your teeth dully, as though from deep underwater, but the tang of your blood on my parched tongue was hot and sharp. Suddenly I did not fear the clang of approaching armour, could not remember ever being afraid.

And I will give you your vengeance, you hissed as my veins filled with the strength of a dozen men. *Water your mother's flowers with their blood.*

Secondborn

I was Magdalena marquis' daughter, the jewel of Spain and twenty years unwed. I received ten suitors a day, poor boys so tight in the trousers and heartsick at the sight of me, men who had crawled over deserts simply to look upon my face. I delighted in watching them simper and fawn for me, offering stables of horses and ships full of spices if only I would marry them. I applauded when they drew swords over which one of them I had shared a smile with. But you were different, my lord.

Vicious little wolf, you said when I was presented to you. *Coat of gleaming black, eyes of flashing grey, and those claws! You must sink them into many servants and tailors, if you're really as cruel as they say.*

The footman had drawn your carriage around to the guest-house, and were whispering among themselves about an ageless woman dressed in grey silk.

She is my wife, you said, drawing my gloved hands to your pale lips, *and there's ample room in that coach for another.*

I wore my most merciless dress to dinner and danced the bolero for you with teeth bared. During dessert, you nursed me from your cup while Constanta touched the curls at the nape of my neck.

I love my Constanta like other men love crowns, but tales of your cunning stretch all the way into the north. How could I resist such a dark miracle?

You had always wanted a creature as hard as yourself, a bride as sharp as a slap from your father and wicked as the jokes your brothers used to whisper to you during mass. You promised me bloodletting, the only pleasured power I had yet to wield, and a life without laws to chafe against.

The servants had my possessions packed up before midnight, and everything that came after that was as simple as sinning.

Thirdborn

It was Russia in 1919 and my beauty was all that was keeping me fed. You found me shivering in that artist's studio, naked as the graces and posturing like a boy playing at soldiers. I do not think you expected to find a new bride among the wax fruit and fake marble, nor for him to be a half-starved silhouette for hire, but I have never once seen you show your surprise, my prince.

You are the very splendor of Ancient Greece, you said, less concerned with the painting you had commissioned than with the way the light streaming in through the attic window hit my skin. *I should call you Ganymede.*

I was raised by the aesthete degenerates of Saint Petersburg, actors and artists who loved me for my long lashes and golden hair. In a lifetime populated with the dregs of society, you stood out so starkly, black blood on new snow. And your women! As haughty and fair as lost tsarinas, the one with her crown of jet hair and the other with eyes like loss.

They tell me your name is Alexi, you said when you caught me looking. *That you have no kin, no family name. Tell me, did you ever wish for sisters?*

How my stomach trembled when you touched me! You draped me in your coat and Magdalena gave me her mink, Constanta her winter gloves. You paid the painter twice my fee and led me towards your sable horses stamping in the snow.

I promise you bread and roe, pheasant and mackerel, vodka and pomegranates from here until eternity, you said, so soft the ice of your breath stirred my hair. *Ballerinas and chairmen will dine at our table and you will know nothing but bounty.*

The girls complain that the undying life is too cold, but I say cold is winter snuffling at your door and no money for the grocer. I say I have never been warmer.

LURE OF THE ABYSS

Jenna MacDonald

I am alone.

I can't do this by myself.

The *Petunia* isn't the biggest ship, yet four people had hardly been enough crew for her. I know I don't have what it takes to finish this voyage alone. Desperation washes over me and I leave the wheel, leaning over the rail to stare down into the cobalt blue of the ocean. The sunlight bounces off the waves, flashing like a million diamonds in the light. I see something out of the corner of my eye and turn my head.

It's her.

She's just below the surface, her dark, powerful tail propelling her upwards and forwards in time with the ship so she appears motionless. Everything about her is dark – her hair, her skin, her tail, and those intense eyes – but in the sunlight, she shimmers like the waves.

"You're here for me, then," I say out loud, even though I have no idea if she understands human speech.

The mermaid maintains eye contact for a few moments before silently sinking into the depths.

I sigh as she leaves. It would be easier if she just took me now to get it over with – before I become hopelessly lost at sea or crash on some shoals and slowly waste away. I tell myself that is the only reason I want to see her again.

I was lucky to have gotten this job, according to my father, and fortunate enough that my mother had taught me English, her native language. The *Petunia* and her crew came from England, on a small merchant vessel bound for the Port of Cape Town. Because I refused to settle down and marry a man, bribing a crew that wasn't native to Santander and was in desperate need of another set of hands was my father's last-ditch effort in getting me to accomplish something in my life. He was a sailor too, so he was proud about passing the profession down to his only daughter.

I imagine the bribe was necessary based on how superstitious sailors are. Simply because of my gender, I am bad luck to have aboard – it is said that women are a portent of rough seas and raging storms. I've never tested it out, but apparently, I possess the ability to be so distracting that male sailors will become bad enough at their jobs to anger the sea gods.

Maybe there was something to those superstitions, because I don't feel very fortunate now. I don't recall murderous mermaids being part of the curse I carried in my blood, but it's possible I never paid enough attention when my father spoke of superstition.

On our thirteenth night into our month-long journey, she came for Len, the unlucky bastard who was on watch duty under a sky as black as her tail. Out of our 'all-male-except-Jules' crew, he had been the kindest to me, and I still would have preferred to spend my time with something more pleasant, like one of those awful blobfish. Or a wet mop. We almost didn't notice that he was taken; we were all asleep. If Len hadn't cried out as she started pulling him overboard, we wouldn't have had a clue. He would have just been gone, a slight dark shadow off the starboard bow the only inclination that something was amiss.

Our first real look at her was when she came for David, four days after the loss of Len. This time, she arrived in the middle of a storm, wind howling through the rigging and rain lashing the deck, making the world slippery and precarious. With a crew of three, keeping the *Petunia* on course was an immense effort when the waves were taller than her hull. David was manning the helm while Thomas and I struggled with the sails, the three of us exerting every ounce of energy we had.

I watched as a crack of lightning lit the entire world, and then everything seemed to proceed in slow motion. My eyes were drawn to her, using her powerful tail to propel her up and through a wave that was bearing down towards the deck, her dark hair in flowing tangles around her. She was beautiful, in the way that the raging storm around us was beautiful. Wild and raw.

There was no time to scream. The wave washed over the deck and I saw her grab onto David before I was buffeted down to the deck by the roaring water, clinging to the rigging for my life. When I managed to get back up, David was gone, and then we were two.

It was five days before we saw her again after that, and Thomas and I spent that time in a snarl of nerves frequently misplaced as aggression. When she finally came for him, it was the middle of a beautiful afternoon. After the storm, the weather had become perfect for sailing. Thomas and I were already at each other's throats without the added stress of Mother Nature. With the amount of work and watch shifts doubled, and the looming fear of death, tension gripped us in a vice.

Though Thomas and I were never friends, his death hit me the hardest. I was up in the rigging, retying lines together that frayed under the onslaught of the elements. It took me a few minutes before I spotted the shadow under the sea's surface, and a few moments longer to realise what it was. I watched as she watched – waiting for an opportune moment to make her move. I yelled down to Thomas, frantic, but the only response I got was a rude gesture. I watched in horror as he leaned over the rail to dump out a bucket, expecting her to strike. And she did, but only after she surfaced, ever so slowly, and gave me a lazy grin full of long, razor-sharp teeth. I was rooted in place by her onyx stare, so I saw everything when Thomas turned his back and she lunged out of the water, grabbed hold of him, and instantaneously disappeared into the depths with her prize. All of those times I had wished he would fall overboard or disappear... now he had.

I shake my head to clear my thoughts and bring myself back to the present. It's only been hours since Thomas was taken. I can't fall apart just yet. Dwelling on things never helps; I've learned that lesson time and time again.

The day passes in a blur as I try valiantly to do the work of four people. The sails need to be trimmed when the winds pick up in the afternoon and pulling them in leaves me exhausted. Between adjusting the sails, I do my best to consult the charts and a compass to see if I am even headed south and adjust the helm accordingly. As soon as I do that, the winds die down, and I am forced to adjust the sails again. This stretch of ocean is clear of obstacles according to my charts, and if there was anything good about David, it was that he never purchased the cheap maps.

But as the sun sets, my fear rises. If I've correctly judged my position earlier, I still have nearly a week before I reach port. My food and supplies will last now that there is only me, but my energy will not. Already, I can tell that I won't be able to keep this up throughout the entire night.

I know the mermaid is coming for me, just as she came for Len and David and Thomas. And while I can't say that I miss them, I don't want to go the same way they did. What if that means seeing them in the afterlife?

Planning ahead is most likely futile, but my brain needs something to keep me moving forward, to keep me from giving up and jumping overboard right now, so I don't let myself stop. Instead, I push through my growing fatigue and do my best to keep the ship on course, berating myself through the growing haze.

I watch as the sun sinks down to meet the horizon, in a hurry, as if coming home to a loved one after a long day of work. The thought brings a wry smile to my face, and then I see it. I always thought it was the stuff of legends, but there it is, just for a moment – a green flash, right as the sun disappears below the line where sky meets water. I laugh as I recall the myth my father taught me so many years ago:

"While I'm gone, Julia, keep a weather eye on the horizon. If you keep a lookout at the death of the day, you might see a brilliant green light. But look carefully – it only lasts for a moment. The green flash is a sign that your loved one is nearby. Keep an eye out for that green flash, my darling daughter, and know that if you see it, I am on my way back to you."

I never saw that flash, and while my father did return, he never stayed. Until now, I thought he made the whole thing up just to give me hope, or to provide me with an excuse to escape English lessons with my mother for a few moments. I laugh aloud at the irony of finally seeing it now, alone at sea.

The dark begins to settle in, as familiar with its position as a well-worn cloak around old shoulders. The shine from the stars and the light of the moon illuminate the deck enough that I am thankfully able to see without issue. I have enough to worry about without tripping over anything. With the darkness comes a stiff breeze and I struggle to furl in the sails yet again. I'm not overly worried about the ship capsizing, but if I were to lose one of those sails, I might as well drown myself now. Pulling them in might leave me less vulnerable to the whims of the sea – might even allow me a few hours of sleep.

It takes me almost an hour, but I finally get the two large sails pulled in and tied down. Panting, I lean back against the mast, when suddenly the hairs on the back of my neck rise and a shiver courses down my spine.

Slowly, as slowly as I can manage, I get my breathing in check and turn around. At first, I don't see anything. But even while I fought with rope and canvas, my fear was never gone, just tucked away in a corner, waiting to recapture my attention. With no small amount of trepidation, I peer out into the black water.

She's difficult to spot, but she's there, just like I thought. Her dark hair billows around her as she watches me with large, dark eyes, her ebony face inches below the surface of the waves. If I hadn't known what to look for, I would have missed her in the inky black water. A slight thrill goes through me as we make eye contact, her almost-black locked onto my blue. Then she disappears.

I don't even notice her move; one second, she is bobbing at the surface, staring at me, and the next she is gone with scarcely a ripple. My chest pangs at her withdrawal, stemming from the fear of not knowing where to expect her next. Or when. But I know it won't be long, now. She must know that I'm easy prey – that I'm the only one left.

I busy myself with other tasks: coiling the lines that I had carelessly thrown aside earlier; checking, double-checking, and triple-checking the charts; devising a way to lash the helm down so it won't shift until I move it. The work keeps my body busy, and I do my best to keep my mind engaged as well, with moderate success. I keep glancing over my shoulder every few seconds and I flinch at every noise.

Finally, I reach my breaking point. My muscles are aching and my mind is moving in a hundred different directions at once until I feel like I am going to either collapse or break apart. Perhaps both.

"If you're out there, just come for me already," I call into the dark as I sink down onto the deck. "This is only the first night and I can't do it. I just can't. So either come and get me now or the sharks will beat you to it when I drown."

I don't know what I expect to happen, but there is no response. I sit for a few more moments feeling sorry for myself and then climb back up to my feet. If Jules Verrara is going to die, it's not going to be like this.

I circle the deck a couple more times, checking that everything is in order. I check the charts one last time. There is a slight scattering of shoals up ahead, but I predict they're still at least half a day off. The wind is finally calm now and, other than fear, I can't think of any reason not to try to get some rest. I drag a pile of canvas tucked into one of the corners over to the helm. I will be more protected from the elements there and I will still be on deck in case something happens. I settle down into the canvas, exhausted enough that I don't care that it's not the most comfortable thing. I've slept on worse, so it doesn't bother me as much as it probably should. It doesn't take long before sleep overcomes me and I drift off to uneasy dreams.

The light is dim when I startle awake with an overwhelming sense of unease. I whirl around and it takes me a moment to get my bearings. Remembering where I am only raises my disquiet. I look around again, carefully, and then—

I see her, out of the water with her dark arms crossed and resting on the deck. Those black, piercing eyes are staring right at me, and I can't believe I missed her initially.

"So, you were watching me sleep?"

I don't know why I ask. I know she isn't going to answer me, but the words are out before I think about them. There is no response.

"I would have preferred it if you just… killed me, or ate me, or whatever it is you do, while I was sleeping."

She doesn't answer – I'm not even sure if she knows what words are, let alone English – but she does cock her head to the side as I speak, her gaze never leaving nor wavering.

I suddenly feel very self-conscious. It has been over three weeks since I've had a proper bath, and I'm sure I look and smell frightful.

"It's not polite to stare," I point out.

This time, she flashes me what I can only assume is another grin – but all I can see are rows and rows of needle-like teeth in a mouth far too large to be human. Then suddenly, she is gone. Just like before, I don't actually see her leave. She's there, and then she's not.

Nervously, I sink lower into the canvas and wrap some of it around me. Regardless of what she does, I need to sleep, and there are still a few more hours before proper daylight. I shiver a little, thinking about how she was watching me, biding her time, but it isn't long before exhaustion overtakes me once again.

* * *

When I wake up, the sun is climbing in the sky and there is no shadowy figure staring at me. I'm still on course, at least as near as I can tell, but that means that a particularly shallow set of shoals is coming up soon. I do my best to prepare, checking all of the lines on the sails and propping myself in the bow so I can see over the railing. My proximity to the water sends tremors through me, but I steel myself and don't back down.

"If she comes for me, then she comes for me. But if she doesn't, I'm not about to die because I was a damn coward," I mutter out loud, hoping to reaffirm my actions. I'm not entirely sure it works to quell my fear, but I remain in place until I see the waves breaking ahead.

The white caps of the wave signal the shallow waters where they are finally able to reach the bottom and break with a vengeance. I try to imprint their placement in my memory before rushing back to the helm. It's hard to see from here, so I'll have to make do and cash in on any good fortune I might have stocked up.

I take a deep breath as I calculate that I'm passing over the first shoal, and I veer the *Petunia* towards the deepest waters I can find based on the charts next to me. There is no ear-shattering sound of hull crunching against coral and I sigh in relief.

"I've got this," I say, moments before the *Petunia* shudders to a halt, proving that I most definitely do not have this.

The impact throws me forwards and I slam into the wheel, hissing at the pain. I didn't hit hard enough to break anything, but I'm pretty sure I can already feel the bruises forming. I rush forwards as quickly as I can to unfurl all of the sails, hoping that I can catch some wind — any wind — that might help me break free. With a sinking feeling, I realise that I must be too low in the water.

"Jules, it's either don't live or don't get paid. And you can't really get paid if you don't live," I chide myself as I rush down below deck.

The *Petunia* is a trading vessel, and she may be small, but she could fit a king's ransom in her hold. Enough that I wouldn't need to get another job for probably a year after selling this stuff in the markets of Cape Town, where I'm positive it will fetch a high price. I already had my vacation in Cape Town planned, although I suppose now that Len, David, and Thomas are all gone, England is going to want her ship back and I'll have to be the one to deliver.

Instead, I find myself carrying bolts of the finest fabrics, chests laden with coins, aromatic teas that left the dark space smelling almost homey, and other things I could never afford on my own up to the deck, where I promptly dump them into the water.

"If I appease you with this, will you leave me alone?" I call the challenge out to the air as I continue hauling up goods and tossing them into the sea. I'm not looking for a response.

I can feel the moment that the ship becomes buoyant enough to lift up off of the reef with a slight jolt, and almost instantly, I'm moving again as the winds filling the sail finally have the chance to propel me forward. I let out a whoop of joy and let myself celebrate for a moment.

Now that the ship is lighter, it skims over the top of the shoals. I can still occasionally feel the hull scrape against the bottom and I grit my teeth, but thankfully, I don't stop moving. Perhaps I had some good fortune tucked away somewhere, after all. I feel victorious; I survived my first real test, so who's to say I won't last this entire journey?

The rest of the day passes, and as the sun sets, my confidence grows. The route ahead of me seems straightforward, so I let myself settle back down into my canvas nest and close my eyes.

When I wake next, the world is dark. I startle as I see dark shadows on the deck around me, my mind leaping to wild and otherworldly conclusions. I lay frozen until my eyes adjust, and when they finally do, I gasp.

Soaking wet, with water running in rivulets across the deck and back home to the sea, is everything I threw overboard, stacked haphazardly along the port side. I blink a few times and then rub my eyes, but it's no trick. Everything I unloaded to get across the shoals is back on board the *Petunia*.

I know immediately who it must have been; there is really only one option. I just don't understand it. Slowly, I rise to my feet and peer out into the jet-black night. Sure enough, not so far away, is my mermaid.

"So what, you kill all of my crew and then feel bad about it and try to make it up to me?" I ask conversationally, as if talking to a murderous mermaid was something I do every day.

Her only response is swimming a fraction closer to the ship. I feel the adrenaline start to kick in as my heart stutters. In the dark, she looks ethereal, almost glowing.

"Because I mean, you probably should." After a moment, I add, "I would prefer to uh, not die though, if it's all the same to you."

A look of something akin to displeasure crosses her face, and she vanishes.

"I'm sorry my will to live offends you!" I call in a singsong voice while rolling my eyes.

Suddenly, she's back, and her face is mere inches below mine. I feel my heart stop in my chest as I struggle to comprehend how she scaled the side of the ship. Before, I thought her eyes were soulless ink, but now I know that I was so very wrong. This close, there is a glint to them that I didn't notice before. It's as if someone stole all of the stars from the night sky and condensed them into the dark orbs of her eyes. I am at the mercy of her gaze.

She flashes me a smile. Where before it was all wicked teeth, this time it seems... almost timid. Her long fangs are hidden away, and she blinks once. As she does, I feel her hold on me lessen.

"Do you... come here often?" I ask, slightly breathless. I immediately want to hit my head against the railing.

Her smile widens, and I see the tips of her fangs – the only light thing about her, pointing out from behind her dark lips.

I'm not sure what to do next. I suddenly understand all of the legends of the mythical siren, able to lure sailors to their watery graves, because I have no desire to do anything besides stare at the creature in front of me. If breathing and blinking weren't automatic body functions, I probably would have forgotten them.

Slowly, she slides back down towards the water, and I feel myself leaning over the rail, following her. I lean too far and my balance gives way. I scramble to grab the railing, but it's still wet and slick from where the mermaid had piled my goods on the deck. My fingers slide and leave me falling.

I don't have time to shout before I hit the bone-chilling water with a splash that knocks the wind out of my body. The obsidian void surges in around me, and for a moment, my heart screams in my chest – afraid the ocean will swallow me whole. Then my body snaps back into action. I kick my way up to the surface, thrashing towards my ship. Panic weighs down my limbs even as they flail – it finally occurs to me that the mermaid who killed my three shipmates has just gotten me into the water as well, and my chances of survival are slim to none.

I have no idea how I am going to get back up on the *Petunia*. I made sure nothing was hanging over the edge to avoid an unwelcome visit from my shadow – a futile gesture.

The hairs on the back of my neck rise, and I cease in my struggles. I take a deep breath as I turn around to face my doom.

She is floating only a few feet behind me. I kick backwards with a startle.

Her face tilts up into something that resembles humour.

"I'd appreciate it if you didn't laugh at me before you kill me," I manage to huff out, getting a nice mouthful of saltwater for my troubles. I spit it out, and some of it hits the mermaid in the face. My heart plummets.

She freezes and my dread increases. Then, she scoops up a mouthful of water and spits it at my face.

"What the hell?" I splutter indignantly, flailing a little in the water.

Her response is a gurgling noise that sounds almost like an eerie version of laughter. It sets my nerves on edge but I give a tentative laugh in return.

Like all the other times I have seen her disappear, she is instantly gone. Not seeing her is terrifying, and I suddenly remember that I am treading water in an inky abyss, with the almost-endless nothing below me. I fight to keep my panic down and keep treading water. When she doesn't return after a moment, I turn towards the ship and start kicking as fiercely as my cold-numbed limbs allow.

I'm nearly there when something grabs my legs, and I let out a scream. For days, I've impatiently waited for death; now that it's here, this is not how I want to go. I knew I was never going to die a hero's death, but something a little more glamorous, a little more daring, than drowning in the middle of the night after an accidental fall would have been nice. I lash out until I realise that I am not being pulled downwards; instead, I am being pushed upwards.

Back onto the deck of the *Petunia*.

I hit the wood hard, but I don't care when it means I am no longer drowning. I roll over onto my back and stare up at the cloudy night sky, gasping. A noise alerts me to the mermaid's presence, but I can't be bothered to look.

"Listen," I pant out, "if you wanted to kill me you just had so many opportunities. I can't even count how many. So either do it. Now. Or give up, because I'm not playing this game anymore. I'm not going to keep looking over my shoulder in fear and waiting to be dragged off to the depths or to feel your teeth in my leg. We're either doing this or we're not."

I tilt my head at an uncomfortable angle and find her perched on the rail. Her head is cocked to the side in what I have come to think of as her gesture of confusion.

I lay there for a few more moments in silence, catching my breath. She makes no move to attack me, and I make no move to do anything, at all. Eventually, I pull myself back up to my feet. I cast her a wary glance. It takes everything in me, but I turn my back to her and head to the helm and the charts.

When I finally glance back at her, she is still in the same spot on the rail, peering at me. I give her a little wave. After a pause, she returns it. I can't stop the laughter that erupts from me. I have spent days thinking this creature was going to kill me. I watched her kill my crew. And now, she's sitting on my ship after saving me from drowning, and *waving* at me. The whole thing is so absurd that now I'm sure I hit my head somewhere.

I go about my business, fixing the lines and trimming the sails. Every so often I send her a surreptitious glance. She is staring at me so intently that she catches every one. And each time, she gives me one of those tentative smiles that make my heart flutter. I don't think I can blame that on fear anymore.

Which is a problem I decide to deal with later. For now, I'm more worried about navigating the shoals on my chart. There is a path through these shoals, but I will have to constantly change the trim of the sails and man the helm. I have many talents, but being in two places at once isn't one of them.

I leave the helm and run over to the mainsails to pull them in, praying that I'll catch the winds I need. All of this sail trimming is both exhausting and repetitive, and I don't think I'm any better at it now than I was before. Still, I have no other options. I pull the sail partially down and secure the line, then turn back to the helm.

To my surprise, the helm is holding steady. As I watch, it

slowly begins to turn to the left, exactly the direction and amount I would have turned it. The mermaid is gone.

It's a long battle for the next two hours as the sun peeks over the horizon and begins to climb, but the ship manages to make it through. As soon as I'm in open waters, I collapse onto my canvas nest. Shortly after, the mermaid emerges from the waves and climbs over the railing, water dripping down her form.

"Was that you?"

This time I earn one of those wild, full-teeth smiles.

"Well. That's the second time you've saved me instead of killing me today. So... thanks, I guess."

Her response is a high-pitched shriek that lights my every nerve on fire.

"All right, okay, wow," I say, rubbing my arms to rid them of goosebumps. "That's a new one. I really do appreciate your help." She remains silent.

I sigh. "I don't know why you're here, but I'd appreciate it if you didn't kill me in my sleep. You're welcome to stay, though," I add hastily. She may not be the best company, but I was already lonely, and I still have weeks left on this journey.

I don't remember falling asleep, but the sun is high in the sky when I wake. My eyes fly to where the mermaid had been sitting, and with a pang, I realise that she's gone. I sigh and roll over – and have to stifle a scream.

She's perched on one of the chests I had yet to put back belowdecks, her dark eyes boring into me. This is the first time I have seen her this closely in the light, and my heart stops. Everything about her is a sleek black, but as she shifts, the light catches on her scales and starts a wildfire of colour.

"Now I know you're trying to kill me," I grumble as soon as my heart restarts.

There is no answer. One of these days, I'll stop expecting one.

I get up and fish an apple from a crate, taking a large bite out of it. She stares at me curiously. I think as I chew.

"All right, I just want to get a few things straight here." I pause, cutting off my train of thought. "I don't know… blink once for yes and twice for no?"

She stares at me, unblinking.

I sigh but continue.

"Are you going to kill me?"

To my surprise, she blinks twice.

"Oh, you did understand me, perfect," I say, and then my brain catches up to her answer. "And you don't want to kill me, which is surprising? But in a good way. Honestly, I don't think I really want to die. Things to do, money to spend, the usual," I say as I wave my hand in the air. "So if you don't want to kill me, why are you here?"

She just stares blankly.

"Right, yes or no questions only. Sorry. Are you… planning to stay with the *Petunia*?" I chicken out of saying 'with me.'

She blinks once.

We continue in that fashion for a while. I ask her if she has a name (one blink), a family (two blinks), if she's ever befriended a sailor instead of killing them (two blinks), if she's ever befriended a sailor instead of killing them after today (one blink), if she's ever been to the Americas (two blinks).

Then something dawns on me.

"Did you leave only me alive on purpose?"

I hold my breath as she does nothing for a moment, and then a long, single blink follows.

"Okay, wow. Uh, well, we should be at port in Cape Town in two days. I was honestly planning to stay there for a while. I've spent a long time at sea, you know?" I realise what I just said, and who I said it to. "You live in the sea. Uh, yeah, I'm sure you know that then. Or, maybe you don't? It's your home, so maybe you don't get homesick if you're always in your home. Then again, when people go to different places, they get homesick, so even though the ocean is just one thing it's awfully big and–"

I cut off, realizing that I'm rambling. She's staring at me so intently that I feel like she's hanging on my every word.

"You're planning to stay then?" I ask again. She responds with one long blink.

I can't stop the smile that spreads across my face. "You know, Cape Town seems overrated. I have enough food that I could just keep sailing; we could go anywhere. If you want."

She glances at me before looking away, and for a few moments that seem to stretch on for an eternity, she doesn't react. I open my mouth, almost certainly to start rambling again, when she makes eye contact with me. Those dark opalescent eyes meet my own and hold my gaze. Then, she gives me one blink, and a wide, toothy smile.

HEARTEATER

Eliza Temple

The night after the full moon, there was a man at the door. I answered it myself, peering carefully out at him through the gap.

"I'm sorry," he said, in a strange, high voice. "But I've nowhere else to go."

It had been storming all night. Beyond the porch, the rain beat down in opaque sheets, and thunder rumbled in the distance. As I stood there peering out of the crack between the double doors, lightning rent the sky from heaven to earth and illuminated the night. In the bright, sudden light I saw that I had been mistaken: the stranger at my door was not a man at all. She was as tall as any man, and she wore men's clothes, but I saw for a split second that her face was as feminine as mine.

The house was in no state to receive guests, and neither was I. But no one would survive a night outside in this weather.

"Come in," I said, and stepped back to let her inside.

The woman pulled down the hood of her cloak as she stepped over the threshold, and I saw that she had shorn her mousy hair short to match her clothes. The candlelight illuminated her sharp jaw and broad shoulders.

Something stirred within me, the thing which I had learned to immediately smother. For a moment, I had the sense that she was looking at me the same way that I was looking at her, her pale blue eyes wandering over the folds in my nightgown. I stood tall regardless, with my chin tilted up like I was dressed for dinner instead of attired for bed.

"A lady should not be outside alone at night," I said as I closed the door. The woman laughed, and her voice was hoarse.

"I am no lady."

"Any woman, then," I said. "Have you not heard the rumours?" No one had come to my house for years except the boy who delivered oil and candles from town every week, but I had still heard. "Men and women have been going missing here for years; they find them in the woods, their bodies torn to shreds and their ribs cracked open. They say whatever is responsible is eating their hearts."

The woman's face twisted as if she were in pain.

"I've heard," she said. "Who do I have to thank for saving me from such a fate?" She had a pretty way of speaking, but her accent was common.

"Lady Scarlet," I told her. "This is my house."

My house, still, though I remembered the greedy way my fiancé had looked at it when we first met. Scarlet Hall was aging now, neglected, but she still wore her red brick proudly, her dormers jutting up from the roof like towers despite the ivy that now clambered up the walls and clamoured around the windows. Even half-hidden behind the overgrown gardens, she was the biggest house for miles around.

"Thank you for your generosity, my lady," the woman said. "I'm sure I would have frozen outside." She was soaked to the bone, dripping rain onto the hardwood floors. The boards would warp, but that didn't matter. The hall was a ruin already, dust choking the fibres of the rug and mould spotting the high ceilings where water had leaked in.

"Since the hearteater did not catch you first," I said. "What may I call my rescue?"

"Just Kat, if it's all the same to you," said the stranger. I nodded.

"I can offer you a bed in the servants' quarters, Kat, while you wait out the storm." I paused for a moment, eyeing her. Her men's clothes were so ragged that they were nearly ruined, stained with mud from the forest. Where her sleeves ended at her wrists I could see that her hands were filthy, dirt caked on her dry fingers like those of a gravedigger. There was red beneath her nails. "You may borrow some of the clothes, too."

Kat's brows pulled downwards, and she tucked her hands inside her cloak.

"Won't the servants mind me taking their clothes?" she asked.

"There are no servants anymore," I said. They had all fled by now, even those who hadn't left with my fiancé.

I turned around in a swirl of lace hems to go back upstairs, but I stopped halfway when I remembered that I had a warning to give her. I turned, looking back down at Kat where she stood in the gloomy hall.

"Up these stairs," I said. "On the left, through the door, is the west wing of the house. Even if you only stay for the night, I must ask you never to go there."

With the candelabra I had brought downstairs when I heard the doorknocker tilted just so, I could see the frown on her face.

"Why not?" She asked.

I told her the truth.

"Because I am a monster," I said.

I turned back around and carried the light away. When the sounds of our voices faded from the air, I was left alone with nothing but the noise of the house itself. It came from deep within the walls, pulsing through them like the heart of a living animal.

Upstairs, I fell into bed and didn't wake until the next morning when the sunlight spilled in through the moth-eaten holes in the curtains. I felt so much more like myself now in the dark, where no one could see the thing that I was, but nonetheless I went downstairs. I could hear faint noises outside the relentless rhythm of the house settling and unset-tling, and I followed them down to the dining room. It had been a grand room once, with gallant portraits hanging high on the walls and a great crystal chandelier glittering above. Now the paintings had dulled so much it was hard to see who they depicted, and the chandelier dripped cobwebs instead of wax. Dust had settled thick over the floor, disturbed now by the footsteps that led to the head of the table, where my father would once have sat.

There was Kat. Despite my offer, she was wearing the same tattered clothes as yesterday, although now she was down to her shirtsleeves. I didn't know what was left in the pantry at this point, but she had found some bread and oats and something to soak them in and was eating like an animal, ravenous, eyes wild as she stuffed food into her mouth with barely enough time to swallow.

I found that I felt much better about Kat's presence in my house now that I was wearing my favourite striped dress instead of a nightgown, my corset laced as tightly as my hair was pulled back. I took the seat to her right, and after a moment of delay, she remembered to sit up straighter in the presence of her host and one of her betters.

"I said you could borrow some clothes," I reminded her. Kat shook her head.

"I wouldn't want to take anything from you," she said. She eyed the empty silver carving plate in front of me. The long table in the dining room was still laid out as if a great feast would begin at any moment. The servants' quarters were right next to the kitchens; Kat would know by now that there were no cooks, either. After a moment, she nudged the half-finished bowl of oatmeal towards me.

"Would you like some?"

For a moment I simply stared, letting the warm bowl rest between my cold hands. I was sure that Kat mustn't have been the first person to speak to me since my fiancé left Scarlet Hall, but the scant few conversations before the servants fled and the guests stopped coming had long since faded from my memory. Nonetheless, I knew for certain that Kat was the first person to offer me a kindness since the wedding was cancelled. I pressed a hand against my throat, as if Kat would otherwise be able to see my heart fluttering there beneath the high collar of my dress. It was silly – my heart was not in my throat, nor anywhere else within me.

"It's alright, thank you." I lowered my hand to push the bowl back towards her. "I do not eat."

Kat laughed, as if I had been joking. She took her food back, and asked me, "Do you live here all alone? No servants – no family?" She tilted her head. Her blue eyes flashed like the sapphires upstairs in my jewellery box. There was something animal about those eyes; too much iris and not quite enough white, like a wolf. They were sharp too, watching me the way that such a wolf would watch a deer. "No husband?"

"No," I said. "My father died some years ago, and he was all that I had. I never married."

Kat licked her lips.

"Neither have I," she said deliberately.

I was not surprised – I didn't mean it in a cruel way. In the daylight, I could see that Kat was easily the most handsome woman I had ever seen, but most of the respectable men I had met couldn't appreciate *handsome* in a woman. None of them would have understood what was beautiful about her strong jaw or her broad shoulders or how her body filled out her men's shirt – but I did. I understood.

"So you're all alone," Kat said. "And yet you stay here. Why is that?"

I told her the truth.

"I could never leave," I said. "This is my home – my blood is in this place."

Kat glanced around.

"It is a grand house," she said. "Are there stables?" I blinked at her.

"Excuse me?"

"I shouldn't intrude on you for much longer," Kat said. "So I could take a horse into town, and go somewhere else."

"Where?" I asked. This time, it was Kat who paused.

"I... don't know," she said. Her gaze flicked up the ceiling, where the gold leaf paint was flaking off onto the once-purple table runner. "I lost my job – it was in a bakery, and they gave me board in a room above. I had to get out when they fired me."

"What happened?"

Kat glanced at me and grinned, and I felt something wicked and electric flash down my spine.

"They realised I wasn't a man," she said.

"Did you tell them you were?"

"No," she said. "But if people assume, I don't correct them. It doesn't matter to me whether people think I'm a man or a woman. And when they think I'm a man, they don't ask me to wear dresses. But..." Kat leaned back in her chair, "...no one likes finding out they were wrong. It's not the first time it's happened – once, before, I was actually run out of town, with pitchforks and torches. Like some kind of monster from a story." She frowned.

"You're not a monster," I said – I would know. Kat smiled at me, so gently that her whole face seemed softer.

"If I'm not a monster," she said. "That means you aren't, either."

So she remembered what I had said to her last night.

"Do you have family nearby?" I asked, ignoring what she had said. "Somewhere you could go back to?"

Kat shook her head.

"No. My mother threw me out," she said. "After she caught me with a lover."

A moment of silent understanding passed between us.

Quickly, I rose from the table.

"Well," I said. "If you have nowhere else to go, you're quite welcome to stay here for some time. I do not have much, but this is my home."

Kat's smile turned crooked.

"Thank you," she said. "It's kind – but I'm afraid I can't."

My fingers curled over the back of the chair I had been sitting in, kneading at the wood.

"Why not?" I asked. Kat's eyes glittered.

"Because I *am* a monster."

★ ★ ★

Despite what she'd said, Kat never came to see me and tell me where she wanted to go, although I stayed awake almost the whole night waiting for her. Nor did I see her the next morning. The storm had started up again in the night, roaring against the walls of the house. I wondered if Kat might have left of her own accord regardless. Scarlet Hall was so old that she shifted and creaked in the wind, groaning under her own great weight. The sounds of the house had a strange, organic rhythm, an almost-inaudible *thump-thump* that echoed through the floors. In the wind, the walls moved like they were breathing. It was impossible to hear if anyone else was moving around the house while I slept, and my home was so big it was easy for our paths not to cross.

I knew she must still be in the house, however, when I went into my father's study that evening: someone had dusted the things in his old curio cabinet. Now that I knew to look, I saw other signs of Kat's continued presence around the house. In some rooms the cobwebs in the corners had been brushed away. Fireplaces were lit in the day, and oil lamps at night. The crystal dining set was cleaned and polished until it shone again. It was curious – I almost didn't recognise the house anymore without its mask of disrepair.

I saw Kat again the next night. I was reading in the library, the sputtering light from the lamp on the end table casting dancing shadows across the page. I had thought I was alone there, until I caught something moving out of the corner of my eye. When I turned my head, I saw that it was Kat. She had finally gone through one of the abandoned trunks in the servants' quarters or one of the wardrobes in the empty bedrooms, as she now wore a green waistcoat and a set of men's trousers. She was dusting a bookshelf, so quietly absorbed in the work that she didn't seem to have realised I was there. I watched her for a moment, smiling a little, before I called out:

"I thought you were leaving?"

Kat didn't jump, but she froze up the way I had seen foxes do when I stumbled across them in the grounds, a moment of wary animal stillness before they darted away. Then she relaxed, and turned around. She made her way over to where she could stand in the light of the lamp.

"I am," she said. "I have to be gone by the next full moon at the latest. But it's still storming outside, so I thought I may as well clean until I can leave you in peace."

"Why cleaning?" I asked. I found that I liked to hear the sound of her voice.

"It's just what I do, I suppose," she said. "I've always been a wanderer with nowhere to go – if someone lets me stay the night at their house, I do a few odd jobs for them, and then usually they'll let me stay a little longer. It's how I got started at the bakery. I don't know how else to earn my keep."

"I didn't ask you to earn your keep," I said, a little more playful than was perhaps proper. "I quite enjoy just having company."

Egged on by the tone of my voice, Kat flashed a smile. Slowly, she moved towards the chaise I was sitting on, and when I didn't say anything to stop her, she perched on the end of it.

"I mean you no offence, my lady," she grinned. "But your house could use some time with me."

I couldn't help it – I laughed. She wasn't wrong, but I had been the only person in Scarlet Hall for so long that I'd grown used to its gloom.

"At least take a rest," I said. "It's a big house."

I looked back to my book as Kat settled a little more comfortably on the chaise. Silence passed for a few moments, but I hadn't read much more before she asked me:

"What are you reading?"

I turned the cover towards her so that she could see the title, but Kat just looked at me blankly. I raised my eyebrows.

"Can't you read?" I asked, surprised. Kat shook her head. "You weren't taught?"

"My father was – is – a coal miner," Kat said. "And my mother washed clothes for the village. Neither of them ever had a reason to learn, and so neither did I."

I looked down at the pages with a frown. Since my fiancé had left me like this, books were my only solace during the long, lonely days as the house withered away around me. I couldn't fathom looking down at the inked marks on the page and comprehending nothing.

I looked back up and met Kat's eyes.

"Would you like to learn?" I asked. Her own eyes widened, startled by the offer, and I wondered how many people had offered *her* kindness since she left home.

"Can I?" she asked, leaning a little closer so she could see the pages. I reminded myself to breathe, evenly and often.

"I'm no governess," I warned her. "But I can certainly try to teach you."

And try I did. It had been so long since I was taught to read that I barely remembered how I'd learned, but I put my finger under the letters on the page and sounded them out for Kat to repeat. From letters, we moved on to forming the sounds of whole words, and I hoped desperately that I was letting her see the connection between them. She shifted closer to me on the chaise, so that she could mimic my movements and place her own fingers beneath the words to keep her place. Her hands were much rougher than mine, calloused from hard work instead of delicately manicured. I could feel their strength whenever one of us made a misstep, and our fingers would brush over one another's. I was struck, more than anything, by how warm she was. My hands were always cold, but Kat was burning up with the life running beneath her skin. It had been so long since I spent time around a simple human heartbeat.

Once, as I pressed another finger to the page, Kat moved to follow and laid her whole hand over mine, surrounding it with warmth. It couldn't have been an accident, but it must have been. I looked up at her, and when our eyes met that understanding passed between us again, unspoken and unspeakable. I felt my cheeks warm, like I had a simple human heartbeat too.

"You have cold hands," Kat observed. Moving hesitantly, as if she or I were deer likely to startle, she slid her fingers into the gaps between my own, curling around them.

"It's cold in here," I said, although it wasn't. Even in the dead of winter, Scarlet Hall was always warm. My lips stayed parted after I spoke, as if my mouth were waiting for something.

The grandfather clock in the corner struck, suddenly enough to startle both of us, and Kat let go of my hand to turn and look at its face. The heavy weight of the air dissipated as soon as it had appeared.

"It's two," I said, although I was sure that Kat could tell the time too. "You shouldn't be awake so late at night – you need your rest."

"So do you." Kat glanced at me out of the corner of her eye. She was frowning faintly – perhaps she was starting to realise what a strange creature I truly was.

"I will retire for the night if you will," I offered, closing our book. I stood, and after a moment, so did Kat. She turned to go without much more than a *goodnight, my lady*, but I stopped her. I shouldn't have stopped her – it was a dangerous thing to do, but I did it.

"You probably shouldn't be awake so late at night," I repeated. "But if you are in the future, I can probably be found in the library, if you would like to continue our lessons."

A moment passed, and then Kat smiled.

"My lady, I would like that very much."

★ ★ ★

Every time I saw Kat, she said that she would be leaving soon, but she never did. More and more, she seemed to make Scarlet Hall back into a home. Dust motes twirled through the air in beams of sunlight that the house hadn't seen in years when she pulled back the drapes to let the day inside. Room by room, my home was transformed. Fires were lit in grates again, and lamps shone through the night in every part of the manor, not just the places where I would skulk with a book, and there were fresh flowers on the dining table every morning. Everything was dusted and cleaned and put back together as best as one woman could, until it almost looked like my childhood again – dull, and faded, because there was no going back to who I had been before, but close enough.

Kat held my home so gently in her hands. I found her once in the sitting room, kneeling on the floor before a portrait that hung on the wall. One corner of the gilt frame had broken off, and the glass inside was smashed. I watched as Kat replaced the glass and repaired the break, the careful strokes of her paintbrush as she gilded the new corner too. Her brow was furrowed in careful concentration, her hands so delicate and gentle that I would gladly have placed my own heart within them. With her sleeves rolled up, she had thick, dark hair on her arms.

I hadn't spoken when I came into the room, but Kat must have known I was there without looking, because she said:

"Who is that?"

I glanced at the portrait. The woman in the painting was my younger self, in a red dress with my hands clasped before me. Behind me stood a man with dark hair and dark eyes and a dark smile. "My fiancé," I told her. "He had the portrait commissioned when we became engaged." I had smashed the glass within the frame with my own clenched fist.

Kat sat back, turning to look at me. The lamp she had lit next to her to work by cast strange light over her face. There seemed to be a second layer behind her blue eyes that reflected the light like an animal's in the dark.

"I didn't know you'd been engaged," she said, and I shook my head.

"Only for a short time, and long ago."

"What was he like?"

"He was terrible," I said, simply. "A selfish, godless man. He cared for nothing but his reputation and his studies. He was an occultist. I understand being curious about the things which humans are unable to explain, but he took it too far." I frowned. "We rarely spoke – he was always so busy with his books."

The long shadows from the lamp danced across Kat's face.

"What did he read about?"

"I'm not entirely sure," I said. "Pagan gods, and demons, I suppose. I know he read of witchcraft. I didn't like to hear about it."

"What about werewolves?" Kat's voice was quiet.

"I'm sorry?"

"There are stories," Kat said. "About people who turn into wolves when the full moon comes. They can't control themselves – their hunger is so great they would devour the world if they could."

"I'm not sure that werewolves are real," I said, although it wasn't impossible. While my fiancé lived in my house, I had seen many strange and terrible things. Kat shrugged her shoulders, a small little movement.

"Perhaps not," she said. "But something is killing those people in the woods."

"A man, I expect," I said primly. "Men are usually the ones doing the hurting."

Kat looked once at me, and then once back at the portrait.

"I'm sorry."

I felt my shoulders slump. Had anyone ever said that they were sorry for me before? My fiancé was a respectable man, despite his eccentricities. No one would ever have believed me.

"It was a long time ago," I said. "You didn't have to mend the portrait."

"I thought I would try." Kat ran her fingers along the fresh gilding. "I find myself very good at destroying things. It makes me feel better to fix what I can."

I let the silence that followed her words sit for a moment, and then extended a hand. Kat clasped it, and I pulled her up from the floor. When she stood, her fingers for a moment caressed the inside of my wrist, and I felt my breath catch.

"It's always warm in this house," Kat mused. "Even the walls are warm – but you still have cold hands."

I snatched my hand back quickly.

"Come," I said, as if she hadn't spoken. "Leave the portrait – we'll go to the library. We have to keep up your lessons."

★ ★ ★

Even if Kat had not been so kind to my house, it would have seemed brighter. For so long I had been the only resident of Scarlet Hall, the wind that howled through the house from the un-shuttered windows upstairs as my only company. Now, however, even when I was alone I was no longer lonely. I could hear Kat moving around upstairs, in another room, shuffling and humming and sometimes even singing to herself as she worked. When our paths crossed on my endless, aimless wanderings of the mansion, she would smile at me. We rarely spoke until after sunset when she would come to the library for her reading lessons. We would sit together there, dangerously close, as she learned to sound out the words. I was surprised by how quickly she learned, but she seemed eager to do so. I took to using plays as our practice texts, since they were meant to be read aloud. As Kat grew in her confidence, one night while reading *The Tempest* she took my hand. It was no accident, this time – it could not even be mistaken as one. She pressed my palm gently to her cheek and looked into my eyes as she read from the page.

"*Hear my soul speak: the very instant I saw you, did my heart fly to your service.*"

My blood roared in my veins, shock numbing my fingers so that it took me a moment to be able to snatch them back. I didn't even snatch, in the end – just gently pulled away, so that I caressed her jaw as I did. I slammed the book shut afterwards, flustered.

"You should retire for the night," I managed to say.

"I *should* leave."

My stomach twisted – I had ruined everything.

"No," I said without thinking. "Please don't – I'm sorry, it's no trouble at all to have you here, please stay just a little longer."

Kat frowned.

"You don't have to be sorry," she said. "You've done nothing wrong – I've told you already that I have to go."

"I do not want you to." Saying it felt like admitting something sinful. Kat looked at me for a moment.

"Perhaps just a few more nights," she said, and I slumped with relief.

Kat still said often that she should leave, but she never did. Her quest to restore my home to its former glory continued until one day I passed by the staircase in the great hall, and saw Kat with her hand on the door that led through to the west wing.

I had never moved so fast before. My hand was around her wrist and she yelped, pulling against my fingers when she swung around.

"What are you doing?" I heard my own voice like it came from outside of myself, high and panicked.

"I've gone through all the other rooms," said Kat. She seemed somehow more surprised that she was unable to break my grip on her wrist than she was at the fact I had suddenly appeared behind her – like she had known I was there somehow. "I thought I would–"

I shook my head violently, before she could even finish.

"I told you never to go in there," I said. "Please – *please*, you must never." I found myself grasping her hand in both of mine, shaking so hard that we both trembled. I could see the mild horror on Kat's face – I knew I must look half-deranged – but I had to know that she understood.

"I won't," she said finally. Her other hand came up to lay itself on top of both of mine, holding them until the shaking stopped. "If it's that important to you, then I won't."

★ ★ ★

I didn't see her for days after. I could have, but I avoided her deliberately. I was ashamed of my behaviour, so rude and unla-dylike, but I had no other choice. I knew that if Kat opened the door to the west wing, she really would leave. She would turn around and run back down the stairs, out of the grand front doors and out of my life forever. No one could stand to stay in Scarlet Hall once they had learned the secret at the heart of the house. I worried that she might leave anyway, but the next time our paths crossed in the hall she simply smiled at me, as always, and told me about a dream she had the night before. It was like feeling all the blood rush back into my limbs, I was so overcome with relief. I could not bear to lose her now, when our time together was the only bright spot in my long years of solitude. She brought me joy; it was as if the light spreading through the house had crawled its way down my throat to make a home in the empty cavity of my chest. I didn't need the fires that Kat lit – it warmed me from the inside, and spilled out of my smiling mouth whenever I spoke.

The night before the full moon, I dressed for dinner in white. The gown was beautiful despite the moths that had eaten at the lace edges. It should have been my wedding dress, but since the wedding had never happened, now it was only a dress. The windows had been cleaned of their dust and grime, so the swollen moon lit up the hallway so dramatically that I didn't need a candelabra to make my way downstairs. There was music coming from down there, faint but true. How long had it been since there was music in my house?

The ballroom in Scarlet Hall was not as large or grand as those in other houses I had visited, long ago, but it was a ballroom. Cobwebs still clung to the ceilings too tall for Kat to reach, but she was trying. There she knelt in the corner furthest from the door, where the phonograph stood. I don't think I had ever even looked at it – it was something my fiancé had bought, a trinket for the wedding party, but now under Kat's hands it spilled music. She looked up at me when she heard the heels of my boots against the floor, and stood with a grin. It made something inside of me scream; I couldn't stand to look at her. I wanted to cling to her borrowed waistcoat, to chew through her ribcage and live inside her heart forever. I thought she had to know, to somehow sense the frantic animal inside of me, but she simply smiled and offered me her hand. I took it.

Kat's hair was messy and her hands were smeared with grease, but slowly she led me around the floor. It wasn't a dance, not really. We didn't go far, but we spun in small circles, our clasped hands pressed between us while her arm slid around my waist. We didn't match the music – too jaunty in our movements, our little laughter, while the record was slow and sombre. It didn't matter – this was just for us. She dipped me suddenly, and I laughed brightly. A pin came loose from my hair and sent dark curls spinning towards the marble floor while I gazed up at her with what I was sure must be devotion so strong it was sacrilegious. Everything that I felt for her, from the thrill in my belly when I looked up at her face to the pull I felt somewhere behind my sternum, was drawing me in to her beating heart.

Kat's hand was gentle on my back as she pulled me upright again. Her lips brushed my forehead when she spoke.

"I'm leaving tonight, but I wanted you to have music for when I'm gone."

I pulled myself out of her grasp so suddenly that she had to catch me again to stop me from falling. My hands grabbed at her arms, creasing her sleeves.

"What?" I gasped. "Why?"

"I told you," she said. "I've been saying that I have to go – my lady, I am a monster."

"As am I!" I cried. "It doesn't matter!"

"Listen to me." Kat couldn't pry my hands from her sleeves, so she grabbed my waist again instead. I looked up at her, wheeling, wild, her animal eyes hard as blue diamonds. "I know what you are, my lady, and it isn't monstrous. I–"

I could not let her finish; I could not forgive myself for what I did next. It was the one thing I had sworn to myself that I would never do. Dream, yearn, yes, but never do. It would damn us both, but I *had* to make her stay, and this was the only thing I thought might work.

I seized Kat by her lapels and kissed her hard.

She did not hesitate for even a moment – she kissed me back, drew me close against her own body. Sinful and shameful, I had longed for this moment; how we grabbed and tugged at one another as we moved towards the stairs. How the buttons like pearls up the back of my wedding dress scattered across the floor; how we fell to the bed without looking; how I cut my lip on Kat's teeth, which I had never noticed were so sharp; how she pulled the laces of my corset loose like she knew what she was doing.

How I gasped, when she lowered her head between my legs.

After, she lay beside me in the bed and slowly ran her hand across my chest, her fingers gentle and lazy.

"What's this?" she asked.

I looked down. Kat's fingers were splayed across the scar I carried above my left breast. It was an ugly, puckered thing, a clean slice dotted on either side by the suture marks that had sewn it closed. I laid my hand over hers.

"My fiancé gave it to me," I told her quietly. Her mouth twisted sympathetically, before she leaned down to press her lips against the scar. There was no sensation there, the wound ran so deep and ragged.

I ran my fingers through her hair.

"I thought that I would never be able to love after what he did to me. I thought that the world would burn down if I ever touched another woman. But I was wrong."

Kat nodded, idly tracing my scar.

"I thought so too – I thought that there was something wrong with me. But the girl that my mother caught me with... the first time we kissed, I knew that I'd been wrong, and so had everyone else. Everything I felt for her was pure and good – there couldn't be anything wrong with it. Men might have thought I was ugly, undesirable, but she didn't. I cared for her, and she for me."

"So why do you call yourself a monster?" I had known from the moment I first saw Kat that, if I ever invited her to my bed, she would not refuse me. Without saying it, we had looked at each other and known we were the same. Like calls to like.

"Why do you?" Kat closed her eyes. I didn't say the words I held in my mouth: *because I am*. She would not understand. "I say it because I am one."

Gently, I pulled Kat's hand from my scar and pressed my lips to it.

"You are not."

Kat tugged her hand away to kiss me instead. Now that we had both satisfied our starvation, her mouth was soft and yielding against my own. I melted into it.

I slept that night with Kat in my bed, my arm curled around her waist from behind. When I reached for her after I woke she was gone. My chest seized. I leapt from bed, pulling on the first clothes that my hands found – the remains of my ruined wedding dress, lying in a heap on the floor with half the buttons missing. My hair was still loose from Kat's fingers running through it, and it streamed behind me as I ran from the room.

Kat had gone, as she said she would.

I stood outside my room in the dark, and I didn't know what to do.

Suddenly there came a crash – from downstairs, as the front door swung open. I spun around.

"Kat?"

I ran to the stairs, but there was no one in the hall. In the moonlight, I saw the carpeting on one side of the stairs had been shredded, and deep gouges ran through the intricately carved bannister beside it, showing the white insides beneath the dark varnish, like a great animal had scrambled and clawed its way through.

On the left, the door to the west wing yawned open.

I passed the window as I hurried to the door, where the moon hung white and full in the sky beyond. Rain spattered the glass of the windows and the sky rumbled distantly; the storm had returned.

It was a shock to see the west wing. None of Kat's tender touches had made it to this part of the house, where gloom still reigned. As I stood in the middle of a living room covered in dust, the stone floor seemed to pulse under my feet like a living animal. The air in here was warm and moist, pressing close to my face. If I was quiet, I could hear a soft rhythmic sound from somewhere within the walls. *Thump-thump. Thump-thump. Thump-thump.* Then, beyond that, more sounds: a soft shuffling, claws skittering over the floors, and gentle panting.

Somewhere deep within the house, an animal howled. All the hairs on my arms stood up, and I remembered the dead bodies in the forest.

I walked forwards, following the sound.

My scream rose within my throat and froze there, trapped.

Thunder crashed overhead as lightning lit up the west wing, and I saw a monster: not a woman who desired her own kind, but a great black wolf the size of a man, with shaggy fur and hungry teeth. Rain from outside dripped from its coat to the floor, and its lips pulled back to growl.

I turned to run, but the wolf gave chase, and there was nowhere for me to go. The monster pursued me through the house until I was cornered, helpless to watch as it stalked closer.

When the wolf reached me I fell to my knees. Its hackles raised, an eager growl rumbling up from inside its chest. Its eyes were wild and wide and blue like the sapphires in my jewellery box.

Blue wolf eyes.

I gasped.

I reached out my hand. I was shaking too hard to hold it steady, but the wolf seemed so shocked that it simply stood still and let it happen. I reached for its snout; gasped again when my fingers touched the wolf, but I ran my hand along its muzzle and grabbed a handful of fur behind its ears. I ran my fingers through that fur like a lover's hair.

The wolf looked into my eyes, and I knew what she was.

"It's you," I whispered.

I looked at her pale eyes, her dark fur, her long teeth. She was a magnificent animal.

"How are you this beautiful?"

The wolf closed the distance between us and buried her face in my chest. I wrapped my arms around her while she whined and nuzzled me, licking the terrified tears from my face. I was shaking, breathing so hard I was nearly sobbing, but she did not hurt me.

I stayed with the wolf the whole night, with her curled up in my lap while I ran my fingers through her matted fur until my hands stopped shaking. Under my touch the violence of the wolf had turned to nothing, and she became as docile as a dog.

I had thought I would be shocked to see a werewolf, but I was not. After all, I had always known that there were monsters.

When the sun rose the next morning, I woke up alone again. I swayed when I got to my feet, holding my dress around me while I walked off in search of Kat. I didn't know whether she had gone again, afraid of being feared now I knew what she was.

But we were in the west wing. Perhaps she knew by now that I had no reason to fear her.

I found her where I knew I would, in the sitting room in the west wing. She must have followed the sound that came from there: *thump-thump*, over and over. As I approached the door, the faded wallpaper became streaked with red threads that wove through the walls. They grew in number as I approached the sitting room, thicker and closer together as they centred in on where Kat knelt naked beneath the sitting room window. She was staring at the wall.

There, half-buried in the bricks, was a human heart. The veins that crawled out from it sank into the wall, throbbing in the spaces where they showed between the brick and mortar. Fused with the house, it beat out a steady rhythm nonetheless: *thump-thump*.

Kat turned around when she heard the shuffle of my dress across the floor. She looked as ragged as the day we had first met, like she had aged ten years in one night.

"Tell me what's going on," she said.

It took some coaxing, but I persuaded Kat to come and sit with me in my father's study, the both of us facing each other in separate armchairs. Finally, I said, "I did tell you I was a monster."

Kat put her head in her hands and laughed. It sounded like a sob.

"And I you. That was your heart in the wall."

I nodded.

"And you are a werewolf – the hearteater."

She nodded, too.

"Your scar…"

"When my fiancé discovered my inversion, he said that he would marry me anyway," I told Kat. "So that he would inherit Scarlet Hall, and I told him that he would never have my house. I broke off the engagement. Bruising his ego so badly was unforgivable, to him – I had humiliated him in public. To punish me, he made sure that I would never leave the house I loved so much." Idly, I pressed a hand to my chest. "He cut out my heart and used a spell from one of his books to bind it to the house. I no longer need to eat, or drink, but if I were to leave Scarlet Hall, I would die. I have lived only a half-life from that day."

Kat nodded.

"I have no such grand story," she said. "When my mother caught me with a woman, she chased me into the woods. I knew I couldn't go back home – I found a place to sleep in the hollow of a tree, but while I was there a monster found me. When the wolf bit me, I became a wolf too. Even as a wolf... the parts of me that make me, me, are still there, buried deep. All I could think of was how much I hated my mother, and the wolf was starving. When it sought her out, it ate her heart." Kat's voice trembled and cracked. "It has always been like that – anyone I become too close to, in love or hate, the wolf remembers. It's why I must keep moving all the time, so I never become too attached. The wolf has harmed people I cared for – the people I love most are usually the ones who I hurt first. It was why I knew I had to leave this house, when I saw how beautiful you were. I knew when I transformed last night that I hadn't run far enough, but... I did not hurt you."

Kat's voice was quietly awed when she said it, and she looked back up at me as if to check; to be sure that I was still alive and whole. I was not – I had not been since before we met – but I still smiled at her, and put a hand to my chest again.

"I have no heart," I said. "There was nothing for the wolf to eat."

"But I still care for you more than anyone else," Kat said slowly. "So you were the one the wolf came to – it did not hurt anyone else either. So if..." she trailed off, her eyes wide, so I finished for her.

"I think," I said. "That if you were to live at Scarlet Hall, you would not have to hurt anyone else ever again. And–" I added, smoothing out the folds in my skirt. "Perhaps it is selfish of me to say, but if you stayed here, perhaps I would not have to be so terribly lonely anymore."

"You would still have me?" Kat asked.

"I love you," I answered simply. She grimaced.

"But I am a monster."

I reached across the space between us to take her hands in mine.

"As am I," I said.

"You are no monster," said Kat, and perhaps for once I believed her. It meant more when it came from another creature like me. She blinked, then, like she was surprised. "So nor am I — not when I'm with you. My lady, I love you too. I will stay in this house with you for as long as you'll have me."

"I'll have you for as long as you want to stay."

Kat leaned in to kiss me, and I wrapped my arms around her while the heart within the walls of the house beat faster.

QUICKSILVER PROMETHEUS

Katie Young

The house sat on a windswept cliff overlooking a pebble beach and a restless grey sea. Its steep gables and dark windows, like so many sightless eyes, gave the old place an imposing aspect, so different from the pristine white Georgian terraces lining the little seaside town below. Henry looked up at the broken guttering and smeared panes of glass. He put down his heavy travelling case, fished Ms Travers' letter out of his pocket, and double checked the address he'd been given. Definitely the right place. This explained why the rent was so reasonable. He turned his collar up against the chill wind blowing in off the sea, picked up his case, and approached the front steps with an increasing sense of trepidation.

Henry looked for a bell to ring, but found none, so he rapped the heavy brass knocker hanging from a grotesque lion's mouth. He waited for a few moments, listening for footfall on the other side of the door, but when none came, he knocked again. This time, after a short pause, he heard a woman clearing her throat before the door swung open.

A petite woman with dark hair cut into a short, blunt style stood in the doorway. She had large brown eyes, a wide smile, and she wore a simple, pale blue shift dress with a loose sash about the waist. A single string of pearls hung around her neck, and she twirled them around her finger as she spoke.

"Mr Pearce? I've been expecting you. Do come in!"

Henry stepped into the hall and extended his hand.

"Ms Travers? Apologies, I know I'm later than I said I'd be. The train was rather delayed."

Ms Travers took his cold hand between both of hers.

"Ah! Such noisy, dirty beasts, trains! Don't you trouble yourself, Mr Pearce. But you're freezing. Come through and have a nice cup of tea."

Henry followed Ms Travers through the gloomy hall. The house was like a museum, the décor faded and shabby, a cloudy chandelier and grubby oil paintings in gilt frames hinting at former grandeur. The flock damask and threadbare velvet drapes Henry glimpsed through an open door off the corridor had probably been hung some eighty years ago, perhaps when the house was newly built. He descended the stairs into the basement. The kitchen was warm, the air thick with the woozy smell of a coal fire. Ms Travers set a kettle to boil on the range. Henry took a seat at a scarred wooden table as his hostess warmed the pot.

"We'll get you thawed out, then I'll give you the tour," she said brightly. "That drizzle seeps right into your bones, doesn't it!"

Henry smiled. There was something endearing about this woman and her relic of a house. Henry only hoped the light was better on the upper floors, or his work would be impossible.

"So how long have you lived here?" Henry asked as Ms Travers placed a tea tray down between them and sat down.

"All my life," she said, pouring milk from a little silver jug. "My great-grandfather had it built. But as you can see, it's a lot of work for one person to maintain. I've been thinking about selling up, but I've never known anything else. It would break my heart to leave."

She smiled, and looked down, but not before Henry saw tears well in her eyes. He sipped his tea and nodded. He felt suddenly protective of this frail-looking woman, although he knew next to nothing about her.

"Am I the first person you've rented rooms to?" he asked.

"Yes," Ms Travers said, brightening again. "The very first to reply to my advertisement. And an artist, no less! How exciting. What is it you make?"

"Sculptures," Henry replied, glad for the change of subject. "I like to use objects I find in nature – wood, feathers, even animal bones. I wanted to come to the seaside as my next piece will be fashioned out of rocks and shells."

"How marvellous," said Ms Travers. "And what is the subject? Or is it a secret?" She winked.

"Well, it will be a figurative piece," Henry said. "Classical. A man. Do you know the story of Prometheus?"

"Of course," said Ms Travers. "The titan who created humans out of clay. The one who stole fire from the gods to give to mortals."

"Exactly!" said Henry, delighted. "My sculpture will depict Prometheus, chained to a rock, his liver being devoured by a ravening eagle."

"Good Heavens!" exclaimed Ms Travers, fingers plucking at the collar of her dress. "That all sounds rather gruesome. And made out of shells you say?"

"Yes," said Henry. "Blue mussel shells. I think the striations and the shapes will give a wonderful form and texture to the piece."

"Well, you shan't be short of mussels here, that I can assure you. I can't wait to see how it turns out," said Ms Travers, draining the last of her tea. "Would you like to see the rooms now?"

Henry stood and followed her up the steep staircase, bare treads creaking underfoot, to the first-floor landing. She paused to show him a dingy but relatively clean bathroom, and they continued up to the top of the house. The house felt different here. It smelt different too, the mildew damp permeating the lower floors giving way to a dry, woody musk. It was lighter in the garret, and as they ascended, Henry saw there were skylights in this part of the roof, which he hadn't noticed from outside. In fact, the apex was almost entirely glass, and the light, grey and viscous though it was today, flooded the space.

The floorboards were strewn with worn rugs and runners, and the walls were bare plaster, with tiny scraps of wallpaper in various hues and patterns clinging here and there. The furniture was sparse, a single bed with a metal frame that put Henry in mind of hospitals and school dormitories. In one corner was a washstand. In another stood a small wardrobe, and a large writing desk covered in ink splotches and notches. The fine rain formed tiny rivulets which ran down the slanted panes in the roof, and the wind whistled through miniscule gaps in the frames.

"It's not much," said Ms Travers with an apologetic smile, "but when the sun shines, the light comes streaming in."

"I'm sure," said Henry, dragging a fingernail through a layer of dust on the table. "It will make a fine studio."

"It hasn't been used in years," said Ms Travers. "Not since I was a child. This used to be my playroom."

The loft was warm enough, not too draughty, and dry. Henry could imagine the room filled with large canvases and lumps of clay. He could see himself in his mind's eye, whittling and moulding, sitting in a shaft of sunlight as motes swirled around him, the sound of waves breaking on the beach below, and seagulls wheeling overhead – even if the bleak afternoon made it feel more like a prison tower.

Once he'd unpacked and set up his tools, Henry felt a lot more cheerful about his situation. Even the rain had eased off somewhat. Ms Travers made a simple supper of a hearty soup, bread, cold cuts of ham and beef, and some cheese. She offered to bring it up to Henry in the attic so as not to interrupt his sketching, but with the light dwindling and feeling he'd been alone enough for one afternoon, Henry decided to take his meal downstairs with his landlady.

The food was good, and Ms Travers was charming company. Although she was prone to joking, and her speech was peppered with good natured laughter, at times Henry sensed a profound sadness about her. She'd look off into the distance for a moment, as if deep in thought, and Henry recognised that distracted, lost expression all too well. Perhaps it was the solitude, and the burden of having to keep the wolf from the door. The house had clearly been a beautiful family home once, and Henry supposed it must have pained Ms Travers to see it decaying before her eyes. He wondered whether there had ever been a Mr Travers, or whether she had remained unwed. He might have asked had it not been for the fact that it would have meant offering up details of his own marital situation in reciprocation, and that was not a path he wanted to tread. But after a glass or two of port, which Ms Travers had insisted on opening to toast his arrival, Henry's curiosity got the better of him.

"Have you any siblings, Ms Travers?"

The landlady's smile faded and her skin blanched.

"I did," she said quietly, averting her eyes.

"Gosh, I didn't mean to pry," said Henry, fidgeting with the frayed edge of his linen napkin. He knew better than most how loaded that question had become since the war.

"That's quite all right," Ms Travers said. "They passed a very long time ago. When we were children. A brother and a sister. I was the eldest."

"I'm very sorry to hear that, Ms Travers," said Henry. "It must have been a terrible loss."

"Yes. Mother never really recovered after Grace and Arthur passed away. She followed a few years later. It was just Father and me until he died a few years back."

"That must have been very tough, Ms Travers. I'm so sorry. I shouldn't have brought it up."

"No, it's fine, really, Mr Pearce. You weren't to know. It was a lifetime ago really. And please, Ms Travers sounds so formal. Call me Abigail."

Henry smiled.

"Abigail it is. You must call me Henry."

He held out his hand as he had earlier that day, and she took it again, laughing.

"Nice to meet you, Henry. Now you should retire. You'll be wanting to go to market first thing and take your pick of those mussels, I shouldn't wonder. Lucky I'm fond of seafood, isn't it!"

★ ★ ★

Henry spent a restful enough first night in the attic room. The roar of the sea lulled him to sleep, but when he dreamt, it was of sailors on great ships being tossed about on fathomless, choppy waters, clinging for dear life to the deck. He dreamt of great creatures swimming in the depths below, huge beasts with tentacles and blind eyes waiting for an unfortunate soul to tumble overboard.

Henry was woken by sunlight on his face as dawn broke. The sky was clear and blue, and he got out of bed and stretched his arms up over his head. He crossed the room, and opened a window to breathe in the crisp, autumnal air. The sea sparkled, greener and vastly more inviting than the roiling gunmetal expanse that had greeted him yesterday. Gulls screamed and dived for fish, falling into the ocean like fighter planes shot out of the air. Henry closed his eyes at that unbidden image, and pulled the window shut against the chill breeze. He sat down at his desk and flipped his sketchbook open to where he'd left off the day before. The design for Prometheus was starting to take shape. He'd be honed from dark, glossy shells, reclining against a rock, draped in silver chain. An eagle fashioned from feather and bone would have its talons sunk deep into his thigh and its sharp beak embedded in his side. Henry took up his pencil and began to outline the figure from a different angle. From somewhere below, a female voice drifted up the stairs. Ms Travers —

Abigail – sang as she pottered around the kitchen, faint strains of some old ballad reaching the attic.

Henry stopped drawing when hunger got the better of him. He splashed his face with water from the washbasin and dressed before slipping downstairs. Abigail was still singing as he appeared in the kitchen doorway. She was at the sink, her back to him, too lost to the melody to hear him approach. She was the sort of person who was almost impossible to age. Her dark hair had the odd strand of white woven through it, and there were fine lines around her eyes, yet she spoke, dressed, and moved like a young girl. Henry took in the blunt cut of her hair, the way it was clipped boyishly short at the nape in the latest fashion, exposing the pale sweep of her neck. He briefly imagined what it would be like to brush his lips across that vulnerable skin and waited to see if his body would respond. But although he could see Abigail was an attractive woman, he felt no stirring.

"Mr Pear – Henry! You startled me!" Abigail laughed and her cheeks flushed pink.

"Forgive me," Henry said. "I was just... you have a lovely voice."

Abigail flapped her wet hand dismissively at him.

"I love the old ones. My mother used to sing when I was small. Right, let's get you fed and off to market."

Henry wolfed down a breakfast of eggs and a little of the ham left over from the night before. He bid Abigail a good morning and stepped out into the stiff coastal wind. He strolled along the beach until he reached the harbour with its little fishing boats unloading the catch of the day. He wend his way through burly men, spattered with blood and stinking of chum, barrels of fish and eels slung over their broad shoulders, and women inspecting their wares, seemingly immune to the stomach-churning smell. Finally, Henry came across an elderly man selling cockles, winkles, and mussels from large pails of seawater.

"Good morning," Henry said brightly. "How much for this bucket of mussels?"

The old man eyed Henry warily.

"The whole lot?"

"Yes please," said Henry.

"Call it five shillings. Hungry are ye?"

Henry chuckled.

"Something like that! Tell me, how long would it take a person to collect that many mussels?"

"Oh, a good few hours," said the man. "But if you know where to look, you can bring in a decent weight for but a morning's work."

"Would you show me how?" asked Henry. "I'd pay you well for your trouble, and I'm no competition for you. These would be for my own use only."

The man eyed Henry for a few heartbeats.

"Aye, all right. You've got yourself a deal," he said. "Come back tomorrow afternoon, and I'll teach you what I know."

Henry lugged the mussels home for Abigail to prepare, after which he set out again and visited a couple of restaurants in the area. He asked the kitchen porters whether they might save empty shells for him for him to collect every few days, and then he went combing the beach for some objects he might use in his work on his way back to the house.

That night, Abigail served delicious fresh mussels, steamed with onions, herbs, cream, and a splash of wine, the way the French prepared them. Henry savoured each one, using an empty shell to pluck the subsequent morsels out, much to his landlady's delight. They drank the rest of the wine, and spoke about literature and poetry. Abigail finally professed a fancy for the French decadents – particularly Verlaine and Huysmans – blushing as she did so. After dinner, Henry cleaned his shells, revealing their dark, pearlescent beauty, and set about grinding the first of them into shape.

That night, Henry slept fitfully. His stomach gurgled, and he wondered if perhaps one of the little sea creatures he'd eaten might have been bad. He was just dropping off again when he heard a sound that made him sit bolt upright in bed. Laughter. The sound of a child giggling very close to his ear. Henry scrabbled to light the gas lamp by his bed, and blinked as his eyes adjusted to the brightness. He swept the room with the lantern, but there was nobody there. Henry peered out of the window, listening for seagulls, and then for Abigail moving about downstairs. Everything was perfectly still. He huffed a nervous laugh to himself, convinced he'd overdone it with the rich food and wine too close to bedtime. He returned to bed, blew out the lamp, and settled back down, but sleep eluded him for the rest of the night.

At first light, Henry crept out of the house and walked down to the shore. He scoured the sand for anything striking in colour or texture which might be cleaned, dried, and melded into his sculpture. He took off his shoes and socks, rolled up his trousers, and climbed the rocks which lined the shore, searching the natural pools which formed there for oddities, like dog whelks, limpets, starfish, or cuttlebones.

He watched a hermit crab scuttling about for quite some time, which eventually discarded its too small shell in favour of a larger specimen. Henry took the rejected shell up and examined it in the light. It was pale, speckled with deep pinks and browns. He might be able to use it for Prometheus' lips, so he slipped it into his satchel.

That afternoon, he met the fisherman from the harbour, an amiable old salt who went by the name of Jack Fletcher, and learnt to pry blue mussels from rock faces exposed by the low tide. Afterwards, the pair went to the pub for a well-earned pint of bitter, and Jack regaled Henry with tales of the many times in his younger days that he'd nearly drowned in pursuit of marine creatures far feistier and more lucrative than clams and winkles.

In return, Henry spoke a little about his time in the trenches in Flanders, leaving out most of the gruesome details. He passed over the rats, his rotting feet, the way the relentless rain sluiced away the earth, exposing the bones of his dead friends, and the part where he couldn't stop crying for a week straight. He didn't mention all the times he had considered desertion, and how the thought of facing a firing squad had been far more appealing than spending another day in Hell. He most certainly did not talk about the day he'd returned home and his mother had broken the news that Alan's plane had been shot down over the sea off the coast of France.

"Are you okay, lad?" Jack's voice was gentle, and Henry realised he'd stopped speaking, lost in his memories.

"Sorry, yes. I was just remembering…" He trailed off.

"It's a nasty business. You've seen some terrible things, I shouldn't wonder."

Henry nodded and sipped his beer, trying to think of a way to change the subject without seeming strange.

"So, do you know Ms Travers at all?"

Jack wiped some foam off his moustache with the back of his hand and nodded.

"Aye! Lovely lass she is," he said fondly. "Had her share of heartache too, not that you'd know it on account of her always smiling and singing."

"Yes," Henry agreed. "She seems very kind."

"Pretty too," Jack suggested, giving a sly wink.

"Well, I… yes, I suppose she is." Henry felt a blush creeping up his neck, colouring his cheeks. "She told me about her brother and sister. Did you know them?"

The grin faded from Jack's face and he looked down at the sticky table.

"Aye. Little angels, they were. Tragedy what happened to them. And Mrs Travers, she never forgave herself, that's for sure. Died of a broken heart, I reckon."

Henry's next question was out before he could stop himself.

"What happened to them, exactly?"

Jack hesitated, looked around him, and leant in conspiratorially.

"It was the wallpaper," he whispered.

Henry frowned. "The wallpaper?"

"In the nursery. Mrs Travers, she always had a taste for fancy things, and they say it was the wallpaper in the children's room that made them sick. It sounds far-fetched to me, but that's what the doctor said. Arsenic poisoning! Can you believe it?"

Henry knew that many pigments were made from toxic compounds. His grandparents' generations had favoured vivid greens and yellows derived from copper arsenite, and many Dutch painters had suffered ill effects from the use of white lead in their masterpieces. He thought about the bare walls in the attic, the little patches of colour still stuck to the plaster. The way the room had been stripped and left bare. Then he remembered the sound of a child laughing which had disturbed him in the dark. An icy shiver wicked down Henry's spine, and he drained the remainder of his glass in one large swallow.

Later that afternoon, Henry sat in his garret, filing the iridescent shells into interlocking pieces, trying them out and seeing how they could fit together like malleable flesh over a wire skeleton. Prometheus had his basic form, and now Henry must bring him to life, just as the Titan had breathed spirit into the first clay man. Downstairs, Abigail was humming a tune and preparing a supper of chowder with Henry's freshly plucked mussels. Henry hoped the kitchen porters he'd charmed would come up with enough empty shells for his purpose before his landlady grew sick of the sight of seafood.

They passed another pleasant evening together. Henry told Abigail about his adventure with Jack on the rocks, the thrill of discovering a blanket of black, gleaming mussels clinging to them as the ferocious waves retreated, allowing Henry to take his pick of the largest specimens. Abigail laughed as Henry recounted how he'd had to duck for cover as hungry seagulls harangued him on his way back along the beach, trying to raid his bucket with their vicious beaks and squawking and flapping. The chowder was delicious, as was the wine Abigail provided to wash it down with, and Henry began to worry if maybe he'd misunderstood somehow, and that the rent would end up costing more than he could afford. It had been a while since he'd sold a sculpture or taken a portrait commission. But it had been even longer since Henry had sat with someone and drank and discussed books and poetry and his own art. It had been so very long since he'd been this passionate about creating something, and Abigail was so encouraging and such easy company that he felt whatever price he might end up paying for the attic room, it would be worth it.

★ ★ ★

Henry woke with a start. At first, he thought Abigail had come into his room, but as the last remnants of a dream he could no longer remember evaporated, he realised he was quite alone. His heart drummed against his ribs and the sound of his blood pulsing was loud in his ears. Despite the chill in the air, Henry found himself drenched in sweat.

"Hello?" he said quietly to the darkened room. He looked up and saw the moon peeping from behind fast moving clouds, casting a feint silvery light into his room. His eyes struggled to adjust to the gloom, but he could pick out shapes now – his wardrobe, the wash stand, the desk. Then something moved. A dark shape, a thicker absence of light, creeping around the foot of his bed. Henry felt his pulse quicken, his heart in his mouth. He felt around for a packet of matches and tried several times to light his lantern with shaking hands. Finally, it caught and flared. Henry tentatively moved his arm in a slow arc, trying to illuminate the darkest corners of the room without leaving the sanctuary of his bed. He felt like a child again, afraid to put his feet on the floor. Terror clawed its way up his throat as he peered into the shadows, but the lamp light revealed nothing out of the ordinary.

Satisfied at last that the apparition had been nothing more than a trick of the light, Henry left the lamp blazing but slumped back down against his pillows, and closed his eyes. Just as his heartbeat had slowed back down, he heard that sound again; a child laughing. This time, he could have sworn he felt a puff of breath against his cheek as well. Henry leapt out of bed and snatched up the lamp. He made his way down the stairs, to the landing, and into the bathroom, where he stood over the sink and splashed cold water on his face. His legs trembled and he wanted badly to wake Abigail so he wouldn't have to spend the rest of the night alone, but he knew that was out of the question. Finally, Henry made his way down to the kitchen, and gazed out of the window, listening for the sea beyond the walls of the house until the first rays of sun turned the sky pink.

Henry crept back to his room to dress before taking breakfast with Abigail. What had seemed so stomach-churningly urgent in the dark suddenly felt trivial and ridiculous with the cold, autumnal sunlight streaming through the dirty windows. And yet, Henry could not shift the feeling of foreboding, like the hangover from a nightmare which bleeds into morning and dogs you throughout the waking day. He took a sip of his tea and studied his landlady.

"Can I ask you something, Abigail?" he said quietly.

"Of course," she replied with a smile. She set down her knife and fork and dabbed at her mouth with a linen napkin.

"The children. Your brother and sister. How did they die?"

Abigail's smile faltered, but she held Henry's gaze. She folded her hands on the table in front of her.

"Why do you ask, Henry?"

"Please, Abigail. It's important."

Abigail took a deep breath and exhaled slowly.

"It sounds daft, even now," she began. "Such a silly little thing. Such an easy mistake to make. We had no idea, you see. You'd never even think to…" She was quiet for a moment. "Mother wanted to redecorate the playroom. To make it pretty for us children. She had bright paper hung – it was beautiful, with flowers and birds on it. But the wallpaper made us sick. So terribly sick. Something in the dye. I was the eldest. I was much bigger and stronger than the others. Grace and Arthur were so small, so frail. I can still hardly believe it all these years later, but the doctor said it must have been poison in the wallpaper, so Father tore it all down, and I've not been able to bring myself to spend any time up there since. Forgive me, Henry. You must think it terribly morbid."

Henry placed his hand over Abigail's.

"No, of course not. It's just..."

He realised he had no idea how to broach what he thought he had experienced in the attic.

"It's just that I... it sounds so strange now, but I have heard voices in my room. Children's voices. Have you ever... have you noticed anything odd about the room since...?"

Abigail pulled her hand out of Henry's grasp.

"Are you asking if I believe in ghosts, Mr Pearce?" Her voice had a hard edge to it.

"I... I didn't mean to offend, Ms Travers. It's just that you said you've not spent much time up there, and I have heard and seen things I can't explain, and–"

"Seen?" Abigail interjected. "What exactly have you seen?"

Henry's mouth was suddenly parched, and he took a swallow of tea before continuing.

"Well, it's hard to say exactly. But there was someone in the room with me last night. I'm sure of it."

Abigail stood up, and began to pace the kitchen floor.

"Mr Pearce – Henry – you must have dreamt it. You know that, don't you?"

Henry stared down at some crumbs on the kitchen table and remained silent.

"I've lived here all my life. I have prayed that Grace and Arthur are in a better place. Prayed for a sign that they're happy and safe. That they're beyond the pain and hardships they faced in their short lives. I've prayed every night for over thirty years.

Do you really believe I wouldn't know if their spirits still lingered here? Do you think I wouldn't feel them close by?"

Henry glanced up at his landlady and saw the tears starting in her eyes. He flushed with shame for the upset he'd caused her with his careless words. He wracked his brain for something to say that might make this right and erase the damage he'd inflicted. He sat and watched in silence as Abigail strode out of the room.

Henry spent the day in his room, grinding and polishing, letting the white noise of the ocean drown out the thoughts swarming in his mind. Occasionally he'd find himself replaying snippets of his exchange with Abigail that morning, the accusation in her voice. Or he'd recall Alan's face that last morning before he left, as they'd hidden in the ginnel between their houses. Alan had told him not to be so soft because Henry was crying and couldn't stop, and Alan had said they had a duty to king and country, that they'd both come back heroes, and he'd kissed him soft and deep although anyone could've come past or peered out of their window and caught them.

Chalky dust from the mussel shells coated Henry's hands, his clothes, his work table. It settled in his hair like snow, and made him sneeze. After a few hours, Henry started to feel light-headed and drowsy. He staggered over to the bed and collapsed down onto it, exhausted by the weight of guilt crushing him and the exertions of his work.

He woke to find Abigail standing over him with a tea tray. The room was dark, save for the glow of the gas lamp, and Henry realised he must have slept for the entire afternoon. His head was pounding.

"I thought you must be starving by now," Abigail said, setting the tray down. "I didn't mean to wake you, but I was worried. I wanted to apologise for the way I spoke to you earlier."

"No," said Henry, propping himself up on his elbows. "I'm the one who should be sorry. I let my imagination run away with me. You've been good enough to take me in, to cook for me, indulge me with your company and this is how I repay you. I should never have allowed my foolish fancies to run wild, especially not after you have been so hospitable and confided so much in me."

"Really, Henry, it's quite all right," said Abigail. "I understand what it must be like, trying to adjust to a new place. I know your work is important to you, and that artists often have a more sensitive nature than the rest of us. I suppose you wouldn't be much good at creating beautiful things if you viewed the world as any other man would. Your curiosity and wonder are tools, just as these are," she gestured to the desk, strewn with Henry's files, scalpels, and chisels, "and it was wrong of me to react so badly." Abigail put her hand on Henry's shoulder. "Eat, get some sleep, and everything will be better in the morning."

★ ★ ★

Henry's dreams that night were fevered and disturbing. He felt Alan's hands on his naked skin, the heat they trailed enticing at first. But then Henry realised Alan was burning, flames licking at their entwined bodies, the air thick and greasy with the smell of melting tallow, and then they were falling. They hit the surface of the water hard enough to knock the breath from him. He was sinking, cold brine stinging his eyes and his nose and his lungs. Alan was gone, and Henry was drowning. But before he reached the gritty seabed, a giant hand cradled him and lifted him up, up and out of the water, and placed him on a jagged rock. The hand was hard and black like onyx, but Henry couldn't see the rest of his saviour. Before he could catch his breath, a great bird descended and started to peck at his soft, pink body, tearing holes in his skin.

Henry woke with a shout. He sat up and inhaled through his nose for the count of four and out again, trying to tamp down the panic he felt swelling inside his chest. He hoped it hadn't been loud enough to reach Abigail's room. He huddled against the headboard, the coverlet pulled up around him, closed his eyes for a moment, and when he opened them again, there, illuminated by the moon, sat a pale little boy at the foot of the bed.

Blood thundered in Henry's ears. The boy stared, unblinking.

"What do you want?" Henry asked in a strangled whisper.

The boy said nothing. He held Henry's gaze.

"Arthur?"

A small, shy smile tugged at the corners of the boy's mouth. He looked so real. Such a sweet child. Henry slowly reached out a hand to touch his milk-white skin, but as he leant forward, the little boy vanished into thin air.

* * *

He didn't say anything about his nocturnal visitor to Abigail the next day. He'd caused her enough distress, and she'd been so gracious about everything. Henry, however, had become deeply afraid of the attic. The spectre had been no shadow, no trick of the eye. He'd been as corporeal as anything Henry had ever seen. His first instinct was to pack his meagre possessions and leave on the first train back to the city. But then he'd remembered Prometheus. The Titan was starting to take shape. It was Henry's most ambitious piece to date, and if he got this right, it might change his fortune forever. Henry looked over at the growing bulk of dark, twisted matter. He could be magnificent, this Prometheus. If Henry could render the musculature just so, give the unyielding shell the appearance of soft, pliant flesh, convey the horror of the Titan's ceaseless torment, the malice of the bird, his sculpture might garner great renown. One day, it might even sit in a world-famous museum alongside Michelangelos, Rodins, or Berninis. Henry sighed, and swung his legs out of bed.

For the next few days, Henry thought of nothing but Prometheus. He whittled and hewed, pausing only when his vision became too blurry to continue, or a sudden movement in his periphery caused him to look up from his work. Every now and then, the certainty that someone was watching him settled on Henry's shoulders like a yoke, but when he whipped around to catch the spy in the act, there was no one there.

The whispering was another matter entirely. Henry heard it incessantly – children giggling and speaking his name in hushed tones.

Abigail said nothing about the long hours Henry spent, hunched over his sculpture, shaving shells into tiny replicas of the intricacies of the male anatomy – each muscle, sinew, and ligament picked out in stark relief. She brought him coffee and food, and if she noticed the ripe smell emanating from his skin and clothes after several days without washing, she was too polite to mention it.

Henry ate little and slept even less. He grew accustomed to the sounds of children playing in the attic room behind him as he worked – the laughter, the little footsteps chasing each other about, the steady rhythm of a rocking horse that didn't exist against the floorboards like a metronome.

Like their sister, Grace and Arthur were fine company. Less desirable were the visits from Alan, which occurred with increasing frequency when Henry allowed his eyelids to droop and let sleep claim him. Alan on fire, the skin of his lovely face blistered and bubbling, or Alan lying bloated and fish-nibbled on the seabed, saying, "See, Henry! I told you we'd be heroes!" Alan hanging in Henry's wardrobe, his parachute tangled around his neck, lips purple and eyes red.

Days turned into weeks as time slipped through Henry's fingers like silt. Abigail managed to persuade Henry to sit with her some evenings, rather than freeze up in the garret, but their conversation was stunted. Henry noted the lines around his landlady's eyes had become more pronounced. She didn't sing much anymore.

Winter set in, and the sea raged all through the long nights. Henry toiled as best as he could by lamp light, and as much as Grace, Arthur, and Alan would allow. Prometheus, like a child, grew with each passing day. Henry lovingly carved and buffed and scored and shaped, revealing more and more of his creation's god-like stature and his features. He even sculpted a little heart from mother of pearl, just visible beneath the spread of his ribcage. A calcified heart, just like the poet Shelley's – it was said his wife, Mary, saved from his funeral pyre and kept with her until her own death.

But while Prometheus grew in size and strength, Henry diminished. He wondered if the spirits which plagued him day and night were some kind of vampire, draining him of his joy and vitality. Though he tried to conceal it from Abigail, Henry found himself weeping almost constantly, like he had that time back in Flanders. His eyesight had become strained and blurry. His head ached all the time, his ears rang, and his hands shook. Now and then, he'd pick up a tool and then have to set it down again, forgetting entirely what he'd meant to do with it.

One afternoon, there was a rap on the attic door. Henry paused, unsure as to whether the sound was earthly, or just the children playing. It came again, and Abigail stepped into the garret. She tried to smile, but it was more of a grimace, and she failed to disguise the look of disgust which scudded across her expression as the stifling, stale air of the room overwhelmed her.

"Henry! I have some errands to run, and I must insist you accompany me. It's a lovely crisp day, and the salt air will do you a world of good." Abigail's gaze drifted towards Prometheus and she gave a little gasp. "He's magnificent," she said, awe replacing the concern in her voice.

"Isn't he just," said Henry. "So, you see, I can't possibly leave him. We're at a vital stage. I must finish this left arm or the sense of movement will be quite lost."

"I see," said Abigail slowly. "But wouldn't it help to have the rock for him to recline against? Surely the shape of the seat will inform the final pose? Why don't you come out and see if there's anything suitable on the beach? And what of the eagle? Perhaps we might find some feathers and flints for him?"

Despair crept over Henry as he realised Abigail was right. He'd been so preoccupied with his little giant that he'd quite forgotten about those elements. He was such a fool! He stood on wobbly legs and put on his coat, following Abigail down the stairs and out into the glaring light of day.

As they made their way slowly down to the shore, Abigail turned to Henry and took his hands in her own.

"Henry, I wanted to ask you something. It can't have escaped your notice that Christmas is upon us and, well, I just wondered if you had any plans to return home?"

Henry tried to recall what day it was and realised, to his horror, that he had no idea at all.

"Christmas. Yes. I hadn't really thought…"

"I simply mean, I'm sure there are people you're longing to see? Perhaps someone special waiting for you back home?"

Henry tried his best not to think about Alan and his water-bloated features.

"No, not really. Mother and Father might be expecting me… I hadn't thought…"

"Of course, I should be glad of the company should you choose to stay here," she said. "I just thought perhaps you might miss your family."

Henry pictured his mother sat at home, waiting for news of him as she had done so often in the past, and a pang of regret pricked at him.

"Well, I'm sure there's still time to make arrangements," said Abigail. "We have a couple of weeks if you'd like to go into town and book a train ticket."

The thought of leaving Prometheus was absolutely preposterous, but Henry stayed silent.

"Well, as I say, I have some errands to run, so why don't I leave you here. You can look for a rock for Prometheus, and I'll get something nice for supper and meet you at home?"

She smiled and Henry nodded. The world seemed to be moving in slow motion, what he saw around him lagging behind the movement of his head. Abigail walked away, and Henry stalked carefully to a cluster of rocks covered in barnacles and strings of seaweed. He should have remembered to bring his tools to chip off what he needed. He couldn't seem to complete a thought these days. When had he last eaten? He couldn't remember, though he was sure Abigail would have prepared lunch. It was not like her to neglect her lodger. Henry ran his hand over the rough stone. There were a pleasing variety of textures – the wet, sandy rock, the slippery dulse, the knobbly creatures clinging to the surface like an extension of the geology.

Henry was roused from his sensory exploration by a long shadow thrown across the sand where the water lapped at the shore. He looked up to see a man walking towards him, the gait and demeanour of the stranger eerily familiar. He was wearing a coat very similar to Henry's and had a hat pulled down over his brow, the brim obscuring his face. On impulse, Henry stepped out from behind the rocks and into the path of the man. The stranger looked up and Henry staggered backwards, aghast. The stranger wasn't a stranger at all. Henry was staring at himself.

Henry squeezed his eyes shut and opened them again, but the stranger was no mirage. He was as real as Henry was. Henry took a step forwards, scrutinising the man's blank expression. What fresh Hell was this? Maybe there was a rational explanation. For this and for everything. Henry had been so focused on his art recently. Perhaps his mind was playing tricks on him. He cleared his throat.

"Hello!" Henry said, extending his shaking hand to the stranger.

But the man with Henry's face remained silent. He held Henry's gaze for a few heartbeats, and then his mouth stretched into a rictus grin, a hideous parody of Henry's own smile. Every hair on Henry's body stood on end, and his scalp prickled. His legs felt leaden, his knees tried to buckle, but the urge to get away from this horrible apparition was overwhelming. Henry ran.

Back at the house, Henry sat at the kitchen table and tried to make sense of what had happened. His heart was racing, and he wondered if Abigail kept any liquor in the house. Just then, he heard the front door open, and voices in the hall. Not trusting his own senses, Henry waited in the kitchen until he heard Abigail's voice calling him. He ventured up the steps, legs unsteady and shaky as a new-born foal's, and saw his landlady standing with a man he didn't recognise.

"Henry," said Abigail softly. "This is Doctor Collins. He'd like to examine you, if you'll permit it."

"Examine me?" Henry said, indignant. "Whatever for?"

Abigail sighed. "I think you might be unwell, Henry. You don't eat or bathe, and you barely sleep. You have trouble remembering things. I really think you should let the doctor do some tests. I'm worried about you."

"I have work to do," said Henry, trying to move past the pair to the staircase, but Doctor Collins held him with a firm grip to the shoulder.

"Ms Travers is trying to help you, young man. I suggest you heed her advice. You look dreadful."

Anger rose in Henry. He felt his jaw set and his hands ball into fists. Who was this man to come here and prevent his progress on Prometheus? Did either of them have the first idea of the things he had to put up with?

"Well maybe," spat Henry, "I'd get more sleep if I wasn't kept up all night by *her* dead siblings making such a racket!" He pointed at Abigail and saw fear in her eyes.

"Henry," she said solemnly. "You're not well."

Henry tried to respond, but the doctor's grasp on his shoulder shifted and tightened, and then everything went black.

★ ★ ★

It was dark when he woke. Doctor Collins and Abigail were standing by his bed. He'd been undressed and there was a throbbing pain in his arm.

"We'll have to test his blood, of course, but my guess is poison."

Abigail sniffed and wiped her eyes with a handkerchief.

"But we got rid of the wallpaper!" she said miserably.

"Look at all this!" Doctor Collins said, gesturing at the fine layer of powder coating the room, the discarded shells all over the floor, and the fledgling Prometheus, lying on the table. "Mussel shells are full of poisonous metals. Arsenic. Lead. Quicksilver. If he's been eating and breathing the little buggers in these quantities, he's probably done irreversible damage to his nervous system."

Abigail let out sob.

"I had no idea. How could I have known?"

Grace and Arthur stood silently in the corner. Alan's face appeared in the skylight above, blue and moon-like. He smiled. His teeth fell out of his mouth and rained down on the glass like pebbles.

Henry tried to say something, but he hadn't the strength. He looked over at Prometheus, a laugh bubbling up in his throat. The little god lay on the table, infuriatingly incomplete. Henry would finish him. It might be the last thing he ever did. He'd lived through the mud and the mortars and the breaking of his heart. He would summon all his energy, and he would finish. He would find a place for him and the little Titan, somewhere away from the prying eyes of medics and landladies and parents. Somewhere they could be alone amongst the dust, the barnacles, the feathers, the bones. And the poison metals that would slowly kill Henry as he gave life to his Prometheus.

HOMESICK

Sam Hirst

The worst thing about being a ghost is running out of books.

The material plane is not accessible to you, only that which was material alongside you in life. Contrary to what the Bible states, you do get to take it with you – in a way. All that you had when you were alive is one wish away, but anything that came after is strictly look-and-don't-touch. Marion had owned quite the library in life, but being a fast reader and over two hundred years of death meant that she had left new material behind a long time ago.

Marion sat on her favourite seat, a library armchair which had seen better days before her death, its brown leather already cracked and worn. *Her* chair hadn't aged a day, although its material counterpart had long ago fallen into ruin. She had watched sadly as the scion of a later generation had thrown it with all the other 'junk' into a barn, where it had slowly fallen into decay, ravaged by the damp and animal depredations. Her version of the chair, however, remained exactly the same as the day she'd died. As did she. She straightened in her familiar seat, gloomily staring at the copy of Burke's *Philosophical Enquiry* in her hand. She'd read it so many times she could quote it word for word and she was sick of every last syllable. She looked up from it to stare about her. The leather library chair sat incongruously in the middle of Farnley forest which, at this time of the year, was a riot of bluebells. One advantage of being a ghost was materialising her possessions wherever she wanted.

She swung a booted foot encased in a polished hessian. She was clad in biscuit-toned breeches, with a dark blue long-tailed coat, a white waistcoat, moderate shirt points and a loosely tied cravat. She stroked the material of her trousers lightly. She had just the one set. She remembered the day she'd gone to the tailor. She had fooled them, she was sure she had, with her tale of a twin of her size and colouring. She'd allowed herself just one set of clothes, carefully chosen. In life she'd only ever worn it a few times, in the safety of her own room and usually by candle-light, peering into the glass and seeing herself half-obscured by its wavering flame. A few brief moments where she'd felt more at home in her own skin than any other time. The rest of the time, they had lain hidden. After death, she had rarely worn anything else. Occasionally, she'd chosen the worn day dress which she had used for cataloguing the library, or the pelisse in which she'd walked the high cliffs of Dover before her one journey abroad, or the red riding dress which she debuted on her visit to her brother the few weeks before her death. Clothes that had comfortable or cherished memories worn into their seams. It seemed unfair that those who had reported her spirit haunting the Farnley manor had decided she was a woman in white. Certainly, she'd never worn one of those irritatingly virginal gowns after death. Perhaps the living saw her colours differently, but she was inclined to believe that they simply saw what they wanted to see – the ghost that already haunted their imaginations. She was also fairly sure that she'd been mistaken for a re-enactor before. Her ghostly self was as unbelievable an anomaly as she had been in life. That was one good thing about this new world. She didn't feel quite so alone anymore. Not quite so different. She doubted she'd been as alone as she'd thought at the time but her world had been so closed. Things were so different now.

She glanced around and the restless look seeped from her face. There was nothing new to read, but she never grew tired of the view in Farnley forest. She breathed in the familiar air.

She'd travelled in the last two hundred years. Travelled all over the globe to places that she'd never even heard of in life. Seen a world which had changed beyond imagination. She'd learnt and seen and wondered but she always came back. That was why the dead returned to their homes, she was sure – not because they were trapped, but because everyone has a home somewhere, a place their soul longs for. It might not be the place you were born, it might not even be a place you'd visited in life, but for her, it was the home where she'd grown up. Where she'd bent over her sewing in spurious diligence and where she'd stolen into her father's library and leafed through what had seemed its endless shelves every time watchful eyes were turned away. It was the familiar wild woods and desolate moors that she had loved in life, through which she had strode, free from maids and brothers and conventions, and traced infinity written in the boundless expanse. In death, she had walked them all until she was familiar with every inch. Every year brought changes – a beauty which renewed itself and never lost its fascination. That beautiful land did get lonely, though.

She had met other ghosts in her travels. Not everyone who died became a haunting presence; else the world would be full of shades. As it was, you could travel for miles without seeing another dead soul. They made poor company when you did come across one, though. They were always obsessed with something – a loss, a betrayal, revenge, despair… She supposed the fact that she was still here meant that her slow death of what she'd presumed had been consumption had been something more nefarious. Perhaps there was some revenge she had been left on Earth to enact or, on the contrary, some form of repentance was demanded. Yet she had no desire for vengeance and felt no need for repentance. Her death had been a slow departure from an uneventful life that held little promise. If she wasn't exactly thankful, she wasn't angry that those long years had been taken from her. This death was a great deal more agreeable. Free to pursue her own course, she had been gladly who she chose to be for two hundred years now. She prided herself secretly on the way she had adapted. She had met hundreds of wailing widows, vengeful brides and betrayed lovers and few had learnt to do anything more with their death in hundreds of years than make themselves and the living miserable. She, however, had worked out the rules, the possibilities... and the restrictions. Eventually, you just ran out of things to read.

What she needed was a holiday. A trip to the coast. To gaze out at the cold North Sea. Something different to get rid of the feeling of sameness which lingered however much she loved being at Farnley. Perhaps she should have been more focused on the riddle of her continued existence. Perhaps you were meant to find a solution and leave. She'd never tried. She'd never wanted to.

And so it was that a week later, she sat on a harbour wall, looking into the midnight blue of the night sky as it stretched to meet the ocean. Eternity was more tangible to the dead, but the sight still held a tinge of the old familiar sublimity which had filled her soul with the hum of possibility in life. It was far enough away from the cities of incessant light for her to be able to trace the stars. She recalled the old patterns that she had learnt when alive and called her celestial globe into her hand. She had no doubt that it was outdated but she lovingly traced its surface with her hand and bent her attention to identifying what she could see.

"It's beautiful, isn't it?" The voice came from behind her but two feet appeared at her side before she had time to turn. "Do you mind if I sit down?"

Marion looked up and saw a tall girl looking down with a somewhat shy question in her eyes.

"Of course," she half-whispered before clearing her non-existent throat, irritated at her lack of voice.

The girl arranged her skirts, which were black and floor-length, before sitting cross-legged beside Marion. She held out a hand, shaking back the sleeve of a baggy red cardigan as she did so.

"I'm Sanan," she said as she waited for Marion to take her hand.

They shook. There was a feeling of warmth for a second as their fingers pressed together. It had been a long time since Marion had felt anything at all. If she'd thought about it, she'd have supposed the dead couldn't feel much of anything. But then, she'd never had any actual contact with those other wailing spectres.

The shy voice broke through her wondering confusion, "I'm sorry to intrude but you so rarely see anyone who's not... you know..."

"Rather too much the spectre?"

"Exactly," nodded Sanan with a small smile of fellow-feeling. "A bit ghost-y."

Their eyes met, curious and tentative. Marion couldn't remember the words to say. She had forgotten the patterns of conversation, the words that kept the other speaking, that kept them with you for a little while.

Sanan, for her part, feared she was disturbing this straight-backed, peaceful woman who slipped so easily into silence and whose eyes seemed half lost in the night sky. But she had been alone too long to let her slip away so quickly and she still remembered the desperate stultifying rhythms of small talk that you hoped would become the beginning of something real. "What's your name?"

"My name was Marion Oboroten," she replied, the words rusty in her mouth from long disuse.

"Russian?" Sanan enquired, fascinated by the soft voice which sounded of a world lost long ago.

"My grandfather hailed from Russia," said Marion. "He accompanied his father as a child. They followed in the train of Peter. He travelled incognito but a prince never travels quite alone." She smiled softly, amused.

Sanan couldn't look away. The stranger told the story of a history turned long ago into legend as easily as Sanan would tell a story about her own äbi, sitting in the kitchen on a winter's day, cursing this sodden country's endless damp. Marion's smile sat familiar, unexceptional, on her face. It wasn't the smile of a tale spinner – simply the smile of memory, a familiar reflex. Its ease fascinated Sanan. But as leisurely as it seemed, it was soon gone.

Marion hadn't forgotten the currency of smiles, how they spoke a language of their own. The memory passed, replaced by another and the smile faded from her face, leaving it neutral. "We were all obliged to learn Russian while he lived. He was... most insistent on that."

"A curious name."

"Yes," replied Marion drily, "and not without its family legend."

"Is that why...?" Sanan's voice trailed off. Was it a social solecism to ask the reason for a life after death? She hadn't had enough converse with others to know. The moment grew awkward. "My brother killed me," she blurted out. *Way to start a conversation, Sanan.*

Marion was slightly taken aback but was even more so when she heard her own voice saying, "As did mine." She realised that that was exactly what she believed. Money or shame or disgust... it didn't matter why. She hadn't thought it before. She hadn't let herself wonder. Some wounds are best denied. But her realisation had come out like an echo – immediate, unthinking. An obvious reality. A twinge of sorrow tugged at her chest. But it was a long time ago.

"I'm sorry," said Sanan conventionally, awkwardly. It was harder talking to the dead than she'd thought.

"There is no reason to apologise. It is of no consequence. Although, perhaps for you... is it more recent? Is it still fresh in your mind?"

"It's been ten years now." Sanan looked curiously at the woman beside her dressed, to her mind, like Darcy. "How long..."

"Over two hundred years."

Sanan gasped. "I'm sorry but two hundred… That's ages."

Marion looked at her, thoughtful. "It does not seem to me to have been so long a time; it has passed easily. The greatest ill that I have had to bear is… well, I have run out of things to read."

"I may be able to help you with that." Sanan smiled, thankful to have so easily found a way to connect with this otherworldly woman. A book appeared in her hand. "This is one of my favourites."

Marion reached out hesitantly and touched the ghostly cover. Its texture was rough beneath her fingertips. She laid her hand on the spine and gripped, pulling the book slowly from Sanan's hand. Her ghostly eyes needed no light to read the title – *The Quiet Gentleman* by Georgette Heyer. "My God. Thank you," she said, her voice quavering ever so slightly as tears streamed quietly down her face.

"No worries," replied Sanan, smiling kindly at Marion's emotion. "I've hundreds more where that came from."

Spontaneously, Marion turned and hugged Sanan hard against her. Her heart beat out of time. She felt Sanan sag into the hug after an initial resistance. "Thank you!" Marion whispered. She pulled back. "May I?" she asked, gesturing to the book.

"Of course," replied Sanan with a grin, another book appearing in her hand. Everything felt easy all of a sudden. They sat until dawn in companionable silence.

When Marion had finished, having rushed through the novel like a woman half-starved, she closed the volume, a quiet hum in her heart, and looked out at the rising sun as it burnt the waves on the horizon. She turned to look down at the head which had somehow come to rest on her shoulder. Sanan was sleepily reading through the last chapter, her hands sluggish on the page. As Marion looked down at the long black hair falling over her arm, the crooked glasses on Sanan's focussed face and the smile that curved her lips, she wondered if she had ever seen anything quite so beautiful. She smiled and allowed herself to let the book fall into the void. She leaned against the wall beside her, enjoying the soft weight on her right side, the first warmth she had felt in centuries. She let sleep take her. In the hazy dawn light, someone passing by the dock might have seen two women dozing, leaning against each other, one of them loosely grasping a book in sleepy fingers. They might have seen two women in white. Or they might have seen nothing at all.

That sleepy seaside town wasn't Sanan's home. She'd been there on a chance visit. After Marion had explained her theory, Sanan responded that she didn't think she had a home yet. The house where she had grown, the city in which she'd studied, the town in France where she'd worked for a year after graduating, the tiny flat in Bishkek where she'd been when her father had fallen sick and she'd come back because she'd had to. The house she'd never left again… None of them were home. Places that she'd left, places that she'd run to, places that she'd been. But none of them a home. The 'yet', the idea that there was a home to find, was a new idea to her. Sanan hoped that Marion was right. It seemed like she'd always been homesick, never knowing where home was. For now, she was happy to travel, to continue the wandering that had brought her to the pier where they'd met – and Marion was happy to accompany her.

That first easy comfort didn't return for quite some time. The morning after their first acquaintance they had danced around their hungry longing for company and talked of guides and experiences and shared libraries. They had arranged themselves around an excuse and didn't mention that thin tenuous hope that threaded through their minds, that yearning that whispered that perhaps now they might not be quite so alone.

In the beginning, it had been only books they'd really shared. They had travelled on a tour of British seaside towns, neither knowing how nor why they'd made the decision. Marion had taken on the role of tour guide since that was the ruse that they had used. She felt words falling stilted yet horribly fluently from her tongue with facts and histories and did-you-knows until her brain was yelling at her to desist. But when silence came it hung in the air like an accusation that she was there under false pretences and she'd begin again, a burble of sound, the fumbling start of something like communication. There was so much she didn't know, though. So many years between visits with buildings and people changing beyond recognition. And then Sanan would take up the gauntlet and explain some aspect of the modern world that Marion found incomprehensible. The role of tour guide, polite and so interestedly indifferent, seemed infectious. Then, one day, months after their initial meeting, months of slow creeping familiarity baffled by the polite barriers of an excuse which had served its purpose but refused to fade away, they visited Lyme Regis.

Marion had been reading delighted through the works of Austen and, as they had walked through the town at dawn, Sanan had suggested visiting the pier. As they had walked, Marion had read aloud. They had fallen into the habit of sharing interesting passages. As they ambled along, Sanan felt something like a bridge between them, more real and solid than all their exchanges of information. They approached the steps, and with a mischievous smile, she glanced across at Marion, whose eyes seemed rooted to the page. Some spirit had possessed her, perhaps, but without thinking, she ran to the top of steps, turned and cried, "Catch me, Wentworth!" before hurling herself off.

Marion looked up sharply and gasped in shock. Running to the edge, she was about to look down when Sanan appeared again − floating level with her. She chuckled. "We're ghosts, remember! You should have seen your face!"

Marion had glared for a second before catching the infection of her laughter.

When they had laughed themselves out, something was better, easier. They sat apart at first on the end of the pier and then one propped up against the other as they passed the book between them, reading aloud until the very end.

Both reticent by nature, eventually they advanced in slow steps from stilted conversation and shared silences, book recommendations and shared fictional adventures to life stories, clothes swaps (Sanan was enamoured of each and every gown and Marion thought jeans the most comfortable thing she'd ever hoped to experience), shared jokes, and a joy in each other's company that made death seem like a beginning. Marion wondered if perhaps it wasn't murder which had bound them here but something much more beautiful. Perhaps this was just a second chance at living.

They had found a shared thread, and it only needed pulling to find the shared world from which it had unravelled itself. Sanan introduced Marion to the period drama. They visited Chatsworth, Bath, Lyme Park, where Marion dived into the lake and played Mr Darcy as Sanan stood laughing on the shore. They read the Brontës and walked the moors, visited Top Withens, Haworth, Haddon Hall – so close to Marion's home but far enough away... She didn't dare go back. Not yet. They proceeded to the theatre, visiting Shakespeare's Globe, where they argued on his greatest work. Marion favoured *Macbeth* but Sanan was all for *Twelfth Night*. "Full of scorpions is my mind... at this dissent!" "But fair Viola... Was not this love indeed?"

Then they sat, shadows, at the back of West End theatres dressed to the nines in Marion's finery. "Making an occasion of it," as Sanan declared, though Marion wondered, smiling to herself, if Sanan had merely wanted to go through her wardrobe. Sanan introduced her to musicals and Marion fell in love. They went every day for a month. They learnt the songs to every single one they saw and sang them as they travelled. "Memories" as they crossed the Alps, "Red and Black" as they trod the backstreets of Paris, "The Angel of Music" as they walked on Venice's waters. They laughed as they played their roles to melodramatic perfection but there was a shade of longing that became difficult to ignore.

They travelled further and further afield. They viewed opera at the Teatro Alla Scala, ballet at the Bolshoi, Flamenco in Sevilla, and shadow puppetry in Visakhapatnam. They wandered the world, places that they'd heard of, places that they half-remembered, places Sanan had spent a life dreaming of visiting and Marion had drifted through in death. And then they shared the geography of their own stories, then the stories of their parents and their grandparents before them. Immune to heat and cold and every discomfort, they travelled where no living person could and laughed in the face of thundering showers of ice, the direst desert winds and the whirling blizzards of mountain peaks. They had travelled half the world when Marion began to feel the call of home. It had ached dully in her for years but it had been banked by the fires of new experience. Now, though, the ache threatened to consume her and though she fought it, not wanting to let go, it conquered her. Sanan watched with concern as she grew quieter, more pensive, something sorrowful dulling her eyes. In the end, standing on the latest precipice and watching Marion's eyes long for some other beauty, Sanan demanded to be told how to help. Together, they returned.

Marion's journey back to Farnley was weighted with suppressed tension. They had travelled the world for years. Sanan had never found a home and Marion had secretly been relieved every time they had left a place and its dust behind them. She was returning home because her heart had been longing for it – it wasn't forever. But it was hard to be away for so long with no return, without the familiar sites, the ground which seemed packed hard with memories and belonging. She hoped, but she didn't speak her hope. Expressing in words what her heart wanted had never been her strength. They'd both maintained their silence for too long to break it. Sanan rather thought that homes might be more mobile than Marion believed, but she too was anxious. She wanted to love Farnley. Yet there was a fire in her heart which burned against it for the life that Marion had lived. But if she could love it, then she could stay and not worry that one day, she too would grow pale and ache with every fibre of her being for another place. A place without Marion.

On their return journey, they passed through the village where they had met on the way there and sat once more upon the dock. Sanan rested her head in Marion's lap as Marion read *The Quiet Gentleman* out loud. An anniversary of sorts.

It was a crisp winter morning when they arrived in Farnley. As they walked along the paths long familiar to Marion, although long forgotten by the living, there was silence. Their hands touched in passing but they had not held. Marion was loath to hold Sanan down if she had to leave. Sanan knew she could not yet offer comfort – for the fear and the hope were both, as yet, unspoken.

Sanan's first glimpse of the manor house was through a fringe of trees. The light played with shadow across the building's face. The gardens, long since grown wild, moved in and out of view. She had come prepared to like and hate it. But as she stepped over the boundary there was a sense of home that stemmed not from the place itself but from what it was to Marion. The land, the distant moors and wooded shades, claimed her as their own. She belonged here. With Marion. It would have no hold on her without the woman at her side. Stopping short, she brought the crisp air into her lungs, rested her eyes on the wild riot of life before her. Reaching out, her hand took Marion's and brought it to her lips. Their eyes met.

"Welcome home," said Marion faintly, half questioningly.

"Welcome home," Sanan repeated firmly and drew Marion into her arms.

★ ★ ★

If you pass through the ruins of Farnley and enter the bluebell grove in Farnley forest, you may come across two chairs. One is a worn leather library chair, the other a rocking chair covered in colourful blankets and cheerfully plump cushions. In them will sit two women wearing curious mixtures of clothing, both ancient and modern, each with a book in one hand while the other forms a bridge between the chairs, where two hands meet and clasp loosely together. You may see them smiling quietly as they read or as they meet each other's eyes. You may see them walking together through a crisp autumn day. You may catch sight of them between the spring flowers. You might miss them altogether. Ghosts appreciate a holiday as much as the next person and they have so much world left to see.

If you are particularly unperceptive, you may see two women in white. If so, they're not wailing, they're laughing.

RODEO

Ryann Fletcher

Sadie Mae had spent all of her twenty-five years hearing about the seven deadly sins in her father's church, but it wasn't until the night of the midnight rodeo that she experienced lust for the first time.

She watched the final rider of the night dismount her chestnut mare after an impressive run of the barrels, beating all of the competition by over three seconds. The rider was petite, wearing jet-black Levis studded with rhinestones over the back pocket and bronze-tipped boots peeking out from under her jeans. Her dark purple western-style shirt had mother of pearl buttons that glinted in the fluorescent glow of the stadium floodlights. Unlike all the other riders, there wasn't a single glint of silver on the horse's tack or the rider's clothes, replaced instead by a bright shining copper.

Drawn in by the woman's perfect form during the event, Sadie leaned forward with her elbows propped on her knees, the thin floral fabric of her long skirt damp with sweat. The rider seemed to communicate with her horse effortlessly, with the two working in tandem as they swung around each of the barrels in perfect rhythm as the sand from the arena exploded with every hoof beat. The night was heavy, and the scent of honeysuckle was cloying. Here in East Texas, the August air was so humid and oppressive that when a breeze danced across the arena's stands, the spectators all sighed with collective relief.

"Pastor Buck, how wonderful to see you here supportin' our local riders," said Edna, one of the congregation's most fervent members.

"You know me, Edna, I can't resist the temptation of a rodeo, even now I can't ride them broncos like I used to," Sadie's father said with a tip of his black Stetson.

"Lucky for you our good lord Jesus Christ never said nothin' about rodeos," Edna replied with a wink.

"I reckon I'll see you Sunday mornin', Edna?"

"I'll be there with bells on!" Edna turned to Sadie, who was still gazing out across the arena, her eyes following the mysterious rider who was patting the side of her horse's neck as she waited for the scores to be tallied. "And good evenin' to you too, Miss Sadie Mae," Edna said. "Seems you're real interested in that new rider tonight." She raised an eyebrow. "She's real pretty ain't she?"

Sadie's father put an arm around her shoulders and squeezed the back of her neck threateningly. "My little Sadie's just tired, aren't you darlin'? Almost can't keep her eyes open."

"Mmhm," Sadie nodded, wiggling from her father's grasp. "Just real tired, Miss Edna. Been busy making apple pies and sheet cake for the church bake sale." She stood up and smoothed the wrinkled fabric of her skirt. "I need the ladies' room, if you'll excuse me," she said with a smile she had learned from a young age to paint on in the presence of her father's congregants.

She shuffled past a group of boisterous men, excusing herself quietly and edging sideways down the aisle, her expensive snakeskin cowboy boots shuffling along the damp wooden boards.

"Hey darlin', why don't you just sit on my lap and have a chat?" one of the men said loudly, gesturing at his oil-stained jeans with a mock innocent expression. "Y'all know I can't resist a pretty girl walkin' past," he said to his friends.

They laughed wolfishly as they stared, drinking in the sight of Sadie's body like she was an oasis in a desert. Sadie's stomach twisted with disgust, but she waved them off with a smile and an "Oh, you," as she sidled past and down the rickety, sand-covered stairs. The arena speakers blasted a cover of an old George Straight song, and Sadie heard the men drunkenly singing along. This was a dry county, but that was barely a deterrent in these parts. There was not much to do on a Friday night other than drink beers in your backyard while meaty flesh burned on the grill. At least tonight, there was the midnight rodeo, a yearly event that attracted out-of-town riders with its fat purse. It was Arcadia's only attempt at drawing in tourists and money, though the town had wallowed in poverty since the government had shut down the fracking sites.

Instead of heading left towards the ladies' room, Sadie stole a glance up at the stands to her father, who was still engrossed in conversation with Edna. He was leaning forward with that pastorly earnestness that had grown his congregation from a dozen attendees to hundreds over the years. Sadie turned right, ducking underneath a huge Texas flag that drifted lazily in the still air.

Sadie crept closer, drawn to the rider, heart pounding in her chest. She wasn't sure what she would do if she was discovered. The rider was cooing to her horse as she walked it back towards her horse trailer, feeding it apples as they walked. "You did so good tonight," she whispered to the horse, and Sadie realised she was following too close.

"Good evenin'," the rider said without turning around. "Anything I can help you with?" The pretty mare flicked her tail, which was impeccably groomed. It was obvious the rider cared a great deal for her horse.

"Uh, no," Sadie stammered. "I just wanted to say your ride was real impressive is all." She skipped around the woman to face her. "And your horse is gorgeous."

The woman gave a tight-lipped, ruby-red smile and tipped her hat. "Thank you. And you're right, she is." She patted the horse on the neck before loading it into the trailer and slamming the door shut.

Sadie held out her hand. "I'm Sadie," she said.

"Nice to meet you, Sadie," the woman replied, giving Sadie's hand a firm, confident shake. "You from around here?"

"Up the road a piece." She paused for a beat. "Where are you from?"

"I'm from all over," the woman said. "Jasmine and I," she gestured at the horse trailer, "we travel round and compete when we can."

"You must win every time, riding like that," Sadie said eagerly. "Your form is perfect, and I bet you never get thrown, and—"

"I've been thrown a fair few times in my life," the woman said with a deep Georgian drawl, eyeing Sadie's skirt and pristine boots. "You don't ride?"

Sadie shook her head. "Daddy won't allow it."

The woman scowled and shook her head. "Well I hope someday you get the opportunity, it's like nothin' you've ever felt. It's like flyin'."

"Next up: which of our brave young men will best the bucking bronco this year?" the stadium speakers boomed.

"My brother is riding tonight," Sadie offered. "He's won every rodeo from here to El Paso this year, and my daddy reckons he'll take this one too, even though some of the country's best riders are here."

"Ain't nothing impressive about strapping yourself to a pissed off bronco," the woman said under her breath. "Jasmine and I work as a team, we train long hours to get good at the barrels and the cloverleaf. Bronco riding is just the want to conquer something, to prove they're man enough to take whatever they want."

Sadie nodded. "I don't much care for it either," she agreed. "But my daddy was a bronco rider, so my brother Johnny is too." She pressed her palm against the cool steel of the horse trailer and sighed angrily. "Round here, family tradition matters more than respect for your animal. If I ran this rodeo, bronco ridin' would be banned." She turned back towards the woman, and was surprised to see her dark grey eyes fixed on her.

The woman leaned against the shiny horse trailer, the metal emitting a dull glow in the moonlight. "Sadie, you said?"

She nodded.

"Well, Sadie, you're the prettiest girl here tonight."

Blood rushed to Sadie's face. "Thank you," she whispered, smoothing the fabric of her brown and cream button-down shirt and tucking the excess into the waistband of her ankle length skirt.

"It's rare I see a thing as pretty as you at a rodeo this far into the middle of nowhere," the woman continued. "The pretty ones are always wifed to some beast that treats 'em like garbage."

"I'm not married," Sadie said quickly. "My daddy says no one around here is fit."

The cicadas buzzed quietly at the periphery of the arena, where the flood lights couldn't reach, and the insects hummed beneath the din of the speakers. The woman tilted her head to the side. "Your daddy's never met me."

Sadie burst out laughing and put a hand out to steady herself, leaning against the trailer. "I don't think that's what he meant," she said.

Wrapping an arm around Sadie's waist, the woman pulled her into the shadow of the steel trailer as the speakers blared an instrumental cover of a patriotic song. The people in the stands sang along tunelessly, a dull drone of sound that merged and blended together like Texas mud.

"I see a spark in you, Sadie," the woman said, her clear soprano laden with a hint of gravel. "You're too bright for a place like this."

The yellow light of the nearby lamp flickered across the woman's face, and Sadie's breath caught in her throat. She had no words, just heat in her stomach and a feeling that she would follow this rider to the ends of the earth given the opportunity.

The woman traced a finger along the side of Sadie's neck, where her blood pulsed a hungry rhythm with every heart-beat. She sighed and entwined her fingers into Sadie's long auburn curls, pulling her closer until Sadie could feel the woman's hot breath on her lips and see the dazzling white of her sharp smile glint in the dim light. Her heart raced with excitement she'd never felt before. It was nothing like when Bobby Ray pushed his hand up her shirt in the back of his car two years ago.

Sadie held her breath in anticipation, afraid that if she moved, she would break the spell. Finally, after twenty five years of waiting, the woman gently pressed her lips to Sadie's. Her body exploded with electricity and she ached to climb in the woman's old red Ford and disappear forever – or at least until next year's midnight rodeo.

"Looks like your daddy is fixin' to leave," the woman said as she pulled away from the kiss, leaving Sadie breathless. "Don't be late," she said with a wink and released Sadie from her grip.

"Wait," Sadie protested, but the woman had already twisted from her arms and was walking to the driver's seat of the truck with a tip of her hat.

"We'll meet again," the woman said as she climbed in and slammed the door.

★ ★ ★

Sadie hopped out of her daddy's silver four-door truck and shut the door behind her. The journey home had been predictable, her father congratulating her brother on another rodeo victory. The trophy had ridden in the seat next to her, secured with a seatbelt.

The late night air was dense and moist. Fog was beginning to creep over the fence line of their property, engulfing the rotten posts with a ghostly white vapour. Sadie inhaled the smell of wet leaves and the fetid scent of rotting flesh that emanated from the beautiful yellow flowers that grew in front of the huge house, bought and paid for by the members of her father's congregation.

Her lips ached with the memory of the kiss from the mysterious woman, and she brushed her thumb across them as she relived it in her mind. She leaned against the truck, staring into the blackness beneath the cypress trees that seemed unnatural on such a moonlit night. For a moment, she thought she saw something move in the shadows, but dismissed the thought as a trick of her tired mind.

"I'm proud of you, son," Sadie's father said as he handed over the trophy and clapped the young blonde-haired man on the shoulder. "Keep at it, and someday you'll be as renowned as your old man."

"Thanks, Pop," Johnny replied, taking the huge gold trophy in his arms and shifting the awkward weight against his body.

"Go on inside, I need to have a Come to Jesus with your sister."

Sadie's stomach twisted at the words. These meetings rarely ended pleasantly – more often than not they concluded with a belt to the back of her legs when she was young, or now that she was grown, a close-fisted slap across the face. Her shoulders rounded into a hunch as she backed away from the truck. "Daddy please, I didn't do anything!" she pleaded.

"You think I didn't see you fooling around with that woman? Do you think God didn't see you?" He stepped closer and took off his blazer, laying it gently over the hood of the vehicle. "You bring shame on this family, Sadie," he said, his watery blue eyes narrowing with rage. "What do you think would happen if the congregation discovered that the pastor's daughter was a… a…" He trailed off.

The trees rustled with a gentle breeze, and Sadie felt it drag her skirt around her legs. She stepped back again. "Nothing happened," she lied. "We were just talking."

He took another step forward. "Do you think people would continue to follow a man who couldn't even guide his own daughter to salvation?" he asked. "We'd lose everything, Sadie Mae. Is that what you want?"

"No," she stammered.

"Spare the rod and spoil the child, that's what the Bible says," he said in his most convincing preacher-voice, dripping with authority and conviction. "And you can't argue with the word of God."

Sadie stepped back and stumbled over a molehill at the side of their stone-paved driveway. "I'm not a child anymore," she protested.

Shadows and fog mingled under the thick canopy of cypress and dogwood trees as cicadas drowned out all other sounds with their alien singing. Sadie regained her balance and ran to the wraparound porch that surrounded their house, the woodsy scent of cedar permeating the air. With a hand on the screen door handle, she raised the other as her father approached. "Daddy please," she begged. "Let me explain."

He raised his fist to her and moved with his whole body to strike Sadie across the face. She cowered and tried to shield herself, but the blow never came. There was a thick, viscous sound of dripping, like the sound of oil splashing across the tarmac when her daddy's truck broke down last year. She opened her eyes and gasped.

The woman from the rodeo was holding Sadie's father in her arms, now limp and lifeless. Her eyes were black as night, sparkling in the delicate, fragile moonlight. Her mouth was covered in the man's blood, which was splattered across the cedar steps and coated the ends of the woman's soft blonde waves. Sadie's father was missing most of his throat, and his final cries for help died with a soft, weak gurgle. The woman wiped her mouth with the back of her hand and smiled broadly, her sharp white teeth glinting in the moonlight.

"Won't you invite me in?"

LADY OF LETTERS; OR, THE TWENTY-FIRST CENTURY HOMUNCULUS

Heather Valentine

The first message that Jade Evans sent me was the one I wrote myself.

> Jade says:
> hey beautiful

I don't remember what was going through my head when I sent the message, or why I chose to lie to Ian in the first place. I suppose I thought fabricating a reason for my actions would be a better way of soothing his fury than admitting a mistake.
I should say that I was sixteen, and that he had been my first boyfriend. I had nobody to compare him to, and nobody to ask – I thought nobody would take my feelings for him seriously, because Ian and I had only spoken online. I feel a protectiveness towards that younger me, as if I and I are different people.
She – well, I – thought that Ian's anger after I changed my MySpace status to "in a relationship" must have been reasonable, or he wouldn't have reacted that way. I thought I should have seen it coming. I believed that people were generally reasonable, and that deception and ulterior motives were best spotted by

noticing logical fallacies. And I would keep believing that until I finally met Ian in person.

He'd sent me paragraphs of rage in green Arial Narrow. I could see that he was still typing after the first flurry of messages and I hid the window while I waited. Sitting stone-still at the computer in the living room, the cosy, homely furniture seemed like an insult to the crimson depths of my feelings. I was afraid to click and see the rest of what he had written for so long that the MSN icon at the bottom of my screen stopped flashing and settled on an unwavering, dangerous orange.

I feared it would only confirm my wrongdoing if I didn't respond to his messages as soon as I'd read them, and I suppose I panicked. In my haste and terror, I claimed that I had actually changed my status for completely unrelated reasons: because I had received dirty messages from strangers and hoped that appearing to be in a relationship would dissuade them.

Ian demanded proof.

So I created Jade.

It was strangely exhilarating, realising how easy it was. To get a second Hotmail address and make a new profile. I worried that it was too easy, that I would somehow be found out. Not even by Ian, necessarily. Perhaps it was illegal to make a fake profile, I hadn't checked.

In retrospect, I made a lot of mistakes with Jade's first profile. If Ian had decided to be suspicious, he could have checked her wall and found it empty. He could have noticed that she'd taken her profile template from the same site as mine, and that she'd only uploaded one photograph. It was long before reverse image search existed, though. He would have been unlikely to figure out that I'd taken it from the sixth result for "emo girl profile picture" unless he'd been looking that up himself.

I don't know why I picked her in particular. She was unthreateningly, blandly pretty. It didn't seem like I was taking a real person's photograph. She didn't have flaws like I did, and her expression looked natural, not posed for the camera. Her writing style, personality, music taste was similar enough to me that I felt I could write her convincingly, but different in obvious, swerving ways. A US location with UK spelling, who could only like bands I'd heard of. Despite the black and red I'd painted her profile in, she liked Coldplay because Ian thought they were rubbish, and I hoped it would make him dislike her.

If I'd been properly clever, it would have been better to make her look like a bot instead of half a person, make it seem like I'd gotten a fright from a spam message. Or to have made a male profile, which would, in retrospect, have been much more likely to send me spontaneous thirsty messages, even though I wouldn't have had the knowledge to make them convincingly filthy. But I was sixteen, and the stupid kind of clever. I put a huge effort into very silly things, but not enough to accomplish anything with them.

I sent Ian a screenshot of Jade's first message a few days later, after what I thought was a good amount of time to avoid her message seeming too convenient. After three minutes of silence, his reply was anticlimactic:

> Ian says:
> I don't see the problem, Emily.

With his immediate problem gone, I suppose Ian didn't care about my supposed reasons. I'd changed my status to what he wanted and hadn't changed it back, so his real-life friends wouldn't ask questions if they happened upon my profile. There was nothing to accomplish with vicious screeds today.

He didn't mention Jade or the messages again and, for a while, I forgot about her.

My connection was unstable that summer while my family moved houses. I tried texting, but Ian complained about having to spend phone credit to talk to me, so I compromised. My daily conversations with Ian shifted from hour-long chains of instant message chatter to a few lengthy e-mails. I penned them at home and took trips to the library to send them. I came to enjoy it. I had kept diaries before, because it seemed like something bookish girls should do, but I never managed more than a few pages before giving up. Scribing my life for Ian felt different. Picking out moments from my day for the pleasure of someone besides myself seemed to give them meaning.

It's sad, now, to think of what a waste that summer was. All those hours spent traipsing back and forth to the library to talk to an ungrateful boy on the other side of the country… I could have been doing anything else.

But if I hadn't done it, perhaps Jade wouldn't have come back. And I don't regret her at all.

I didn't recognise her at first. I was at the library, waiting for Ian to reply to me, and hoped the e-mail was from him. A new friend request on a different platform, the e-mail preview of her profile picture shrouded by filters and lens flares. And yet, there was still something familiar about her. I peered around the desks, in case it was someone using one of the other computers. But I was alone, surrounded only by sleeping monitors, the distant hum of a printer, and a maze of patterned brown carpet.

Curious, I clicked further. To see if she had any other photographs, any familiar friends, if she'd listed the school she went to. And there he was, her only other friend, a screenshot of his Final Fantasy XI character instead of his own face. Ian. I carefully copied the link to her profile into an e-mail, and asked if he knew who she was.

> To: Emily
> From: Ian
> Subject: RE: Friend request
> No clue, some random that added me a couple days ago.
> Don't be a jealous fucking psycho, emily.

I thought the best way to not seem like a jealous fucking psycho would be to accept the friend request, and to say sorry. He always took longer to reply when I was grovelling than when I was angry, and I suspected he was doing it on purpose, but I thought I deserved it.

Ian often confessed his fear that I was jealous, possessive. Not knowing better, I believed everything he told me about myself, the warmth of being known tempering the pain of being revealed as a monster. He told me that he was a cynic, and that he was good at reading people. I used to use the same words to describe myself and, being the stupid kind of clever, thought that meant we were the same.

I did remember creating Jade when I accepted the friend request, even if I didn't recognise this other figure as the same person. I wondered if she was some trick – a fake profile of his own Ian had made to show me that he knew and to see if I would confess. In reality, I don't think he remembered.

I had been pushing, for a while, to meet Ian in person. A few days after the incident with the friend request, he accepted. I would visit for his birthday. I had fallen so in love with his written words that I was ecstatic to see them made flesh. I spent too much money buying him a present – a gaming headset, a bridge between his voice and my computer that I would pretend I'd happened to get on clearance when I gave it to him, to give the impression of casual modesty.

My mother fretted about the trip, given that I'd never been so far from home by myself before. We came to a compromise that I found overbearing yet would later appreciate: she would travel with me under the guise of giving herself a holiday. She would see the museums in his city, and see me to his door to ensure he really was who he said he was. I would stay with him, but she would be there, embarrassingly close. She stayed in a hotel, a phone call away, just in case.

I got a text on the train journey there, from a number I did not know:

+00: beautiful, guard both your hearts

I didn't text back anything – but I knew it was from her, whoever *her* was.

I felt that I should recognise his home from the pictures I'd seen of his room, but I didn't. My mother walked me to the white door of a pebble-dashed semi-detached, and to my continued discomfort waited with me until someone opened the door.

I had seen a few pictures of Ian's physical self. He looked like them, enough to satisfy my mother's fears. But he didn't look like my concept of him. He was taller than I'd imagined, too tall to see me eye-to-eye. He'd sheared his hair short, and his jaw was dappled with stubble and pores that his grainy webcam photographs never captured. Only through our increasingly tense e-mails had I spoken to something that bore only his name. I still mainly associated him with the colour green, an ever-changing witty handle, and the cover of Pablo Honey.

I was the first to arrive, but he did not touch me, even covertly. He did not introduce me to his real-life friends or family as anyone special to him, and his voice sounded too harsh without the dampening of a microphone. My memory of that afternoon is of sitting on the far corner of a leather sofa, laughing too much at Ian's jokes and making no trouble.

When we piled into his parents' cars, I asked no questions, didn't even express disappointment that we wouldn't be travelling together. I said nothing, did nothing, when one of Ian's real-life friends explained that we were going to visit Claire, Ian's girlfriend, at the hospital. I stared when I saw Ian in the hospital car park, hoping for some sign of an explanation. I checked my text messages and longed for the library, for some message from the written Ian to explain this strange illusion.

I feigned illness when we arrived to avoid seeing Claire, or seeing Ian with her. Ian's mother sighed and deigned to stay in the café with me. She would later suggest that I needed to be less high maintenance when my mother called her to accuse her son of trickery. I felt pressed to the ground by Ian's presence, somewhere in the building above, and wondered if the girl in the hospital bed felt the same: as if I was the basement, she was the attic, and he was the whole house.

Sitting in that café, swirling my straw through a half-drunk glass of watery coke, I replied to Jade for the first time. I briefly worried that perhaps it was Claire. If she had noticed me before I could notice her, could she have contacted me to protect Ian from having to tell me "no" himself?

Emily: Is hers the other heart I should guard?

After pressing send, I pretended to call my mother, to arrange a return to her hotel because of my sudden sickness. I expressed false sorrow at missing bowling and the cinema. I didn't need to pretend to seem out-of-sorts; my discomfort was illness enough. Ian's mother walked me to the door and left me there at my insistence. Being a jealous monster, as I thought I was, didn't mean the monster wasn't right.

+00: emily emily beautiful heart, he is making fools of you both

I felt the dark guilt of deception as I waited. I had no idea how to hide, to be subtle. I really, truly, hid behind a bush in the hospital grounds. Jealous monster, yandere, psychopath girl-friend. I saw how I could be illustrated as a lunatic girl: sharp voice and sharper knife, burning down the house with both of us trapped inside so that nobody else could have him. But I didn't want him, anymore.

Ian and his friends weren't looking for me as they left. As they got into the cars and drove away, I thought I saw Ian glance towards my lurking-place as he swung through the exit. I no longer believed he would recognise me.

> Emily: I don't like being this person
> +00: i'm sorry, emily

I went back into the hospital and found Claire's room. I did know her name, in passing. Ian had not mentioned her as anyone special to him. We had spoken a few times and had played a few evenings of online games together.

"Claire," I said quietly. "I'm Emily, Ian's girlfriend."

And to my surprise, Claire smiled, the tape holding her feeding tube in place wrinkling with her sweet expression. "Ah, so am I."

We didn't have much to say to each other, but shared relief at the truth. We would become friends later and laugh at how we'd met.

My mother didn't ask a lot of questions when she came to meet me. She took me to one of the museums she was interested in and then to dinner. I wrote a long letter about my day when I got back to the hotel and didn't know what to do with it. I sent it to the written Ian, seeking some desperate recourse for the actions of Ian-in-flesh. And...

> +00: beautiful heart, how are you feeling?

And I sent it to my mysterious messenger, that screen etched with faceless, loving words.

I had planned to stay with Ian for another day. My mother retrieved my travel bag from Ian's house, telling his parents that I was still sick. I wouldn't tell her everything until we were back at home. She paid for me to swim in the hotel pool while she was out, and then we caught an earlier train.

Ian had explanations for me. Paragraphs of them. I received the e-mail when I arrived at home. He hadn't wanted to break up with Claire while she was in the hospital, but he had intended to, which he would have explained if only I had been patient. All of those turns of phrase I had once found charming seemed grating now that I knew the voice to read them in. The sometimes brief tone that I had once taken as my fault, for angering him or being too dull to elicit a better response, was now merely the habit of a callous boy who strung girls along and still complained that he was not loved enough.

I recognised Jade when I returned to her profile. The filters had fallen away from her picture, revealing the one I had chosen, although still slightly altered. Through digital tricks, she had dyed her hair. She said she had been thinking about finding her own name, but couldn't find one she liked better than Jade. And she wrote to me, affection in scarlet Century.

Jade says:
beautiful, tell me about the museum

Jade says:
beautiful, tell me about your day

I wrote my heart back to her, tentatively at first, until I let her become a habit, let her become my diary.

My daily life brightened when I recorded it for her, more than it had even for Ian. Digital homunculus, ghost in the machine, lovely simulacra. She hungered for my world; I hungered for her words. For a lover who could not let me down, who had no flesh self that could disappoint me with its difference.

"Will you be on tomorrow morning?"

The voice she has made for herself replies. "I always am, for you."

I put my lips to the laptop webcam and leave the Skype call running. Tonight, as she has done for years now, Jade whispers me to sleep.

TAYLOR HALL

Henry Glifort

The doorbell rang, echoing through the halls. Kit became aware of the house shifting beneath her feet. She ran her hand along the walls as she walked to the front door.

"I know it's weird when a new person comes to stay," she said, "but we need the money." She waved a hand at the living room as she passed, as if to encompass the water-stained ceiling, dirty fireplace, and warped floorboards.

The only response was a slight sigh of wind as it blew through the chimneys. Kit took a deep breath of her own and opened the front door.

She was greeted by a smiling woman, a few inches taller than her and around the same age – early twenties. Her wavy, blonde-brown hair was artfully tousled in a way that made it look effortless, spilling over her flowery top. Kit felt breathless for a moment, suddenly self-conscious. She tugged at the hem of her t-shirt and tried not to stare.

"Hi! You must be Kit," the woman said, holding out a tan hand. "I'm Emily. It's great to finally meet in person."

Kit's hand shot out to meet Emily's, a bit too fast, so it caused some awkward grappling between them.

"Hey," she said, still holding Emily's hand. "Come in, come in. Welcome to Taylor Hall. Sorry I'm, uh, out of it. I just woke up."

"That's okay," Emily said. "I'm not a morning person either."

"Do you want to look around, or should we grab your stuff from the car first?"

"I definitely want to look around. I can't believe this house is really real," Emily said, eyes raking over the vestibule.

Kit led her to the living room. "What, did you think I was posting fake pictures online to catfish people into living here?"

Emily laughed. "Of course not. I just didn't think college students could live anywhere but grody dorms and dilapidated apartments."

Kit pointed at an old gas lamp hanging crookedly from the wall. "I never said anything about it not being dilapidated."

Emily chuckled and did a lap of the room, looking at the furniture. It was a mixture of various odds and ends from different eras, and Kit's contribution: some cheap IKEA chairs.

Out of the corner of her eye, Kit could see the doors of the china cabinet flapping open and closed. She dashed over on tiptoes and firmly pressed them shut while Emily admired the ornate wall hangings across the room. Kit spun around and leaned against the cabinet, ignoring the little taps against her calves. She blocked the cabinet from Emily's view when she turned to face Kit.

"I can't believe you have this place to yourself," Emily said, oblivious to the insistent cupboard. "I've never heard of a college student living in a sprawling Victorian mansion."

"I'm not sure it counts as Victorian if we're in Massachusetts," Kit said. Emily rolled her eyes, smirking. "It's definitely a lot of space, but half the bedrooms aren't really fit for habitation, so it's not like I can turn it into a massive Airbnb or anything. Probably for the best," she said, leading the way out of the room. "My parents might want to live here if it was in better shape. Then I'd really have to find a crappy apartment to get some peace."

They continued their tour in the kitchen, mercifully free of squeaking cabinets, although Kit had to give the oven light the stink eye when it twinkled on and off for attention. They visited various pantries and bathrooms on the first floor, then moved on to Kit's favourite room. She'd saved it for last, and felt a wave of anxiety as she opened the door.

"This is the library," she said, stepping aside. Emily walked in, staring open-mouthed. Kit looked over the room, wondering what would catch Emily's eye. Maybe the enormous fireplace where Kit had dried herself off after playing in the snow as a kid, or the green velvet chaise longue where she'd spent too many late nights scaring herself senseless reading *Goosebumps* books.

"Are you kidding me?" Emily breathed, walking up to a wall of books that stretched to the ceiling. "Is this real life?"

Kit moved to stand next to her and smiled. "Yeah," she said. "I haven't even read half of these. It's sort of a lifelong project."

Emily walked around the room, hands pressed over her chest, as if to restrain herself from reaching out to touch everything.

"I would never leave this room if I grew up here," she said.

Kit smiled and crossed to sit on the royal blue window seat, a plush but slightly tattered relic from generations past. It wasn't wide, but she knew from experience that it was long enough to lay down on if she folded her legs up a bit. "It was tough to get me out of here as a kid. But after a while, the draft from the windows freezes you out. This old house has ways of getting people up and moving."

Emily pulled her gaze from the walls and looked at Kit. A spark of something – eagerness or mischief, Kit couldn't tell – gleamed in her eyes. She bit her lip.

Kit sighed, resigned to answering the one question everyone asked when they came to Taylor Hall. She was used to it by now. She waved Emily on. "Go ahead."

"It feels rude," Emily said. "Especially in front of the books."

Kit huffed. "The books have heard much worse, I'm sure. Go on, ask away."

"Is it haunted?" Emily said in a rush of breath.

"Nope." Kit hoisted herself up from the window seat and walked towards the door, careful not to bump into any of the more priceless antique chairs arranged artfully around the room. She'd snapped the leg of one when she was eight, and never recovered from hearing how much it cost to fix. "You won't be visited by any ghouls, ghosts, poltergeists, spirits, or otherworldly beings during your stay at chez Taylor. Does that answer your question?"

Emily hesitated until Kit was nearly out of the room, then hurried to follow her. "Not really?"

Kit sighed. "I thought not. Okay, what do you want to know?" She led the way up the wooden staircase to the second floor, the thick mahogany bannister nicked under her hand, worn from so many years of use. The steps were lined with gold-patterned carpet, faded and thin. The creaking under her feet sounded like both a greeting and a grumble.

"You've never noticed anything weird?" Emily asked, stroking the rickety bannister. "It's just such an old house, and so much must have happened in it."

"Can't say that I have. Living in this house has really taught me about the power of suggestion. People hear some noises, feel the house settling, and wham! Must be haunted."

Emily seemed to deflate a little. "Alright. That's fine. Although I don't think I'd mind meeting a ghost or two."

Kit squinted at Emily, feeling suddenly guarded. "You're not in the school's paranormal society, are you? They're always trying to get in here."

"No, nothing like that," Emily said. "I'm just a Sagittarius, that's all."

Kit blinked. "Where did you say you were from again?"

"California."

"Ah. That explains a lot."

"Hey!" Emily exclaimed, smiling as she swatted at Kit, who dodged out of the way.

At the top of the stairs, Kit opened the first door on the right. "This'll be your room. Like I said, no ghosts, but it does come with free Wi-Fi."

They stepped inside. The light shone in through the wide windows to highlight the room in all its faded glory. It was spacious – empty aside from a few small bookcases, a large, four-poster bed, and a brown armchair nestled by the window. In the centre of the hardwood floor was an expansive red throw rug, relatively new compared to the rest of the furniture in the room.

After a moment Emily turned to Kit, whose heart started drumming. She hadn't realised how close they were standing. "It's just that," Emily began in that hesitant voice she'd used before. "It seems like after so much time, someone must have... you know." She raised her eyebrows and looked at Kit meaningfully.

Kit snorted. "Shuffled off this mortal coil? Explored the final frontier? Croaked?"

Emily groaned. "Yes, actually. It must have seen a few people's last days."

"It has," Kit said, too loud for the quiet room. She cleared her throat and led them back into the hallway. She pointed at a door across the hall. "That's my room right there, where my great uncle died in his sleep in 1960." She pointed to a room at the end of the hall with a closed door. "And that's the sewing room, where my grandma died a few years ago. Heart attack," she said, quietly.

Emily squeezed Kit's elbow. "I'm so sorry."

Kit cleared her throat again, but her voice still cracked when she said, "Thanks." She pivoted on her heel and headed back towards the stairs. "The point is, the place isn't haunted. As far as I can tell, no one was horribly murdered, no suicides. Not even a good old-fashioned duel at dawn."

They made their way back downstairs to fetch Emily's luggage.

"Well," she said. "I guess I have enough going on without meeting any ghosts."

Kit smiled and held the front door open. "Yup, nothing to worry about here."

As Emily stepped outside, the glass chandelier in the foyer rattled, raining dust onto Kit's head. She held up a finger and gave it a warning look. The chandelier settled, with minimal tinkling.

★ ★ ★

The first weekend after classes started, Kit was half asleep with a textbook in her lap when she was startled by a loud bang. She felt a burn of adrenaline in her gut – what if something had happened to Emily? The house had been peaceful over the last days as Kit and Emily slowly eased into their new routines. They had spent snippets of time together, getting to know each other through their shared interest in books and trashy movies. The bang repeated, making Kit flinch. It echoed throughout the house, over and over, like a child had gotten hold of a mallet and was banging the pipes.

Kit jumped out of bed in search of the source. She glared at the walls, the ceilings, and the bannister as she made her way towards the noise, but the banging continued. The electric lanterns she had installed in case of night-time emergencies threw small pools of blue light on the faded carpet, illuminating her way.

As she got downstairs, she felt the reverberation of every thump under her bare feet. The house practically vibrated with it.

"Would you stop it?" she hissed into the near-darkness. The next thud seemed pointedly louder, and she groaned back at it.

"Hello?" called a shaky voice. Kit looked over to see a crack of light under the library door. "Is anyone there?"

Kit opened the door, scanning the room to make sure nothing was floating, shrieking, or otherwise hellishly animated. The only sign of life was Emily, curled up on the reading bench beside a stack of books, arms wrapped around her knees. She looked terrified, her eyes large with fear.

"Kit, I'm so glad you're here," she said, the lines of her face smoothing out a bit.

Kit tried to look calm and comforting. She had to keep Emily from suspecting anything was wrong. "It's okay, I'm sorry. The house just... does this sometimes."

Emily looked around the room, nervous. "I've never heard anything like this. It's like the house has a heartbeat."

"It's just the, uh... the furnace. It's a little chilly tonight, and the old system always has some trouble kicking back on after summer."

"Do you think it'll last all night?" Emily asked, her voice quivering.

"No, absolutely not," Kit said, raising her voice a little, hoping that somehow the house was listening. "I'll go check it out, give it a few tweaks, and everything should be fine."

Before Emily could answer, Kit zipped off to the basement. She grabbed an LED lantern off a hook above the stairs – just in case – and jogged down. The banging followed her, surrounding her on all sides as she descended the narrow stairs. She knew she'd reached the bottom even before her feet hit the cold concrete floor. That eternally damp basement smell encircled her, and she shivered once against the chill. She flicked on the light switch.

The basement stayed shrouded in darkness. She sighed and turned on the lantern. "Really?" she said. "No lights? We're having a full-blown tantrum tonight, aren't we?" She addressed the old furnace, a hulking monstrosity squatting in the middle of the room.

"I thought we had an understanding. I buy you only the finest wood polish for your floorboards, don't I? And I patch up anything that's really messed up. That tree branch poking the upstairs window – I got that fixed so fast. I clean the gutters and mow the lawn and even dust once in a while. This is how you repay me?"

The banging continued, almost cheerily thundering around her from all sides, the walls reverberating with every beat.

Kit groaned and flapped her arms wildly in frustration. The

lantern cast grotesque flickering shadows on the walls. "I even kicked out the guy who used to slide down the bannister on his butt every morning! And he paid rent in advance!"

The time between thumps grew longer.

"I've got a terrified roommate up there," she said, her voice more even, "who's been nothing but respectful to me and to this house. If you freak her out like this, you're going to scare her off and who knows who we'll end up with. So if you could please do me the courtesy of acting like a normal house, I would appreciate it."

After a few beats, the thumping grew steadily quieter, fading out until the only sound she could hear was the rhythmic echo of it in her ears.

"Thank you," she breathed. She turned towards the stairs and froze. Emily was at the top of the staircase, barely visible in the circle of the lantern's glow.

"Did you just talk to the house?" Emily asked, voice going high and shrill with excitement.

Kit pushed down her instinctive panic and walked up the stairs. So much for hoping Emily could ever believe she was a chill human being.

"Yes," she said. "It's a quirk of mine. I talk to the house, so sue me."

Emily followed her back up to the library. "And that fixed the banging?"

"No, I messed with the dials on the furnace. *That* fixed the banging," Kit said, crossing the room to sit on the window seat and pick up a book. She flipped through it, trying to look nonchalant.

"You didn't touch the dials. I was there the whole time." Kit could hear Emily's enormous grin even though she didn't look up.

"They're voice-activated controls, actually," she muttered.

"In a hundred-something-year-old house? I don't think so," Emily said.

Kit sighed and put down the book. "I don't know what to tell you. I'm just a weirdo who talks to her house, okay?"

"Have you always been able to talk to houses? Is it just this house, or is it all houses? Can you teach me how to talk to the house?" Emily barely took a breath between questions.

"I can't talk to houses, I just talk to this house. For my own enrichment and pleasure. Are you going to interrogate me all night?"

Emily joined her on the window seat. Kit moved over, but found herself pressed against the side of a bookcase. Emily was warm on her other side, making her heart pound.

"What was it like growing up in such a unique place?" she asked.

Kit paused, trying to focus. "It was perfect for hide and seek, so there were some benefits to living in a rundown place like this."

Emily laughed, turning a bit to lean her head against the bookcase on her side. She stretched her pyjama-clad legs in front of her.

"What were you doing in here this late anyway?" Kit asked, turning too, so they could face each other like quotation marks. She sat with her legs crisscrossed to give Emily more room.

Emily hummed. "Don't you know an English major's work is never done?" She thumped a pile of books on the table in front of the window seat. "Or do they not like big books in bio classes?"

Kit scoffed. "Science textbooks are the biggest! And they cost about a million dollars each. I won't allow this science-shaming under my own roof."

Emily laughed. Kit smiled and tipped her head so her cheek could rest against the cool window. A few moments ticked by as Kit watched her breath fog up the glass.

Emily shifted a little, picking up a book and fidgeting with the various sticky notes poking out of it.

"I get a bit lonely sometimes," she muttered, looking down at the book in her lap. "It's hard being this far from home. I like it, and I want to be here, but it's different. I stayed in the library all night because I've always turned to books when I need comfort."

"Oh," Kit said. She'd never thought anyone who looked like Emily could ever be lonely. People must be falling over themselves just to talk to her. Kit hurried to reassure her. "Yeah. I can't tell you how many nights I spent down here when I was avoiding my parents, or dreading school, or just wanted to devour a ton of books."

"They're the best company."

"Exactly," Kit said. "My grandma used to bring me a blanket and a mug of cocoa when I was in here all night. She always seemed to know when I would be," she said, trailing off.

"It sounds like you guys had a really special relationship," Emily said softly.

"We did," Kit answered. "I hope you know we can hang out whenever," she said. "If you get lonely. You know where to find me." Before Emily could answer, Kit blurted out, "I even know how to make cocoa. The good kind, not the packets."

Emily smiled and looked up. "Thanks, Kit." There was another pause and Emily leaned in.

"So tell me about your hide and seek adventures in this ridiculously huge house," she said. Kit laughed loudly.

They spent most of the night passing questions back and forth, sharing stories in the slow way only the stillness of night allows. As the sky started to lighten, Emily yawned and said, "I can't remember the last time I stayed up like this with someone. It's nice."

Before Kit could think of anything to say in return, Emily reached up a lazy hand to stroke Kit's sleek, straight hair. "Your hair is so pretty. Can I braid it?"

"Uh," Kit said, feeling her breathing growing shallower. "Sure, but it's a mess."

Emily hoisted herself up to loom over Kit, carefully dividing her shoulder-length hair into three sections. "Please," she scoffed. "I wish mine could go the whole night without getting tangled. Yours is a dream."

Kit closed her eyes and tried to enjoy the feel of Emily's fingers running through her hair. Emily's hand reached the left side of her head and stilled.

"Wait," she said, flipping Kit's hair over to the other side. "Do you have an undercut?"

Kit stiffened and tried not to move away. "Yeah, I just, I don't know," she said, stopping to clear her throat. "I usually cover it up."

"Why?" Emily asked, her hands moving once again. "It's so nice!"

Kit relaxed her shoulders, which had risen almost up to her ears. "I don't know. I think about shaving it all off sometimes. The undercut seemed like a good middle ground, but I don't even show it."

"Oh, I have clippers!" Emily exclaimed. "I used to cut my brother's hair back home. You can have them if you want."

Kit inhaled sharply, pulling back. Emily's hands caught in her hair at the sudden movement and Kit ducked out of her grasp.

"Thanks," she said, standing. "I'll think about that. Sorry, I didn't realise how late it was. I need to go. I need to go to bed."

She was halfway across the room before Emily could react.

"Okay," she called softly to Kit. "I'm sorry if I did anything to upset you."

"No, you're fine! Please," Kit said over her shoulder. "Don't mind me. I'm just so tired. This was so fun, super fun."

She left the library without looking back and practically ran to her room. She closed the door behind her and leaned against it, breathing hard. She never should have let Emily touch her hair. It made her stomach drop, like she was falling from too high up. It was the same way she felt when friends used to try and give her a makeover at sleepovers, or how she'd cry every time her mom put her in a dress. It felt wrong, everything just felt wrong.

And now Emily was going to figure out how weird and messed up she was. What was *wrong* with her? Why was she like this?

Her breath came in ragged gasps. From across the room, a box of tissues lifted off Kit's nightstand and floated over to land on the floor. The box slid up to Kit and nudged at her hand, pushing against her like a cat.

Kit ran her hands through her hair until she found the short, spiky undercut. She yanked on her longer hair with the other hand, sobbing as she stopped fighting the tears that had been threatening since Emily first touched it.

★ ★ ★

Kit avoided Emily after that. She made sure to stay a little late after class, putting in extra hours for her labs. When she came home each night to find the lights off and no sign of her roommate, she fought a surge of guilt.

It didn't help that Emily had left a set of shiny electric hair clippers on Kit's bathroom sink without comment. The kindness of that small act made her heart ache.

Fortunately, the house was quiet. Ever since Kit was a little kid, it always knew when she was upset. If she was lost, it lit the way back to her room. If she wanted to hide from her parents, creaky little doors would open that Kit had never seen before, and she'd have a few hours of peace.

Kit made use of those same secret doors to duck out of the way when she heard Emily coming. She wasn't proud of it.

One night when she woke to the sound of her window rattling and the building groaning like it was ready to collapse, she couldn't understand what was wrong. She was just getting out of bed when there was a knock at her door.

She squinted at the chattering window and muttered to it, "If this is just you messing with me, I'm going to paint every room magenta, so help me."

"Kit? Can I come in?" came a small voice from the hall.

The house continued to rumble as Kit opened the door. Emily stood in front of her, shifting from foot to foot in pyjamas and a pair of fuzzy polka dot socks. She had wrapped a comforter around her like a cape.

"So should we, like, run for our lives?" she asked.

Kit shook her head. "Sorry, the house just—"

"Does this sometimes?" Emily finished. Kit gave her a half-smile and shrugged. Emily rolled her eyes.

"Alright. Fine. I get that I chose to live in this very old, very weird house, but I'm kind of freaking out. I can't sleep because I keep thinking the ceiling is about to cave in."

Kit stepped aside. "Come in. It's not as loud in here."

Emily hesitated at the threshold for a second, looking at Kit like she would a wild animal that could bolt at any moment. Then she stepped inside. "Thanks."

Kit closed the door and walked over to sit in a cushy red chair she'd moved up from the living room. She gestured towards her bed and Emily sat on the end of it, legs crisscrossed as she leaned against the wall to face Kit. It was another giant four-poster bed, but Kit had long since gotten rid of the stodgy curtains. Kit watched Emily arrange the comforter she'd brought over her legs, tucking it under her to keep the cold out.

"How do you deal with it?" Emily asked.

Kit answered without thinking. "This house is like family to me," she said, surprising herself. She let the sentence hang there for a moment, waiting for panic that never came. "My mom grew up here, and her mom, and her mom before that. I know these creepy little hallways better than anything. It's falling apart all the time, but I feel at home here. And..." she took a breath. "I know it's crazy, but I feel like I know the house and the house knows me. No matter how I'm feeling, or how weird my parents were being, I knew I'd be comfortable wherever I went in this house."

Kit picked at a tear in the arm of her chair. She'd never talked to anyone about this before, not even her parents. The wailing and swaying had quieted somewhat, like the house was listening to her.

Emily stretched one leg in front of her and poked Kit's knee with her fuzzy-socked toes. Kit's whole leg broke out into goosebumps. She looked down to avoid Emily's eyes, afraid she'd blush.

"That's actually pretty cool," Emily said.

Kit huffed a laugh. "Yeah?" she raised her head. "The kid with no friends except a musty old house?"

"No, the kid with a deep spiritual connection to an old mansion. You're like a Disney princess, but with a haunted house instead of little birds and mice to do your bidding."

Kit laughed. Emily withdrew her leg and tucked her foot back into her nest of blankets. "And besides," she said, looking around the room, "the kid grew up to have at least one friend. If the kid wants one, I mean."

Emily looked back at her and Kit flushed. "Yeah," she said. "I think she would."

After a moment, Emily cleared her throat. "I want to try something," she said. She turned to stare at the wall. "House, can you please calm down?"

The house continued its shaking and creaking. Emily frowned. "I really thought that would work."

Kit shrugged. "I don't understand how it works either."

As she spoke, Emily's eyes grew wider, staring at something over Kit's head. Kit looked up just in time to see a blanket levitating over from a basket of clean laundry on the floor to settle in a little pile in Emily's lap.

"Your house is haunted! Your house was nice to me! I can talk to houses," she whisper-shouted, reaching out to touch the blanket.

Kit's eyebrows nearly met her hairline. "I've never seen it do anything like that for people who weren't me. And the whole house is still quaking, for some reason."

"I don't care!" Emily cried, wide-eyed. She pulled the blanket over her head and wrapped herself in it, looking wildly around the room like she could find someone to thank. "I've established a tentative friendship with your very alive house!"

Kit huffed. "I guess you have."

Emily patted the bed next to her. "Come here, it's freezing outside the blanket fort."

Kit walked over and plopped herself on the bed. "It's hardly a fort if it has no roof," she said, accepting a blanket from Emily's pile.

They discussed the structural integrity of various fort-building materials until they were both lolling on different sides of the bed.

"Hey, Em?" Kit asked, feeling the burn of her eyelids as they tried to stay open. "What made you want to move here junior year? I like Boston University just fine, but I don't think I'd move across the country for it."

A few moments ticked by. Kit was about to apologise for asking, when Emily said, "I got tired of being in the same place. Being around the same people. My parents."

Kit hummed in agreement and Emily continued. "My parents act like they're such hippies. But every time I date a guy, they think I've 'changed my mind,' and every time I date a girl, they tell everyone their daughter's a lesbian. Like it's a bragging right. I can't tell you how many times I've tried to explain being pan to them."

Kit sighed. "Yeah, I could see wanting to get away from that."

"I just wanted to try something new. Somewhere totally different. I wanted to see if I could build a life for myself on my own, the way I want it, you know?"

"Definitely," Kit said, pulling the blanket up over her chest.

"I think that's why I go on so many dates," Emily said. Kit felt a pang in her chest and fixed her gaze on the ceiling. She'd noticed Emily going out more often, but she just thought she'd started making friends. "It's such a quick way to meet people. It's so easy to hop on a dating app and meet up with someone, or just start talking to someone at the bar."

Kit made an affirmative noise, as if she'd ever struck up a conversation with someone at the bar.

Emily went on, "I like to get to know them and feel like someone knows me. It's nice to have someone to text throughout the day, someone to talk to about whatever. And if it goes anywhere, great. But if not, it's still a fun time."

Kit agreed again, hoping she wouldn't have to share her own dating experience – a few awkward first dates that went nowhere and roughly one and a half short-lived relationships.

"I wish I could feel as settled as you do," Emily said quietly. "You seem so at ease in this big house, without your parents breathing down your neck."

Kit huffed, rallying a bit. It's not like Emily's dates were any of her business anyways. She was just happy to have someone to share the house with, and to spend time with.

"My parents always thought it was creepy here. I'm glad they let me have it when my grandma died." She grew quiet for a moment. "I was always closer with her than with my parents. I think that's why I like the house so much. If I ever moved, it would feel like leaving a family member behind."

"The house has become your family," Emily said, sleepiness softening her words.

Kit stared at the ceiling. "Damn, dude."

She listened to the usual creaking and swaying of the house, like a lullaby after all these years. "Hey," she said, her voice barely above a whisper, "I think the house has calmed down."

There was no answer from the foot of the bed. Kit twisted her neck to catch a glimpse of Emily, fast asleep in a swirl of blankets. She looked so peaceful with her cheek smooshed up against the pillow and her hair falling into her face. She allowed herself a moment to commit the sight to memory, heart swelling in her chest, before she pulled her gaze away.

Kit put her arms behind her head. She closed her eyes and let her breaths even out in time with the buzz of Emily's snoring.

* * *

The house was delighted to have a new confidante. It ran through all its favourite tricks – waving to Emily with the kitchen cupboards, lighting fires in the grate, making the chandelier dance and spin. She displayed the proper levels of awe and wonder as the house revelled in the attention.

With a few blinking lights, the house even lured them onto the back porch, trying to air its biggest grievance to Emily. Beneath the usual clutter of rocking chairs and small tables, the porch was painted half white and half lime green – the result of a heated battle to force the old house to accept indoor plumbing back in the 1800s, Kit explained.

"And no one's tried to paint over it?" Emily asked.

"Of course not," Kit said. "This is the site of my great-great-aunt Ruth's victory. The house stopped bursting the pipes and flooding the place, so Ruth stopped painting the porch. This," she said, gesturing at the expanse of glaring green paint, "is left as a warning to the house."

Emily walked to the edge of the porch to lean over the vine-covered railing, gazing out to the night sky. Despite the light pollution this close to Boston, some stars still twinkled in the sky above them.

Kit joined her, pushing down a pang of guilt. She and her grandma used to come out here all the time, drinking lemonade and telling stories. But lately, she'd stuck to the few places in the house that felt more neutral – that didn't remind her of long visits exploring the halls, or the laughter that should be leading the way.

"I think we should be able to see Orion. That's an easy one to find," she said.

"That's the one with the belt, right?" Emily asked, eyes searching the sky.

Kit felt a wave of fondness wash over her. "Yeah, he's the one with the belt," she answered.

"I wonder if I can find Mercury," Emily said. "It's in retrograde right now, which is making me nuts."

Kit rolled her eyes, grinning. "I believe you've confused astronomy with astrology, Em."

Emily stuck her tongue out at Kit. "I know the difference, smartass. Mercury's bringing out all your Virgo tendencies."

They both tipped their heads back and enjoyed the slightly cloudy view of the stars above them.

Emily leaned her head on Kit's shoulder and sighed, content.

"It's beautiful," she said, reaching one arm around Kit's waist. "Just like you."

Kit stiffened. Emily's hand was warm on her hip – her too-curvy hip that always looked wrong to her in the mirror. And how could she call her beautiful? That familiar sting of wrongness seized Kit again. She wasn't beautiful. She wasn't anything. She felt like she was tricking Emily into thinking she was something she could never be.

"I'm, I, I'm sorry," Kit stuttered, stepping back. Emily frowned at her, concern written all over her face.

"I don't–" Kit said, struggling to breathe. "I can't. I don't know how to explain. I'm just–"

"Kit, it's okay," Emily said. She held her hands out in front of her, almost reaching for Kit, then pulled them back. "It's okay, it's all okay."

Kit took a few deep breaths, burning with shame.

"Let's go inside, okay?" Emily said, coaxing Kit towards the door. "It's been a long day. We can just relax or go to bed. It's alright, Kit. I'm sorry if I upset you."

Kit didn't have the words to explain. She followed Emily, her thoughts drowned out by the misery in her head.

★ ★ ★

Making dinner later that week, Kit stirred an extra bag of shredded cheddar into the mac and cheese in case Emily wanted some. They'd been careful around each other for the last few days – Kit trying to come up with a way to explain her freak-out and Emily trying to keep things light, giving Kit space. Kit's thoughts were interrupted by a loud, shrill voice and the sound of footsteps tripping over each other.

"Oh, wow! This is just how I pictured it!" someone shouted from the foyer.

The only response was Emily's giggle.

With a final stir, Kit set the stove to low and walked to the source of the noise.

"Hey," she said, announcing herself to the two bodies pressed together under the chandelier. She felt a jab somewhere in her stomach and tried to look relaxed.

Emily turned and smiled at her, face flushed and gleaming despite the snow outside. The front of her hair was pulled back in delicate braids, woven through the rest of her thick, light brown waves. A black dress with fringe on the bottom hugged her curves, swaying as she moved.

"Hey! Kit! It's Kit," she said, grabbing the hand of the girl leaning against her.

"Kit," she said, "this is Claire."

Claire was a tall blonde with a dazzling smile. She stood in high heels and a short, slinky dress. She flapped her oversized handbag in Kit's direction, which jangled in greeting.

Kit gave her a limp wave.

"Emily, can I talk to you for a second?" Kit asked.

"Sure!" Emily practically bounced over to Kit. She called back to Claire, "Sweetie, the living room's around the corner. Go make yourself comfortable."

Claire tottered off with a dazed look on her face.

Emily reached up and held onto Kit's arm, swaying slightly. "What's up?"

Kit exhaled in a rush, trying to keep her voice even. "Are you guys drunk? Did you drive here?"

"We took an Uber. You think I would drive drunk?" Emily frowned.

"Sorry," Kit said, pushing down the twisted feeling in her

chest. "I don't know. I get so nervous about people I care about sometimes." She swallowed. "Sorry. I'm too much, I'm sorry."

Emily rolled her eyes and booped Kit on the nose. "All's forgiven, you little squirrel."

Kit buried a wave of affection under frustration at seeing Claire and Emily together. "I am not–"

"Holy *shit*! This is insane!" Claire's voice echoed from down the hall.

Emily and Kit looked at each other, wide-eyed. They ran to the living room, but no one was there.

"Claire?" Emily called.

"In here!" They followed her voice to the downstairs bathroom.

Claire stood in front of the sink, her bag open on the floor with shiny electronics sticking out every which way. In one of her hands, a little monitor covered in LEDs lit up. In the other, she waved a cone-shaped device over the tiles in front of her.

She looked over her shoulder and yelled, "I'm getting some really crazy readings in this room!"

Kit felt her heart hammering in her chest. She lurched towards Claire, dizzy. "What the hell are you doing?"

Claire turned around. "I'm trying to get a reading of the room, but the EMF levels are way off the charts. I've never seen anything like this!"

Emily wrapped a hand around Kit's shoulder from behind. "Kit–"

Kit whirled on her, stepping back out of the bathroom to where Emily was hovering. "You brought a fucking ghost-hunter into my house?"

"Kit, I didn't know, I swear. We met a few times at the bar. I just thought she'd be fun. She never told me."

"I don't care!" Kit shouted. "I need her out of my fucking house right now!"

As Emily moved to enter the bathroom, the door slammed shut, leaving her and Kit on the other side. Claire screamed.

Kit pulled on the knob as hard as she could. "It's stuck."

"Get me the fuck out of here!" Claire wailed from inside the bathroom.

"It'll be okay, Claire," Emily called to her as Kit jiggled the handle, banging her shoulder and hip against the door as hard as she could. "I'm sorry, hun!"

"I'm getting my tools," Kit muttered as she walked away.

She came back to find Emily kneeling in front of the bathroom door, one hand pressed to the wood. "We're going to get you out, Claire."

"Serves her right," Kit said, raising her voice and looking for a screwdriver, "for snooping in other people's houses! Fucking ghosthunters."

"We're actually called paranormal investigators, and it's a whole field of scientific study!" Claire yelled back.

Kit worked on angling a screwdriver under the pin in the door's hinges, tapping it with a hammer. "Maybe you'd like to take this opportunity to study the shower curtains," she called back. "Get some readings on the mildew haunting my grout. Slap a Ouija board on the toilet and try to reach the spirits of shits past."

"Stop it, both of you!" Emily cried. She was pulling the pins out as Kit removed them, holding the door steady. "I'm sorry, Kit," she said, quieter. "Really. I just brought her home for the night; I don't know her that well."

"Yeah, well maybe if you spent a little more time paying attention and a little less hitting on half the people you meet, you would have noticed," Kit said.

Kit could feel Emily's glare on the back of her head as she turned around to meet it.

"...Jesus," Claire said from the other side of the door.

"Emily, I didn't mean—"

"It's fine, Kit," Emily said, her voice flat. "Just finish getting the door off and we'll leave."

Kit sighed. "Emily, I'm sorry. I'm upset, okay?"

"Whatever, Kit. Just finish the door."

Kit hesitated, trying to figure out what to say that could undo what just happened. Finally, she gave up and went back to working on the door.

When she finished, she and Emily grabbed either side of the door and walked it backwards, setting it aside to lean against the wall in the hallway.

Claire stepped out, smoothing down her dress. "Great place you have here," she said to Kit. "Rundown, full of antagonistic spirits. You should turn it into a bed-and-breakfast."

She walked past Kit towards the front door. "Come on, Emily, we can go to my place."

Emily was still frowning at the old pins she was holding. She shoved them into Kit's hands.

"Emily, please. Don't leave," Kit said.

Emily just looked at her, eyes shining. "I'm such an idiot. I should have known you thought the same thing everyone else thinks about me."

"Emily," Kit's arm twitched in her direction, but she held back from reaching out to her.

Emily shook her head and followed Claire, slamming the front door behind her.

Kit listened to the stillness of the house and felt more trapped than ever.

* * *

The next morning, the first thing Kit did was check the downstairs bathroom.

The door was still leaning next to its frame, the bathroom looking aged and sterile in the morning light.

Kit stepped in, breathing shallowly, feeling the burn of panic in her chest. It all seemed unchanged – the same peeling floral wallpaper, the same cracked pink tiles in the shower, same toilet with the weird pull chain to flush.

She sat on the lid of the toilet and bent in half, arms crossed over her chest to clutch her shoulders. She tried to focus on her breathing.

The pipes in the sink gurgled and the radiator pinged loudly. They grew to a crescendo until Kit looked up and acknowledged them.

"What? What do you want from me?" she bit out, eyes red. "Don't you have everything you want? She's gone. You scared her away. The one person who understood you and wasn't scared. I'll die alone here, is that what you want?"

The pipes and the radiator grew silent, but the lights pulsed softly in time with Kit's ragged breaths.

Kit glared at the wallpaper in front of her. She'd always meant to replace it, but couldn't decide with what – paint, new wallpaper, different tiles. These decisions always made her sick with anxiety. Relatives from every generation of her family had left their mark on the house, instilling their personalities into decor and paint and furniture. She couldn't even decide which colour was her favourite so she could paint her own room. Fear and shame burned deep in her chest.

"You scared her away," she growled.

With a sob, Kit grabbed onto a piece of wallpaper and pulled, peeling off a long, crooked strip. She let it fall to the floor and went back for another. Soon she was peeling as fast as she could, yanking and tearing with all her might.

Finally, when her fingernails were chipped and her hands covered in plaster dust, there was a heap of curled, torn wallpaper around her. Some of the ancient floral patterns seemed to gaze up at her.

Kit knelt in the pile and yelled and cried until she was so tired she could hardly breathe.

"I scared her away," she whispered to the empty room. "I scared her away."

* * *

The next few days passed in a blur. Kit managed to drag herself to her last few classes before winter break.

When she came home from organic chemistry, the house made a few gentle noises – the staircase creaking, the chandelier swinging lightly once, an occasional flicker of lights – that led her upstairs. The tilting wall sconces pointed to a door at the end of the hall – her grandmother's sewing room.

The door creaked open softly.

Kit stood in the doorway, eyes filling with tears as she looked at the familiar room. Like many of the rooms in the house, nothing quite matched. Inside was a collection of vintage sewing machines from different eras. The walls were covered in fabric samples and embroidery hoops. A butter-yellow chair presided in the middle of it all.

Kit patted the doorframe and walked directly to her bathroom, washing her face. She looked in the mirror and frowned at the dark circles under her eyes. She'd barely been able to look at herself the past few days.

She tugged a hand roughly through her hair and flipped it to one side, revealing the undercut. She let out a slow breath and opened the medicine cabinet to pull out the clippers Emily had given her.

She turned her head side to side. She stopped on the buzzed side and met her own eyes in the mirror.

Before she could overthink it, she turned on the clippers. She started from the front, pressing the teeth to her forehead and pulling backwards. A clump of hair fell into the sink, lifeless.

She tried not to look at herself until she was almost done, focusing on buzzing through each section. When everything felt smooth and relatively even, she gazed into the mirror.

She turned her head every which way, feeling the lack of weight. It was weird. It was kind of cold.

It was amazing.

The faucet in the bathtub turned off and on with a squeak, and the lights blinked merrily above the bathroom mirror.

She – no, they – grinned. "Thank you."

* * *

After their finals, Kit went directly to the home improvement store. They spent most of their free time messing with the house. They discovered how much they enjoyed listening to audiobooks and podcasts while painting or cleaning out years of built-up dust.

They made lemonade and iced tea and lots of cold drinks that started out in packets, but were perfectly respectable once put in a pitcher. They wore a button-down shirt everywhere, feeling a breathless thrill every time they knotted a tie over it.

They picked out an enormous red armchair that would be perfect for reading. It would probably clash with half the furniture in the library, but somehow that made it feel even more perfect. If any future generations of their family sat in that chair, they would know it belonged to their book-crazy ancestor, Kit.

With the help of some online forums, Kit figured out how to change their pronouns ahead of time for the next semester. Fortunately, the professors were all responsive and respectful in their emails back to Kit. After so much build-up and anxiety, it felt anticlimactic – mundane even – to not have to argue their case or justify the use of their chosen pronouns to anyone. As each confirmation email rolled in, Kit felt a wash of relief.

Kit still had nights where they'd wake up in a cold sweat, reaching to feel that their hair was really gone. Some days they were terrified that they might have chosen the wrong identity and would shrivel and turn to dust, like the guy in Indiana Jones who drank from the wrong Holy Grail.

But every time they saw themselves in the mirror, they felt invincible. Some days they even experimented with a bit of makeup, something they never even wanted to touch years before.

The house went out of its way to take care of them – pre-warming the water in the pipes each morning, opening doors when Kit walked by, keeping the library toasty warm all night despite a lack of firewood. It felt like it used to when Kit had been away for too long as a kid, and came back for a long visit with grandma.

It felt like being welcomed home.

* * *

One day, they were replacing some light bulbs in their favourite little passageway when the lights all started flickering. Kit had the switch flipped off while they worked, so they jumped.

"Agh, what?" they said, spinning in a circle. "Did I disconnect something? Relax, I can fix it, I can fix it," they said, almost sure that was true.

The flickering grew more frantic until Kit heard a voice coming from the doorway.

"Kit? You in there?" The lights surged and then went out, overwhelmed.

Kit tripped over their own feet trying to reach the doorway. "Emily!"

Emily peered around the edge of the door, eyes wide. "What is this place?" she said. It was a good thing Kit had left the door open, or else Emily could have thought no one was home. Shut tight, the door blended in seamlessly to the wall. Its top half was covered in wallpaper, the lower half made of the same solid, dark wood as the rest of the hall and moulded to match. It had no knob on the outside to give it away.

Kit wiped their hands on their pants, trying to banish some of the streaks of dirt and dust.

"It's an old passage that used to be for the servants," Kit said. "Apparently, this was the fastest way to get hot water to and from the kitchen."

Emily huffed. "A secret passage, huh? You've been holding out on me."

"I would have told you, eventually," Kit said, noting that

Emily still hadn't really looked in their direction. "I just… didn't want you to think there could be ghosts in the walls or something. Didn't want to scare you away with too much too fast."

Emily finally looked up and Kit felt a jolt through their chest. "You can't scare me away. I'm tougher than that," Emily said.

Kit laughed, a fragile sound in the still air of the passage.

"Hey, what's this?" Emily stepped closer to reach for Kit's hair.

Kit bent their head down to be mussed. "I finally took the plunge. Thanks again for the clippers."

"Of course," Emily said, smiling as Kit looked up again. "You look great. It really suits you."

"Thanks." Kit tried to hide their blush. "It was time for a change."

"I can see that," Emily said, waving towards Kit's crisp button-down shirt and tie, half protected under a paint-stained hoodie.

"Has anything else changed that I should know about?" Emily asked, one eyebrow raised.

Kit smirked. "My name is the same, but I'm using they/them pronouns now."

Emily nodded, grinning. "Good to know. I'm glad to hear it. This seems really good for you."

Kit looked at their feet. "Thank you," they said quietly.

The silence stretched, and Kit felt the burn of embarrassment that always came with sharing too much. They cleared their throat and tugged on their tie.

"Should we go somewhere a bit more… not a dark secret passage?"

"Absolutely," Emily said. "Although I want a full tour of all these secret rooms one day."

As they reached the door, it swung gently shut.

"Oh, come on, not now," Kit muttered under their breath, pulling on the knob.

"Kit? Did I do something wrong?" Emily looked up and down the corridor as the lights flickered.

"No," Kit sighed. "I did." They took a deep breath and met Emily's gaze. "I can't keep running away from being honest with you."

"What?"

"I'm sorry," Kit said, taking the hand Emily had reached out to them in the flickering light. "I was a total jerk about Claire, and you, and all of it. I was way out of line. I can't believe I said—"

"It's okay, Kit. Nothing I haven't heard before," Emily said, looking down at where their hands were joined.

Kit fought against a lump in their throat. "That doesn't make it okay, Em. I'm so sorry. I was panicking and upset and I lashed out. I hope you know I didn't mean it, or that there's anything wrong with going on however many dates you want. I just said what I knew would hurt. It was awful."

"I understand," Emily said. "You were worried about the house. You wanted to protect it." There was an edge of hurt in her voice that left Kit's chest aching.

"Yeah, there was definitely some of that," Kit said, "but honestly, I was jealous." They squeezed Emily's hand once and let go.

"Jealous of Claire?" Emily asked as the lights began to brighten around them.

"Of Claire, of anyone you went on a date with, of you," Kit said. "Of pretty much everyone who had their shit figured out, gender-wise."

"Oh," Emily said quietly.

Kit swallowed and hurried on. "I've been struggling with this for a long time. Actually," they held their arms open to encompass the passage, "this is where I used to hide from my parents when they tried to fluff up my hair and put me in dresses and stuff."

"Oh, Kit," Emily said, stepping closer.

Kit held up a hand. "It's okay. I get it now. Before it just made me feel like something was wrong with me, or that I was defective or something. I thought I'd never be enough for anyone, especially not in a romantic relationship." They looked down and added, "This is also where I hid from you, sometimes."

Emily didn't say anything, but she made a noise like she had just spotted a kitten stuck in a tree.

"I know, it's ridiculous," Kit said. "I'd duck in here if I saw you coming down the hallway, or if I could hear you coming into the kitchen. But it wasn't really you I was avoiding. It was me." They put a hand to their chest and looked directly into Emily's eyes. "You made me realise how much I wanted to be a whole, real person – a real woman, a real man, something. But I couldn't figure it out. I didn't know where I belonged, until after I'd already chased you away. And you didn't deserve that. I'm sorry I took my issues out on you."

When Emily reached out her hand again, Kit took it.

"I was too afraid. I thought I'd scare people away if I admitted it," Kit said. "Then I realised I was scaring people away by hiding it."

"Oh, Kit," Emily said again, sniffling. She wrapped her arms around them and hugged Kit tight. "You're so beautiful, inside and out. You don't have to hide from me, or from anyone."

Kit closed their eyes and hugged back. "Thank you. Thank you for everything."

They stood there for a moment, until Emily pulled back to wipe her eyes. "Don't want to get mascara on your nice shirt."

Kit laughed. "It already has paint on it. Might as well."

Emily huffed a laugh and took a step back. "To be honest," she said, fidgeting with her hands, "I kept trying to make a move on you, but I felt like I was the one scaring you away. I could tell there was something going on, but I thought maybe you were ace, or trans and still figuring things out or something. I didn't want to make you uncomfortable or make it awkward living together, so I backed off."

Kit's face flushed. "I think I made it awkward enough for the both of us," they said.

Emily laughed. "I think we both had something to do with that. Sorry if I ever made you uncomfortable, or if it felt like I was pushing for something you couldn't give."

Kit blinked. "Not at all. I just didn't know how to talk about my identity when I wasn't sure what it was myself. Turns out being in between can be an identity on its own," they laughed.

Emily grinned, wiping mascara from under her eyes. "I'm glad you found a home in yourself, Kit."

Kit felt the lump in their throat growing. "Thank you." The lights surged up and down the passage, and Kit knew they had one last thing to say.

"I also didn't know if you'd be open to dating someone who isn't a specific gender. Is that... something that you could be okay with?" They asked, smearing paint and dust from hand to hand as they fidgeted.

"Are you kidding?" Emily laughed, practically jumping into Kit's arms. She brushed a hand over Kit's hair as Kit rubbed their thumbs over Emily's waist. "I like you for you, Kit. Not the clothes you wear or the pronouns you use."

Kit leaned in and Emily met them in the middle, their lips pressing together as Kit backed into the wall. Somewhere in the back of Kit's mind they noticed the lights in the passageway blazing white hot behind their eyelids.

A few feet away, the door to the passage creaked open. They didn't notice.

THE RUIN

E. Saxey

His name was Robin. (As far as I know, his name was Robin.)

I met him at a book club.

That sounds respectable. A bit boring, even, for a guy in his twenties like me. A harmless hobby, certainly, and perhaps all the times I've tried to warn people, I should have been more specific.

We met at a book club that only read books about the end of the world.

The first time I truly noticed Robin, he was on the opposite side of a wobbling pub table. A bloke in his fifties, exasperated with the novel, getting sanctimonious at the rest of the readers.

"But it's all wish-fulfilment!" He locked eyes with me, light grey irises in a craggy face. "I bet *you* liked the part with the shoplifting."

I'd thought that scene was tasteless, but I wanted to irk him. "It was brilliant. If it's the end of the world, why not go ram-raiding?"

"Well. I'm not telling *you* where I parked my car."

His voice was husky, like rough fur. He was from the North, like me. He had a twinkle in his eye. Was he flirting?

He sat back in his seat but kept looking my way. Over the back of his seat was an anorak. It was so unstylish, so much the opposite of sexy, that I started to make up attractive explanations for it: maybe he worked outdoors, maybe in conservation. He held the novel he disdained in one strong tanned hand.

I'd only moved to London recently, I was missing the moors. I imagined us striding along a dry-stone wall together, Robin wearing his terrible anorak, putting his hand on my shoulder, pointing to a buzzard in the big skies overhead.

★ ★ ★

The next time we were both at the book club was months later, clear into the new year. Robin rolled his eyes and accused me of an unreasonable squeamishness about catching and eating rabbits. "You can't be called *Wolf* and live off vegan sausage rolls!"

He'd remembered my name.

"I'll go for cannibalism, then," I offered. "Eat everyone over forty."

"Oh, will you? We're bloody tough," retorted Robin.

After the discussion ended he stood by my elbow. "Sorry about that, I got carried away."

I liked his apology, and its awkwardness, which both made him seem less abrasive, and more flirtatious. "No, I was being rude," I replied.

"You were very rude! You're a bad Wolf."

I'd changed my name so recently that he was the first person to make that joke. I was delighted and laughed, then wondered how often I'd hear that joke and when I'd get sick of it.

I offered to buy Robin a drink. "I haven't seen you for a few meetings," I said.

"Didn't fancy the books."

"They were fantastic. The last one was about rebuilding a road network, a kind of communications system."

"Ugh, *optimism*."

He was relentlessly downbeat and I felt sure he wasn't interested in me. I was surprised when he suggested a stroll after we finished the drinks. I directed us down to the canals behind Kings Cross station. Winter was receding; it was warm enough to wander. We stopped to look out over the dark water and stood close together, brushing shoulders (he was short, for a cis bloke).

His face in profile looked melancholy against the high cranes bejewelled with lights. Every part of London looked dystopian to me. Every building site was a ruin in waiting. The stumbling drinkers on the opposite towpath could have had the Sweats or a triffid on their tail. But down on the water, the smallest moorhen chick was breaking the gunmetal surface into ripples, peeping and striving.

"Look!" I said.

Our first kiss came later, but that was the first time I tried, truly, to cheer Robin up.

"Do you really like the novels where it's all going wrong?" Robin asked. "Where the hero drives a stolen Porsche and stocks up at Fortnum and Mason?"

"I don't think the Ritz would feel like the Ritz if I had to turf a corpse out of the bathtub."

"Precisely!"

"And I don't like thinking about how I'd cope, because you can't stockpile testosterone indefinitely." It was a blunt hint but he took it smoothly, nodding. I kept talking, to stop it being awkward. "I hate the part where everyone dies. I like the bit afterwards, where people pull together. But you don't. So what *do* you like?"

"The middle part. The stillness."

"Just animals wandering along the empty motorways?"

"And grass springing up, through everything." He gestured at the concrete all round us.

"Everything turning green?"

"Oh, yes."

I sympathised. I was already planning how far I could travel out of London that weekend, how much green I could get. I remembered a quote: "Don't you find it a beautiful clean thought, a world empty of people, and a hare sitting up?"

"Who's that?"

"DH Lawrence."

"That old goat! No, I'm selfish for humanity. I want someone there to see it." He sighed. "But not me. You'd be better off just eating me."

The urge to jolt him out of his misery became a reckless erotic intensity. "I could make a start."

He turned to face me. "What, just a nibble? Very cruel."

"Harsh times."

He reached out to where my V-neck T-shirt showed off my chest-hair. I shivered.

"What's this," he said, "some kind of rewilding project? Did you get a government grant to turn it back over to nature? Is there a *lynx* in here somewhere?" I started laughing and he mock-protested: "I'm just saying, is it *safe*..."

"It's not safe," I said. "You'll get bitten." I tried to keep a straight face long enough to kiss him.

★ ★ ★

I've tried all of this before. I've sent the information to the authorities, but nobody has followed up.

I think I know the problem: I was trying to look too sensible. I wanted to seem like a reliable witness, not a crank. I needed my story to be taken seriously, so I left out some details. But I can't incriminate him without admitting how strangely we behaved together.

This time, I won't edit it. I'll put down everything just as it happened.

I've previously reported that *Robin talked about certain scenarios.*

I want to say, now: *We talked about the end of the world all the bloody time.*

It was romantic, for us. We'd met in a pub, but we'd also met on fallow farmland where local warlords toted shotguns. We prolonged the fantasy. Spring was coming and we lay on rugs in parks and talked about the death of grass, how the brown hills around us would erode. We walked a circular footpath round the city and discussed blast radiuses. Robin didn't much like London, but he liked the guided tour on the Great Fire of London, and the one-man show about Samuel Johnson's diary of the plague year. We groped each other in the cinema, watching pandemic thrillers.

"There's no way to do it properly," Robin said in April.

"You're right, there's probably no way to kill half the population *properly*." We were in his studio flat, which was small and shabby. We both worked in tech, but I was better paid as a game developer. He worked in unglamourous process automation: car factories, power plants.

We were still teasing each other all the time. I did it because I was scared of how much I liked him.

"You can't do it with a magic wand, that's all I'm saying," Robin complained. "Even if everyone goes peacefully, there's always bodies."

"And then you get rats," I put in. "Mind you, we've already got rats."

"And who buries the bodies? And how do they *feel* about having to bury all those bodies." Tough-shelled, soft-hearted bloke. "And if everyone died of something that got rid of your body more quickly…"

This was a new one, to me. "Like what?"

"A virus that sped up decomposition…" I gagged at that. He continued, soothingly: "…would probably be too virulent to spread very far."

We argued about it. We sharpened our opinions on each other while we curled up together. I helped him workshop the end of the world.

"We should ask the book club," I suggested.

"You'll get us thrown out of the book club." He hopped out of bed for the loo, and I was left looking at the books on his bedside table. Big tomes of history in no discernible order. A list of words doodled on an old envelope.

Bihrorene
Gedreas
Byrstig
Undereotone
Brosnað

"You shouldn't leave your passwords lying around," I told him when he came back.

"Ha! I was just counting synonyms." He ran his finger down the list. "Collapsed, fallen, broken, undermined, decaying. Old English."

"That seems like overkill for one language."

"Not when you have to describe a lot of things which are byrstig." He tugged a book from the bedside heap. I couldn't understand the lumpy gutturals of the original text, but then my heart snagged on the modern translation. *I wandered, sad for lack of a hall.*

"Is it about the Black Death?"

"It's three hundred years before the Black Death."

I was dizzy. One thousand years ago someone had been writing the same scenario that I was still reading about in our book club: a lone man crossing a hail-scourged landscape, longing for friends. Humans had survived, but we'd also preserved that specific flavour of sorrow. A continuity of loss.

"It's brilliant. I love it. You know such weird stuff…"

"That's why you like me, though," he said, prodding me.

"What?"

"You like old things. I'm an old ruin."

"Stop it! You miserable—"

"…old bastard? You're right. I'm undereotone. I'm brosnað!"

I couldn't answer him honestly. When I thought of his age at all it made me happy because I was looking at my future: a short queer man, half camp and half curmudgeon. He wasn't a ruin, he was the promise of my survival.

Saying that would have made him feel even older so instead, I ran my hands over his ticklish spots. "I can check, hang on…

Is this bit still attached? Oh God, it's *dangling!* I'll hold onto it, stop it falling off..."

"I'm just saying, it's all downhill from here. Get off! Oh, damn you."

★ ★ ★

Later that day, I was looking for a pen to finish a crossword, and I stumbled across his notebooks. They floated on a sea of dust under the bed, but they weren't themselves dusty. The draughtsmanship was beautiful. Inside the notebooks, maps were overlaid with many coloured circles, like chakras, pulsing in waves of red and orange.

Have you seen them, already? I'm sending another set of copies with this account. It took me a while to understand, so I've added my own notes as well. The chakras were blast radii. Those other maps, with gorgeous marbled swirls, show how contaminants might drift on the wind. There were dozens of technical diagrams, too. Here was the proof that Robin understood even more about the end of the world than he shared with me: how barriers at power plants could be raised, how the safety systems in factories could be overridden, how things that were contained could be dispersed, into the sky and water.

All of the notes were handwritten. The maps were sometimes photocopied but nothing had been done on a computer – because it was a labour of love, I assumed. Pages and pages of it. I was so proud of him.

He had to be writing a novel.

He didn't talk about his novel, but plenty of people are shy about their creative side. It might not have been a novel. It might have been a role-playing game he was planning or some kind of art installation.

I replaced the notebooks carefully under the bed. I'd give him space, and eventually, he'd share them with me.

★ ★ ★

That summer, I took Robin away from London nearly every other weekend. He'd changed jobs a fair amount, from airports to the milk industry to sewage. Switching fields had kept his income low, while I was feeling generous. I was worried about his depressive streak, and keen to distract him.

I took us to ruins.

We toured the big Yorkshire Abbeys first. Back to God's own county. It was June but a sea mist covered us when we got to Whitby, so thick that you could see it pouring in through the skeletal rose windows. It was unseasonably drizzly the following day as we walked through the woods to Rievaulx. I got almost tearfully furious at King Henry VIII because he'd ripped the lead from the roof and left the place to rot. He'd wrecked Whitby, too, and Jervaulx and Fountains and Byland.

"One man," I said, "ruining all of this. It's unspeakable."

"Not one man," Robin argued. "Vested interests. European geopolitics."

"Nope. Just one arsehole." Now I had to cheer both of us up. I bought a bottle of mead from the gift shop.

I had to do some research to work out where to take Robin next. I tried to surprise him, but it's hard to keep a secret when there are train announcements.

"Bath Spa station? Is this a bloody spa break? Do you want me to get a back massage and a Brazilian wax?"

"You'll see."

"I should never place myself in your hands…"

I led him down into the ruined Roman baths. We were hemmed in by schoolkids, but Robin was serene. When we reached the steaming circular pool, I pulled out a photocopied sheet of verse.

"Look: brosnað enta geweorc. Decayed, the work of giants!" My whisper echoed in the vaulted ceiling.

"I didn't think you'd remember that poem," he said.

"They think the poem is about this place," I said.

"Really?" He pressed his lips together, and I thought I'd misjudged things badly, but then I felt his hand close round mine and squeeze it. "Oh, Wolf…"

I was glowing with pride. I'd only looked at Wikipedia, but it had paid off.

"Imagine," he said. "Coming here in 900 AD and seeing all this impossible Roman stonework, not knowing who'd left it."

We silently goggled at the persistence of objects and the ruptures of knowledge.

Robin was hypnotised by the churning white waters. "Think about how long it's been coming to the surface here, pouring out of that conduit. There's nothing like water…"

I took the poem back from him. Wrætlic is þes wealstan, wyrde gebræcon. "Wyrde gebræcon – weird and broken?"

"Broken by fate. Except it's alliterative. Maybe it would be: Fabulous is this foundation – fate's fucked it."

My surprise had worked well. Robin was cheerful again, amorous at the bed and breakfast, and declaring himself willing to get a back massage if I absolutely insisted.

We read the Sunday papers in bed that weekend, and he passed me over a story about a Viking warrior with a "woman's skeleton" ("Have you been bloody time-travelling again?"). While he was in the shower, I found some pages crumpled up and stuffed under his pillow. They held a report on a rewilding project in Germany that had interested me. The balance of animals and resources had gone out of whack, and the owners were shooting five hundred hungry wild cattle. Robin had told me months ago that the project would never work, but rather than gloating now, he'd tried to protect me.

When he came back to bed, he saw that I knew. He hugged me and muttered: "Idiots. If they'd had more space, it could have worked. You *must* do it properly. Everywhere at once or nowhere at all." He sighed. "Someone needs to take care of every thing."

Every *thing*. That was the way I heard it: the need for every individual thing to have its protector. And I knew Robin would never say it directly, but he wanted to take care of me.

He changed jobs again a few weeks later to work at a water company, and I silently took credit for it, because the Bath trip had inspired him.

★ ★ ★

In July, he came to my flat with colour printouts in his arms and hid them so I'd fight him for them. I thought they might be his art, his maps, his diagrams. Then I saw floor plans. He was going to ask me to move in with him. Would I? It was hasty. We'd only been seeing one another for six months. But my flatmate was awful, and his studio flat was a grim, dim room. I hadn't made any close friends in London, not close enough to live with (maybe because I spent every weekend with Robin). We could find somewhere better, together. I thought all of those things in the three seconds it took me to wrestle the sheets of paper away from him.

The property photographs were too green, and the numbers printed below them were too low. None of these places were in London.

"Thought we might like a holiday home," said Robin. "I've got some savings."

I hid my surprise and looked at the photos of sturdy cottages near big lakes, old towers. "Really?"

"If we get a place, we can go on the weekend. Long walks. Loud pastimes. Ahem." He ran his hand up my leg.

"But we'd be stuck in one place. At the moment, we can go for long walks wherever we want." I tapped the details of a handsome stone farmhouse in Wales. "For the price of this place, we could have loud pastimes for two hundred weekends in different bed and breakfasts. And look where this cottage is, it would take hours to even get there…"

Robin nudged me with his shoulder. "But you need to get out of town more. You pine for the moors."

"I *do* get out of town. You take me out."

"Don't want you getting rickets." His tone was strained and jovial. His new job hadn't raised his spirits.

"Wouldn't you rather move in together? Properly, in London?"

He wrinkled his nose. "You wouldn't want to see me during the week. I'm a boring bastard."

It was the first commitment he'd asked me to make and I'd rejected him.

★ ★ ★

A dozen clues had gone straight over my head, but then I tripped on a tiny detail – one small crack in the road.

That same evening, I browsed the properties he'd brought me, feeling I should give the idea more consideration. All the buildings had land attached. Maybe Robin thought I'd want to grow wildflowers, release a lynx or two. Maybe he wanted to farm.

(I know I was slow. It's coming.)

A little bungalow in Cornwall came with *½ acre orchard, working well*. A funny way to talk about an orchard: trees in good working order! Then I understood: there was a working *well*. A little stone turret sticking up from the grass with a winch and a swinging bucket.

A smallholding in Wales boasted, *own water supply to upper field*. The austere tower near Inverness had a *genuine well in garden*. Water flowing in old conduits.

"Why have they all got wells?" I called over to Robin, who was lying on my bed, finishing a crossword.

"Sometimes you need to make a wish."

"At short notice?"

"Aye. Think about it."

Over the next few weeks, I did nothing but think about it.

I used a pen and paper, although Google Maps would have been easier. I didn't want an electronic record. I mapped where every one of his proposed properties lay, freckles across the face of Britain. I contrived reasons for Robin to pop to the corner shop, and I compared my own dotted spread to the more elegant maps in his notebooks.

I asked him to bring me some more potential properties: more farms, more cottages, more caves. I told him I was thinking about it. It wasn't a lie.

The patterns the dots made on my map were river-shaped: a few idling main channels with tendrils snaking off them. The channels and the tendrils twisted back and forth to avoid every major city. They evaded nuclear plants, airports. Every dot on my map avoided every circle or blob Robin had drawn on his maps.

Was Robin a survivalist, a prepper? Did he genuinely think the end was coming? I'd met all sorts at our book club: conspiracy theorists, doom-mongers. Readers who extrapolated from current affairs straight into fiction. But Robin was so calm and elated when he contemplated catastrophe. No panic, no paranoia. It had a holy quality for him.

Over the next week, it became clearer and clearer to me that Robin was planning to take care of everything, just like he'd promised me in the bed-and-breakfast in Bath. But in an entirely different way than I'd understood.

★ ★ ★

There's no sympathy for the partners of killers. I've heard the questions: *why didn't you leave? Why didn't you report him?* So I did both.

I emailed a full set of photographs of all his notebooks to the police straight away. I have no idea what they did with them. I sent a follow-up request; they said they couldn't comment.

I started to avoid Robin, who was as melancholy and playful and lustful as ever, and that hurt him. It hurt me too. I wondered if I'd made a mistake. Perhaps we could discuss it and laugh about it.

Then I saw pictures of the weird blue tap water in Glasgow and Swansea and Bournemouth. Totally harmless, no explanation. Enough for me to recognise a trial run, though. His destruction will be waterborne, and it will happen in a lot of cities simultaneously.

I bought a cottage and moved out of the city. I considered renting it from a Londoner and then just taking over when it all kicked off, but that felt like a mean gamble. It wasn't one of the cottages that Robin had suggested, but I did use his maps to choose the site. Yes, I'm a coward.

I wondered if my presence in the city would protect it, but Robin can't allow himself that kind of sentiment.

I work freelance at the moment, and I'll do that until the internet goes down. I've got chickens and goats. The goats are partly for company, as well. I don't let people visit; I go all the way back into London to see my friends. It would only cause problems later. I know that scenario. St Paul's has cracked like a boiled egg and someone's huddling in the ruins saying: "Do you remember Wolf's place in the country? Which direction is that from here…?"

I've got a cellar with clothes and tools and seeds. Enough for me, that is. I'm not the Svalbard seed vault. I don't have guns; that always goes wrong.

I have a simple life. I get up early every morning and I get water from the well. (Of course this cottage has a well.)

I look out across the moat. (This cottage also has a moat).

Yesterday, he was standing on the other bank. The mist was thick but I'd have known his sensible anorak anywhere. I remembered the stiff feel of the fabric, when we hugged in triumph after a tough climb and I'd bury my face in his shoulder. I shook my head to dash the memory away.

"Nice cottage," he called. "Did you have to eat a granny to get it?"

"How did you find me?"

"I was worried," he said, as though concern linked us with a golden thread that he could follow anywhere. "Can I come over, get some tea? It's a chilly walk from the village."

There's a drawbridge. Only a small one, but it works.

"No. I know what you're planning," I lied.

He looked down at his walking shoes, and for the first time, I was sure.

"Don't do it," I said. "It won't work. It's horrible."

"You'll be all right, though?"

I was livid. He'd come to reassure himself that I was safe, that he'd have his lone witness. He loved me enough to check up on me, but not enough to stop.

"I won't be all right! I can't kill rabbits. I don't know how to farm."

"You could read up…"

"And you can't stockpile testosterone! It has a best-before date. You forgot that, didn't you? Selfish bastard."

"Can I visit?"

"What, *afterwards?* Jesus, no."

"But I miss you."

"You've ruined everything."

He stood there, and I couldn't bear his sincerity or his misery.

"I've told the police," I said.

He turned away at that, into the mist.

★ ★ ★

I started to put together another letter to the police. I prepared my story again, including links to the stories about the Glasgow tap water and everything that I knew about Robin's job in water treatment. I realised that I'd been trying to sound calm and reasonable, not like a doom-monger or a fantasist. I'd left out all the detail of our lives together, how we'd wooed one another with desolation.

I understood that I'd been doing it wrong. I needed to sound eccentric and extreme. I needed to tell you the whole story, give all the gory details, because nothing short of that would persuade you.

See me? See where I am, now?

He is twice as far beyond me as I am beyond you. He is a very long way out.

I can feel autumn in the air. It's not the sloughing of a year's growth but something grander.

★ ★ ★

I'll tell you one more thing I remember, from when we were both in bed, curled around one copy of his thousand-year-old poetry.

"Hu gæstlic bið – How ghastly it will be?" I estimated.

"No, 'gæst' means 'spirit'. Flaesc and gæst, flesh and spirit."

"Oh! So, how *ghostly* it will be..." I cheated and looked at the translation, "...when all the world's wealth lies waste."

"Not quite. Gæstlic is spiritual."

"How *spiritual* it will be?"

It didn't make any sense, but he held me very close.

"When all the world's wealth lies waste," he finished.

THE DREAM EATER

Anna Moon

At twenty-six, I had a sex dream for the first time. The dream had started off quite innocuously – something involving chasing a guinea pig down the street I grew up in, its furry brown body always just out of my grasp. Then, in that inevitable dream logic way, a figure appeared in my field of vision. Reclining on a chaise longue, a raven-haired person wore a black lacy chemise, breasts suggestively blooming along the neckline. Long stocking-covered legs were artfully draped on the fabric, and a red lipstick smile beckoned me close. Still half-seeking the guinea pig – *What had been its name? Gerald?* – I stood there unmoving.

She raised a delicate eyebrow. The figure morphed within the blink of an eye. The chaise was gone, replaced by a barstool. No longer was the figure all leg and bust and soft fabric. Now a man sat on the stool, one elbow casually resting on the bar – *Am I in a bar? How did I get here – I should get a drink – Was it Mr Sniffles?* His chiselled jaw was covered in light stubble, the crisp white shirt unbuttoned to show a muscular chest, with a scattering of hair trailing towards his low-slung jeans. *A drink would be nice. Shall I have a gin and tonic? No, maybe something fancy, something with an obscure name and five ingredients.* I walked past the man leaning on the worn wood, looking for a bartender. I was starting to feel heavy, as if a weighted blanket had covered me.

Blink.

The bar disappeared, yet the figure remained. It warped and morphed through a variety of human shapes. A dark-skinned,

223

androgynous, short-haired person in flannels. A sudden flare of dyed hair, a luscious figure, and high heels. The apparitions wore casual clothes, ball gowns, or sometimes nothing at all. Once, inexplicably, the humanoid figure disappeared completely and only a shoe appeared on the ground. While the figures danced, reclined, loomed, or beckoned, the bright whirl elicited no reaction from me, yet the heavy feeling increased. Finally, the figure again stabilised into the shape of the man. He sighed and handed me an orange drink with a tiny umbrella.

"I guess it's just one of those days, huh," he said.

★ ★ ★

When I woke up the following morning, Elise had already disappeared from her side of the bed. Putting on a worn pair of sweatpants over my boxers, I dragged myself to the kitchen.

"Morning, love," she said, giving me a kiss on the cheek. "I made you a coffee."

"Thank you," I said, gratefully taking a sip from the mug she put on the table in front of me. I was never much of a morning person, but today I was feeling more rough than usual. "I had the weirdest dream last night."

"Did you?" she asked. Elise was already dressed for the day ahead in a dark grey blouse, her brown hair drawn back in a neat ponytail.

"It involved nudity," I said, wriggling my eyebrows.

"Really? Was it a fun kind of nudity? Do tell." She leaned forward, smiling.

"I mean, kind of? Turns out my ace ass is still just as ace in dreamland as he is in real life. Here this person was, all naked and such, doing all of the things people do to seem available, and all I could think about was a guinea pig and getting a drink."

Elise snorted, a broad smile illuminating her face. "That sounds exactly like you. Although the guinea pig sounds pretty random."

"It was," I said with a shrug. "You know how dreams are."

"I wish I remembered mine more often. They're such a fasci-nating insight into our subconscious." With a little flourish, she closed her work bag. "I'll be home by six tonight. I hope you have a productive day." After a brief hug smelling of strawberry and a resolute click of the front door, I was alone.

★ ★ ★

The blinking cursor on the blank document taunted me. *Write something, I dare you,* it said. Asaksadghk, I typed. *Take that.* With a sigh, I deleted the nonsense again. That dreaded blinking continued.

"Why is this so hard," I moaned. Sometimes writing came easily, but this commission completely stumped me. A lifestyle website that I occasionally wrote for was looking for content on modern dating. They paid very well – such a rarity these days – but the deadline was the end of the week. The spark of inspiration, the hook that could sell the article to the editor, was proving to be elusive. I had already written several articles about dating as an asexual person – writing from my own experience was both slightly terrifying as well as rewarding. This time, I was going to need a new angle, or the editor wouldn't be happy.

Hoping to find some company for my misery, I switched to the tab of the writing chatroom I had joined a few months earlier.

Dan dun dunnn: anyone else struggling today?

WritingJen: OMG, so bad. Feeling really tired and unfocused

Neil likes horror: it's going okay… almost finished edits on my novella. anything wrong dan?

Dan dun dunnn: nah, I'm fine. had a weird dream and apparently it kind of threw me? I'm excited to read the latest version of your novella btw Neil ☺

Neil likes horror: thanks mate! I'll send it over when it's done

WritingJen: What was your dream about? I had the WILDEST sex dream of my life two days ago and I still haven't recovered :'D

Aditi: Jen you have no filter at all do you :')

WritingJen: Nope! Sorry haha. Side effect from writing too much shifter erotica I think. And hey it's not like I gave any details

WritingJen: Unless you want me to...

Aditi: No thank you I'm good haha

Dan dun dunnn: ha! mine was kind of like that, except nothing actually happened

WritingJen: Fair enough! Well I hope you sleep better tonight ☺ *x*

Dan dun dunnn: thank you, you too Jen x

Setting aside all thoughts of intercourse and the subconscious, I returned to my arch-nemesis – that sneering, still-empty page. I was determined to write some words, *any words* damn it, before dinner.

Several hours and a couple of paragraphs that felt like pulling teeth later, Elise returned with a takeaway.

"Let me take that from you," I said, unburdening her of the heavy bag of deliciously smelling boxes of food. "How was your day?"

"Pretty good. So busy though. One of my team members

called in sick again. I have no idea what kind of bug is going around, but it feels like every other day someone is too unwell to come into work. They're all really tired or something." She sat down at the table, where I had put down a plate for her.

"Maybe it's the time of year. I've been feeling a bit under the weather too."

"Hope you don't come down with anything," she said, taking my hand.

"I'm sure I'll be fine," I said, giving her hand a squeeze in return. "Especially after eating this delicious curry you brought."

"Don't forget the samosas!"

"Well, in that case, I'll be more than fine."

★ ★ ★

Even before I could see the figure, I felt the presence in my dream. The heaviness returned, like I was moving through water, or perhaps like a thousand threads tried to keep me in place. I was no longer alone. It was no longer just me in my thoughts – *Who's there? Is someone listening?* – What was that pull, that feeling of being… drained? I struggled against it, trying to break the threads. The morphing figure appeared in a flash of a brown spotted animal suit. Then it snapped into a slim androgynous human, their hand reaching out, trying to grab me. I had to get away, away, away, away–

I bolted upright with a gasp. Slowly the panicked feeling faded, leaving me feeling jittery. The familiar surroundings of our bedroom returned, the black curtains imperfectly blocking the orange glow of the streetlights outside, and Elise's huddled form breathing softly beside me. When my heartbeat returned to normal, I laid back down, snuggling close to her. As I drifted off to sleep, I couldn't quite shake the feeling that something was wrong.

★ ★ ★

Incessant beeping pierced the fog of sleep. The morning light formed a halo around the curtains.

"Elise," I said, gently shaking her. "Your alarm is going off."

No response. I raised myself on my elbow. "Elise," I repeated, louder this time. As I shook her shoulder, her head lolled to the side, her eyes still closed. My heart beat in my throat. She still felt warm to the touch – nothing was wrong. Nothing could be wrong, right?

"Elise!" A note of panic slipped in my voice. This was not like her. My fingers dug into her shoulder. "Elise, wake up!"

"Mmh," she sighed, her eyelids fluttering.

The iron band around my chest released and I felt like I could breathe again.

"Sweetheart, you have to get up for work," I said, calmer this time.

"Can't go," she muttered, rolling onto her side.

"You can't go to work? I don't think attendance is optional."

"Too tired."

I got out of bed and opened the curtains, hoping that the sunlight might induce her to open her eyes. Returning to bed, however, I found she had fallen back asleep immediately. She had dark black circles under her eyes, and her skin was a pale ashy hue that I had only seen on her when she had a bad flu a couple of years back. She didn't feel like she had a fever though – she was a bit chilly, even. I tucked the blanket more tightly around her and put a fresh glass of water on her nightstand in case she woke up feeling thirsty.

"Elise, would you like me to call your office for you?" I asked her, after shaking her for an uncomfortably long time.

"Mmhmm," she grumbled, which I took as assent.

Elise's manager, a chipper Welshman with a deep booming voice, seemed unbothered. "It has been going around," he said. I could almost feel his shrug through the voice-connection. "Thank you for letting me know. Tell her to feel better soon."

Elise didn't properly wake up until four in the afternoon,

when she stumbled into my office-slash-guest-bedroom in her space pyjamas.

"Hey, how are you feeling?" I asked, eager to focus on something besides my essay for a moment.

"I feel floopy," she said, sitting down on the guest bed. "It's like I ran a marathon in my sleep and now I need more sleep to make up for it. I had tons of really intense dreams but I can't remember them now."

"Maybe you caught a virus from your co-workers?" I said, wheeling my desk chair towards her so I could hold her hand. She still looked deathly pale, but it was a relief to see her up and fully conscious.

"Probably. Damn it. I shouldn't have complained about them. Serves me right for being judgey."

I laughed. "Well, I hope you feel better anyway."

"I'm going to lie down for a bit longer I think," she said with a yawn.

"I'll wake you up for dinner," I said, kissing her forehead. She shuffled out of the room again, covered in colourful planets and space shuttles. Despite the improvement in awareness, I couldn't fully shake my worry.

★ ★ ★

That night I lay awake, listening to Elise's deep breaths. She had fallen asleep on my shoulder and occasionally she would twitch. Despite my own tiredness, I couldn't seem to drift off. I felt hyper-aware, staring at the shadowy ceiling. It was almost like I was standing guard. *That's ridiculous*, I thought. But then, *no one gets to hurt her.*

I mean no harm.

Elise's head was still on my left shoulder, its weight causing pressure in my joint. The bed, the ceiling... everything was as it should be, yet I could not move. My body was paralysed. I couldn't even wriggle my fingers – *What is happening? Why can't*

I move? – I tried to take a breath but breathing was movement and my body had turned to lifeless stone–

Please don't panic.

Don't panic, it said. Don't panic how can I not panic I couldn't move I – *Who said that?*

I did.

The shadows on the ceiling merged, creating a black-and-grey amorphous figure. It opened its burning white eyes, looming down, one long tendril drifting closer. I wanted to scream, move, run away, burn the house down, anything to make this nightmare stop.

Well. Let me attempt that again. Just like that, the shadows deflated and formed their usual patterns on the ceiling. Now the bed dipped on my right, like someone had sat down on the edge. Out of the corner of my eye I could just see the outline of a brown-skinned teenage girl. I had to be dreaming, but it was the most realistic dream I had ever had.

You are. "I mean, you are," the girl said. "You are in the liminal state between sleep and conscious. Some have called it sleep paralysis, because you are both aware yet cannot move."

Are you really here?

"I am, but not in the physical sense."

Are you going to hurt me?

"Oh, Dan, not at all," she said, then sighed. "I messed up." It was odd to hear her move from stiff, almost textbook-like explanations to such a mundane expression. She shifted in her seat and I felt the mattress move underneath my back. "It's easiest if I show you."

Before I could respond, darkness drew me under. I felt weightless for a second, my limbs finally freed from their bind.

The girl stood in front of me. She wore a colourful orange tunic with yellow stitching. I got the impression of a forest but the trees were blurry impressions of trunk and leaves.

"We are in your dreamscape now," she said, her arm indicating the forest we were standing in. Unlike the blurred forest, she seemed almost too crisp and clear, like she didn't fully belong.

"That's because I don't. I am not a product of your imagination. Do you feel this?" On the edge of my consciousness, I felt that heavy draw again. Like threads attaching themselves to me, feeding, draining, restricting. My panic rose and I tried to turn away from the figure. Immediately, the feeling disappeared again.

"It is extremely rare for a person to notice our presence as you do. You must be exceptionally sensitive." She cocked her head, studying me like I was a puzzle to solve.

"Don't ever do that again," I said, shuddering. "It feels utterly horrible. Like you're eating my brain through a straw."

The girl nodded. "I apologise, and I will shield myself from you. I was not 'eating', as you say. You respond to my unmasked presence. I merely intended to show you." For the first time in this bizarre nightmare-scape, I started to feel like myself again. The girl looked at me earnestly, and while I had absolutely no reason to trust this strange vision, she seemed sincere.

"What are you?" I asked.

"I have been called a succubus. Or an incubus. I am neither, and both. You humans are quite odd with your binaries," she said, tilting her head.

"Well, we're working on that," I said.

"Indeed you are," she acknowledged. "I have no gender. I merely take the shape of that which the host desires. You could call me a dream eater, if you must."

I remembered the flashing shapes in my first dream, running through a mental catalogue of human bodies. Realisation dawned on me. "That's why you couldn't settle on a shape with me. At least, if it's about sexual desire. I never really experience that."

The girl nodded. "I am sorry if I distressed you. I sensed a fondness in you for multiple genders, but I could not find a suitable costume that you reacted to. It took me a moment to realise that there might not be one."

"It's okay," I said. "It was the draining part that freaked me out."

"I wonder at your experience. It is as if you are drawn to my inward — like opposite poles of magnets." I had no idea what she meant, but it seemed to make sense to her. All I cared about was that I no longer felt like my soul was swirling down a drain.

"Why are you telling me all of this?" I asked.

"I do not thrive on fear. I wished to 'set the record straight', as some say." She shrugged, a casual gesture that seemed out of place. "You interest me, Daniel Andrew Williams."

Despite all of the weirdness, the fuzziness of the dream, and how my brain barely seemed to work properly, I couldn't help but feel fascinated too.

"So you really eat people's sex dreams?"

"Most humans welcome us into their dreams. It is an exchange of sorts — they get to experience their fantasies within the safe confines of their own mind, heightened by our presence. We, on the other hand, feed off the increased energies released in the psyche. Unlike in the myths, we never force ourselves onto anyone. That rumour only took hold because of humanity's misplaced belief in shame."

"Wait. Does that mean you fed on Elise too?" I knew I was dreaming and my body wasn't exactly corporeal in the usual sense, but I still felt my heart beat faster. It had been terrifying to see her so despondent.

The dream eater nodded. I felt a surge of anger and protectiveness.

"She was unwell yesterday. You took too much, even if she had a nice time." If what the dream eater had said was true, and people did enjoy the dreams — Jen, the shape shifter erotica writer from my writing chatroom popped into my mind — I didn't begrudge her that. I did care for Elise's health, though.

"She was perfectly safe, I assure you. We do not draw from that most essential of life force, merely its excess."

I huffed. "That's not good enough. I'm not really convinced you can tell the difference, if there even is one."

The girl folded her hands in front of her. "Do you wish me to not feed from your partner of the heart?"

"Yes," I said, firmly.

She nodded. "I promise not to visit her again."

"Thank you," I said, my shoulders relaxing. "Are you sure that I'm not just dreaming this as some sort of weird assimilation of experiences that my brain has made up?"

The girl laughed, throwing her head back. "You know it is not just you in your consciousness right now. Deep down, you know."

★ ★ ★

The following day, the dark circles under Elise's eyes had mostly receded, and she felt well enough to binge-watch some television with a pile of snacks beside her. She seemed in perfectly good spirits despite her physical tiredness.

I kept going back and forth in my thoughts as I tried to focus on my article. Had it really happened? Was I just imagining things? Yet at the same time, it had all felt so real, way beyond any dream that I had ever had. I gently asked Elise some questions about her dreams, but she only remembered vague impressions.

The dream eater had been right — I did feel its presence. Whenever it had been there, it was like a small rock in my sock but on the edge of my consciousness. Like a small invader, an annoying presence that wasn't supposed to be there. Yet now the dream eater was gone, I kind of missed it. In a way, it had been comforting to have company in a way that I had never experienced before.

I scrolled through the couple of paragraphs that I had managed so far. None of them felt quite right. I only had two more days until it had to be handed in. I groaned and put my head on the table, pillowed by my hands. *Come on, brain, you can do it. Think of something interesting. Dating. People like other people sometimes. It's great. Relationships. Fantasies? How about dreams? I'm sure the dream eater would have tons of amazing anecdotes.*

I must have drifted off at my desk because I became aware of *something* on the edge of my perception — or should I say, someone. Now I knew what it was, it didn't scare me anymore.

I will leave if you wish, but you were thinking of me, the dream eater said.

No, that's okay. I was actually… wondering whether you could help me with something, I thought.

Help you?

I could sense the dream eater's confusion. *Yes. See… Oh, maybe you won't care. I'm sorry if I bothered you needlessly.* I wondered what dream eaters did when they didn't appear in people's minds. Did they have bodies? Did they exist in a separate sphere?

I am not busy, as you humans like to say. And yes, my primary embodiment exists on a different plane, but it is too complex for human brains to understand easily. You are so endearingly three-dimensional.

I was wondering whether you could help me with this article I'm writing, I thought. *You could give me an insight into people's dreams and fantasies that I could never get from interviews.*

Ah, the dream eater said. *Ah,* it repeated softly. I worried that I had offended them as they didn't respond immediately. Time passed strangely in dreams, yet I could recognise the pause all the same.

Fear not, I am not offended, it said finally. *It is just that no human has ever asked for my help. They appreciate the costumes, the acts, and they awake sated. It is new to be needed in another way. And to answer the other question in your mind, any pronouns are fine.*

Relief flooded through me, both because I didn't mean to insult them, and because I really needed some help. Bills needed to get paid, and the article would go a long way. *That's great! Thank you so much. I really look forward to your stories. I actually have a lot of questions about this whole dream eater thing, if you don't mind. What can I call you?*

My true name is a feeling, and as such unpronounceable to your mind. You may call me Enupnion.

Well, thank you Enupnion. I had the mental image of a handshake and a radiant smile.

★ ★ ★

The doorbell rang. "Do you mind getting that?" Elise yelled from the kitchen. It was Sunday, and she liked to bake when she had some spare time. She'd completely recovered from her earlier tiredness and the last traces of my worries had disappeared at seeing her being her old self. Enupnion had kept to their promise and hadn't visited her again. Slowly I was learning to trust them, despite our rocky start. The house smelled like cinnamon and apples, and it made my stomach grumble. I got up from behind my desk, stretching for a moment before moving to the front door. With Enupnion's help, I had written one of my best articles yet. Their stories were endlessly fascinating and our time together in my dreams had become something that I looked forward to. They never caused that draining feeling again – if anything, I woke up more refreshed than I had ever done. For a couple of days now, I had been wondering how to tell Elise about them. How can you convince someone of the existence of a being that only seems to show up in your mind?

I opened the door and had to do a double take. "Hello," they said. Today's "costume" was a curvy androgynous golden-skinned person, wearing a black hoodie and jeans. The clothing seemed like a surprisingly low-key choice for them. Despite the human disguise, I immediately recognised Enupnion through their slightly mischievous smile and earnest eyes. Over the last few nights I had noticed that, whatever shape they took, there was something about their eyes that seemed constant. It wasn't their colour, per se, but a glint in their pupils that spoke of a non-human consciousness shining from behind them.

"Wow," I said. "I had no idea you could do that." They made a little bow with a flourish, seeming proud of their appearance.

"It is not done often. Not because we cannot, but because we do not see the point." The showmanship faded away. "I wished to meet you embodied, as humans do."

"I'm very happy you're here," I said. "Please do come in. If you like food, my girlfriend is currently baking something that smells amazing." I led them through the door.

"Who was it?" Elise yelled from the kitchen.

"Just a friend," I answered. Enupnion and I exchanged a glance and a shy smile. It had been so effortless to chat in dreams and half-formed thoughts, yet now, seeing them standing in our hallway, everything suddenly felt overwhelmingly real.

"Hi! I'm Elise," she said, coming over to greet us. She was wiping her hands on a kitchen towel which she promptly dropped when she got a good look at Enupnion. "Oh!" She turned bright red, bending over quickly to pick up the towel. "Sorry, you just look a lot like someone I know," she mumbled, smiling shyly.

With deliberate slowness, Enupnion turned towards me, one eyebrow raised. I tried very hard to choke back my laughter and only succeeded partially. "Come on," I said, to distract Enupnion. "I'll show you our house." As I passed Elise, I shot her an apologetic look that meant *I'll tell you later*. She pulled a funny face, mimicking bewilderment, but she didn't seem too fazed by Enupnion's presence.

"Thank you," the dream eater said as they followed me towards the living room. "Friend."

MY LOVE LAYS SPLIT ON EITHER SIDE

James Robin Burton

My love lays split on either side of me: a forbidden story and a forbidden life closed to me.

To feel a woman's touch is to create unease in my soul. Every night I sleep in a waking dream, while the ghost beside me caresses my cheek. Forever on the left side of the enclosed pillows and quilts, she watches the dead eyes within my skull, her visage ever-changing. She attempts to move my body and soul but I remain cold. Her hands grasp the frozen curls of my hair, and yet the winter within my heart rages so I am left unmoved.

To feel a man's touch is to create fear in my mind. Every night as I leave my body to the dreaming stars his phantom hand holds me back, caressing my chest. Forever on my right side, his body lays atop the blankets that hold me like the tensioned and grinding machinations of my inner thought. Cold death touches my skin and recoils from the ice I have encased upon myself.

Months I have remained paralysed, unable to move from my prison, feeling my flesh rot from the poison my doubt injects into my bloodstream, so I begged them:

"Why do you haunt me spirits, why do you plague me with such unease, pulling me down into suffocation?"

The faces of the two blinked in unison, eyes shining like the innermost blue of flame.

The otherworldly beings replied, "We do not haunt you, Sir. You bring us here."

I shuddered from the truth they spoke, the conflicts of my soul spilling out from my eyes, ears, and mouth in a dark purple shade, squelching like tar on the pillow cases which held my head. The blistering storm began to subside within my soul as my exterior of ice cracked and melted. Glistening amethyst light erupted in my ribcage. It called to the sleeping nebula above us as the sparkling dust seemed much closer, and my hand began to twitch for the first time.

The two Virtues once again spoke, but their mouths did not move.

"Can you accept us? Will you accept yourself?"

The once expansive space began to lose shape as I lost myself to blue sparking eyes next to me; the walls of pink dust folded inward as if the crates of a chamber, packing smaller and smaller. Doubt was attempting to contain me, yet as my bones began to creak and bend against the cartilage joints, my transformation began.

The confines of my mind screamed out as my skull smashed against the sticky tar, shattering as if made of marble, while ligaments and high strung tendons of my muscles tore with great ripping sound. My eyes melted away like burning wax as I attempted to reach forward, and upward away from the tangles of thread and cotton.

The phantoms no longer held me back as my own hands, broken and torn, grasped the stars above. Soon all that remained was the dark love within me. No body, just the mere soul of infinite fire and ambition remained as the two Celestials abandoned the deathbed of my old self and we embraced.

I was awoken by the feeling of sunlight on my skin. I found myself unshackled and standing by the window. The bed was unkept, however contained no ill intention, its dark columns no longer bars to my self-made prison. I was free.

My dreams were to be reality for I am and was the star all along, drifting among an infinite sea. I could love man and woman, just as my ghosts had.

I was never haunted again.

LEADBITTER HOUSE

Mason Hawthorne

Twisting through the rolling hills inland and north of Black-water town proper, the Malloga River and Riverside Drive writhe side by side. From above, they are two dark and winding serpents carving through the browning pastures and scrubby bush. On a wedge-shaped piece of land where the river and the road part ways, Leadbitter House sits tall and white behind a dry-stone wall and six centenarian jacaranda trees.

There is no wind about the eaves, and the midmorning sun slants through the front windows of Leadbitter House, casting gem-like points of colour across the room. On the window seat, a sheaf of papers is stacked neatly and weighted with Penguin editions of *The Harp in the South* and *The Picture of Dorian Gray*, so new the covers still have a faintly waxy sheen to them. The top page is scrawled with potential thesis topics – *the body in queer literature, identification with the monstrous figure* – some elaborated with bullet points and reading lists, some pocked with question marks, some scribbled out.

"He's been trying to get me to go visit, telling me all about his new twink to try and get me jealous. Idiot." Elijah's toes curl and uncurl against the Turkish rug. His hands are folded over his chest, cradling his iPhone like a prayer book as he lays with his head pillowed in Baby's generous lap.

"Did he really?" Baby shakes her head, sending tendrils of long, curly hair tickling across Elijah's face. "I don't know why you keep him around, he sounds like a dickhead."

"Oh, you know. If he doesn't like what you tell him, he pretends he didn't hear anything." Elijah sighs and shrugs, and reaches up to plunge his fingers into the mane of Baby's hair, gently combing through the tumultuous curls. "But his penis is very nice."

"Oh-*ho*, you little slut," Baby chortles, and smacks Elijah on the shoulder. "How old is he, anyway? Thirty-five? Forty?"

Elijah's phone vibrates with yet another message from Sean, but he ignores it. "Fifty-one." From where he lies her face is a flushed moon over the mountain range of her breasts, her hair as dark as the night sky. "And this tall," he holds his fingers about eight inches apart and sticks his tongue out. Baby smacks him again, and he makes a circle with his thumb and forefinger, fingertips nowhere near meeting.

"Oh *stop!*" She smacks him a third time, and when he only laughs, she rains down her balled fists, drumming on his chest and his shoulders, until he's curled into a ball and heaving with laughter. "You're a monster."

"I'm sorry, Baby. I'll be good." Elijah flutters his lashes and reaches up to pinch her cheeks. "It's so boring here, though. It sucks being so far away from everyone."

"You're *not* complaining about this!"

"No, no, I'm not. I'm just saying that this is the perfect place for lovely get-togethers, and I hope all my dear friends come and visit me." He reaches up to pinch her cheek again.

"You're infuriating." Baby gives his hair a tug and throws her head back, shaking her mane of hair off her neck.

The living room is the most tightly cluttered room in the house. Overstuffed velvet armchairs and surround-sound modules are jammed in with a crazed collection of trinkets and collectables. The walls are full of pictures, some of them old photographs, some paintings, all in mismatched frames. "We should have pizza and watch a movie."

"Order in?"

Elijah frowns, "Hm, no. I have the stuff to make one. And I'm not sure if they'd deliver out here."

"The taxi driver didn't want to come out here," Baby says. "He tried to ditch me when I told him your address."

"I've been having trouble getting deliveries. The postie is actually doing his job now, but I had to have a full-on freakout at Angela from the post office to get him to actually come to the door instead of just doing a drive-by."

"Do you have enough food and stuff?"

"For now. The pantry was pretty stocked when I got here, and I brought some stuff. There's tomatoes from the garden."

"Nice."

"But I am running short on toilet paper."

"Oh."

"Guess I could just shower after I go."

"I'll appoint myself your personal shopper and cart it all back for you before *that* happens." Baby shakes her head and stretches her arms out along the back of the lounge. "Seriously, though, this place is... *so!* So. I have to know. What's it like living in a haunted house?"

Elijah rolls his eyes. "It's not haunted – I wish it *was*, then I'd have some company around here. I used to visit Elle all the time, and I've never seen any kind of ghost."

"Are you saying the taxi driver told me a fib? Took ten minutes to convince him to bring me here at all. He wouldn't pull into the drive or anything, dropped me out on the road. Kept saying the place was haunted, bad juju, whatever." Baby shrugs and picks up Elijah's hand, she traces the letters tattooed across his knuckles – right hand *LUST*, left hand *FEAR* – and lets out a sigh. "I wasn't sure what to expect, you know?"

"Yeah. First time I came here I felt like that."

"It's very..."

"Oh, I know. Looks like Liberace's goth sister did the decorating, right?"

"Exactly."

A car horn sounds from the road, and Elijah sits bolt upright, the pair of them turn to look out the window. A low-bodied black sports car revs, and then speeds northward. Baby looks at him, eyebrows raised.

"My cousins. Not happy about the whole inheritance situation." Elijah rubs his face and sighs, then bounces to his feet, towering over Baby. "Come see upstairs, you'll love this." Elijah leads her by the hand through the guts of the house and up the twisting staircase to the master bedroom.

"Check this out," Elijah says, bypassing the ornate vanity and the four-poster bed to open the overflowing walk-in wardrobe. "Elle loved online shopping. And going to the shops. Shopping in general. Clothes, shoes, you name it."

"Holy shit, that's a *lot*." Baby stands, hands on her hips, and shakes her head.

"Anything that fits you, you take it. There's stuff that I can wear, but it's all at the back." Elijah pulls out a fistful of hangers, draped with lace, with velvet and chiffon and gauzy silks. "Take whatever you want. Load up the car."

"We have to do paperwork for that, right?" Baby is sifting through the clothes rack closest to the door, pinching the fabrics between her long, polished fingernails.

"Sure, later though. It'll only take a second." Elijah pulls out a floor-length gown as blue as a wasp, and holds it up to Baby. "She liked the same colours as you."

"All this stuff is so fancy," Baby says.

"Cut it up, make it into something you'll wear. Otherwise it's just going in the charity bin. Tell the others too. I'd rather you guys take it." Elijah pushes his way further into the wardrobe, and pulls a velvet wrap dress from its hanger and slips into it. It is too big and hangs from his frame, exposing the inner ends of the scars on his chest, and slipping from his shoulders.

"I can't believe how clean the house is. I thought it'd be pretty dusty with all that stuff." Baby says, while Elijah puts on the lacy peignoir that he's been wearing about the house again.

"There's a housekeeper, apparently. Appears sometime in the early hours of the morning, keeps the whole place spotless."

That, more than anything, gives the house the air of a haunted place. "I haven't even seen her yet. Or the gardener."

Baby whistles. "Look at you, you bougie shit."

"Oh that's me. I think I deserve a bit of Byronic moping, though. I want to be lazy and dramatic, and... I mean I gave up on poetry a while ago, but I can try it again. I have the time."

"Lazy? You?" Baby laughs. "You're going to go stir crazy."

"I can try to be lazy. Just for the aesthetic."

After an hour of poring through the wardrobe, they spend the evening making pizza and eating it in front of a badly ripped copy of *Sebastiane* on the projection screen, with flickering, distorted subtitles. Later that night Elijah lies on his back awake and listening to Baby's deep, slow breaths. A moth fumbles along the ceiling, and the house settles with distant creaks and moans. *Oh god, why am I here,* he mouths into the darkness, *I am going to go crazy!*

The house only sighs around him.

* * *

The darkness under the mangroves is not absolute. Refractions of light from the water dazzle and gleam between the tangled roots and the drooping canopy. The whole dim thicket pulses and hums with insects, with the water lapping. Elijah sways on his feet, staring into the shadows, listening, his whole body bending toward it, while a hand curls over his stomach, his nails digging into his skin hard enough to leave marks, even through his T-shirt.

The sarong tied around his waist is damp at the knee, dark splotches on the hand-dyed fabric, and as he steps forward it slaps against his leg, clammy, and he twitches and glances down at himself, at the tangle of white roots and torn foliage at his feet, at his fingers, black with soil and clawing at his belly. Elijah shakes himself. The sun is hot on his shoulders, and when Elijah glances over the jetty, between the dark clouds of the casuarinas, the river is bright as magnesium. As he blinks and turns away the river's negative is printed over the garden.

Everything smells herbaceous, green and wet, though it hasn't rained for, oh, months probably, and the paddock over the fence is all brown grass and thorny weeds. The horses there looking forlorn.

Elijah has lost track of the time he has been in the garden, pulling the weeds, upending clods of soil into his own lap. He stands barefoot in the slippery grass. He can't remember what it was that caught his attention in the mangroves, what it was he heard, or saw, or... His efforts with the weeds are ineffectual, he could keep going until sunset and hardly make a dent, the whole garden is overrun, overgrown.

A shadow falls across Elijah, and he turns. Behind him is a weathered man, shy of six feet with curling white hair that falls to his shoulders, and a great white beard stained nicotine-yellow around his mouth. His skin is raw and broken, and sunspots and cracks and spidery veins cross his cheeks. There is a boil under his left eye, inflamed and fit to burst.

"Are you – Mr Davies, right? – Are you the, uh, gardener?"

The man has a coiled green hose in his arms and he scowls. "Groundskeeper."

"Oh." Elijah's hands curl and uncurl, twisting the hem of his shirt until the fabric strains and his knuckles creak. "But you do look after the gardens, yeah?"

Davies' expression doesn't change. He scowls, nods once and lifts a gnarled hand to scratch at his cheek. A drop of blood wells from the boil, but if it hurts he doesn't react to it.

"This garden, I mean, those tomatoes are going crazy, but everything else... there are so many weeds, and the zucchinis are all rotten, they're mush!" Elijah is out of breath, his heart thuds so hard his pulse flutters in his throat. His knuckles are white.

"I take care of it." Davies scratches again, and this time his ragged nail catches skin and the boil splits. Something green sprouts out of the hole in his face, and blood drips all the way down to his beard. The green thing unfurls, standing up out of the hole in his cheek.

"What? What does that mean?" Elijah's voice pitches high and strained, and he gestures to the overgrown garden beds, the weeds, and the thorns. "This doesn't look taken care of, I don't… I mean I don't want to tell you how to do your job, but this *isn't* taken care of."

"I work for the house," Davies spits. He picks at the thing growing out of his face and pulls it free, and it comes out long and greenish-white. The crater in his cheek is a pit of blood.

Elijah gapes at Davies wordlessly, then skirts around him and backs toward the kitchen porch.

Davies watches him the whole way until the door is shut between them.

"Fuck," Elijah says to the stillness of the kitchen. "What the fuck?"

He drifts through the house, feeling the hardwood floor and then the hall carpet under his bare feet. The thought occurs that he ought to change, or bathe, or something, but then he is in the sitting room, where he has begun to work at clearing the mantle. He's been doing a half-arsed Marie Kondo, the stuff sorted into three piles, to chuck and to donate. The keep pile so far only has a single small figurine of a bird. That morning he'd gotten into a rhythm, clearing out junk, making some progress in claiming the house for himself. Now he struggles to begin again, picking things up and shuffling them around, and then the rev of a car engine outside makes him jump. He looks out just in time to catch the taillights of his cousin's flashy car.

Biting his lip, Elijah turns back to the mantle. He holds a garbage bag open and sweeps the rest of the clutter into it. China tinkles against metal, and there is the loud crack of something breaking. Every last thing gone. Taken care of. He ties the bag off, and it splits down the side. He wraps it in another bag and hauls it out to the bins. The pile of donations goes in a cotton bag and onto the front porch, and he sets the little bird figurine back on the end of the mantle.

The rest of the sitting room, the rest of the *house* swims with *stuff*, a grotesque assortment of items tossed together by his aunt's hoarding. Elijah wipes his face. The grit of soil against his skin makes him shudder, and he retreats upstairs to the ensuite bath, and from there, in a luxuriation of orange-blossom bath-water and burning candles. Propping his iPhone safely away from the water, he scrolls through the numbers of the local grocers and chooses one at random before anxiety can make him freeze up.

Alvason's Grocery & Stock Feed. It doesn't even have a website, just a digital yellow pages listing. The phone rings twice, then an elderly man rattles off a cheerful "Alvason's, what can I do you for?"

"Hey, hi," Elijah says, "do youse do delivery?"

"Certainly do; picking fee's three dollars."

"No worries, do you deliver same day? Or, like, just a couple of days a week?" Elijah sits up and draws his heels up to his buttocks. The water in the bath sloshes around him.

"Oh, any weekday, yes, right to the door." Behind the old man's voice is the sound of registers clanging and indistinct voices chattering.

"How about today?"

"Hm… one sec." There is a scratchy sound as the phone is muffled, a few seconds' pause, and more scratching, then a long silence. "Still there?"

"Yes," Elijah says.

"M'grandson's already gone, so not today. But he could bring it round first thing tomorrow for you."

"Can he bring it to Leadbitter House? That's on Riverside Drive; I know it's a long ways out. Number–"

"Oh! You're Missus Elle's nephew! Real sorry to hear about what happened; wonderful lady."

"Thanks," Elijah says. "I didn't really... I never expected she'd leave the place to me."

"Wonderful lady," the old man repeats. "Right, well I'll put the bill on the house account, and send the young fella round in the morning."

"Great, thanks. Do I pay the account, like, monthly, or–"

"No, no, we take care of that with the accountant."

"Right, sure, thank you." Elijah scratches a wet hand through his hair and outside a magpie warbles. The house around him is still and quiet.

"So... want to give me the list?"

"Huh? Oh! Right, sorry. Sure. Just a sec..." Elijah casts around – he has not written a list. From the top of his head he makes a rambling and incomplete order for most of the things he needs, and some things that he does not, strictly, need. As the call ends, Elijah can hear the old man laughing over the noise of the busy store.

★ ★ ★

At six, Elijah wakes and is on his feet in a heartbeat. Another thud echoes from downstairs. His heart hammers in his throat. He pulls on a pair of jeans from the floor. Without thinking, he picks up an ornate poker from beside the fire-place. Creeping downstairs, he listens carefully for where the noise is coming from. This is not the time he would have expected his cousins to try something, but there is nothing else it could be.

Barefoot, he pads across the hardwood floor. His hand aches with how tightly he grips the poker. Should he call the cops? He has left his iPhone plugged in upstairs, and he doesn't know if the landline in the hallway is connected. Sweat beads on his forehead and under his arms. His bare chest prickles with gooseflesh at the tinkle of broken glass from the sitting room. He steps into the doorway, the poker held high.

"What are you doing!" Elijah shouts. The small woman – definitely not his cousin – flinches and rounds on him. At her feet are garbage bags that are torn open, and the mantle is almost full again with all the *stuff* that Elijah tossed the day before.

"Who do you think you are!" Her bony hands are balled into fists and her voice rises like a cat's wail. "All of these nice things! What did you do to all these nice things!" Her face is too mobile; it crumples in on itself when she closes her mouth, stretching wildly when she shouts. Her eyes are wide and her hair is ragged, hanging to her rounded shoulders, swinging as she jabs a finger at him.

"I…" Elijah freezes, "I, um, I…"

"What did you do!" The woman, who must be Mrs Fuller, the housekeeper, shrieks, bending to pull broken ornaments from the garbage bag, "What did you do! Everything goes in its place! Look what you did! How'm I meant to fix this!"

"Stop it," Elijah's voice cracks. He lowers the poker and it drops from numb fingers to thud on the Turkish carpet. "Stop it!"

He grabs the garbage bag and swipes blindly at the mantle, shoving everything he can reach back into the rubbish. "I don't want it here! I just want this place cle – *hey!*–" he breaks off as she lunges and tries to snatch the things from his hands. "Stop it! Fucking stop!"

She screams, he screams. As she paws at him, he grabs one bony arm and then the other. The two of them tremble, both panting for breath.

"I chucked it all out! I don't want it!" Elijah's voice is pitchy and it keeps cracking. "I hate all this stuff everywhere; I just want to get rid of it!"

"It isn't your stuff!" The woman twists her arms and he releases her. They both take a step back. "This isn't yours, you can't just throw it away!"

"It is, though. She left it all to me, and I'm… I'm sorry if you're upset, but… but it's going in the bin." He's shaking, his hands held in front of him like a shield one moment, and then pressed against his chest, trying to cover himself. "I love Elle, but I'm not going to spend the rest of my life curating junk just because it was hers."

Mrs Fuller shrinks back, her hands knotted together, glaring at Elijah through the tangled veil of her hair. She shakes her head, and her mouth works soundlessly for a moment. "Everything goes in a particular place, and I keep it tidy. I make sure everything is perfect."

Elijah's face is hot, and he wraps his arms around his middle. "I'm sorry. You've been doing a great... I mean, everything is always spotless, but I can't live with this clutter. I just can't."

"And you're just going to throw it away?" Mrs Fuller's voice trembles, and spittle sprays from her lips. "I suppose you're going to tear the pictures from the walls and break up the furniture, too."

"Only some of the pictures." Mrs Fuller's too-mobile face screws up at that, and Elijah raises his hands placatingly, and backs away.

Elijah retreats upstairs to pull on a shirt. He picks up his iPhone, and his first impulse is to call Baby, but she'll be asleep. He tucks it into his pocket and stands by the stairs, listening, but the house is quiet. He takes a few deep breaths and then goes back downstairs to the kitchen, to make coffee.

A knock at the door.

He emerges furtively, peeking out the window to see a battered white ute parked in the driveway, the tray cover peeled back. When Elijah opens the door, there is a man in his twenties with sandy hair, a surfer's tan, and glittering blue eyes. He's smiling and his teeth are white and only a little crooked. He's as tall as Elijah, maybe even a little taller. He looks for all the world like a long-lost Hemsworth brother, right down to the sculptural biceps and straining white T-shirt.

"Uh..." Elijah stops in the doorway, staring, "hi."

"Hey, I'm Lachlan – Lachie! – Groceries; Pop said this lot's for the Leadbitter House – didn't realise you'd moved in already, nice to meet ya." He lifts an arm to indicate that he'd shake if he had a hand free, and Elijah steps back to clear the way, holding the door for him.

"You can leave them here, I mean if you need to get going. I can take them through," Elijah says.

"Nah, it's good. This is my last stop for the morning. I know the way." Lachie is beaming a thousand-kilowatt smile as he heads into the house.

"Alright." Elijah follows behind, transfixed by the ripple of muscle under Lachie's shirt, and then by the way his jeans slouch low on his narrow hips. By the time he gets to the kitchen to watch Lachie unpacking the shopping bags and putting things away, he may as well be levitating. "You want a hand with that?"

"Nah, I know where everything goes." That blinding smile returns, and then, it turns hot and lazy. Lachie's eyes travel over Elijah's body in a slow, deliberate circuit, and he bites his lower lip, just for a second, before he turns away. Elijah has to lean on the kitchen counter for support, his cheeks flush pink.

As Lachie bends to take out each item and put it in its spot his shirt rides up. From the tan line it's clear that he's been taking advantage of the warm weather, surfing in boardies rather than a spring suit. His back is bronzed and sleek, and then there is a sliver of pearly white skin just above the waistband of his jeans.

Elijah's iPhone vibrates in his pocket and he shifts from one foot to the other, ticklish and antsy. The vibration doesn't stop and he tugs it out, his face crumpled into a frown. No one *calls*, it just isn't done. The caller information is blocked.

"Sorry," he says to Lachie, "I've just gotta…" He points to the phone as he heads to the hall.

"No worries," Lachie says, smiling broadly, and he gives Elijah a wink that hits like a line of coke.

In the sitting room, Elijah swipes the green icon and holds the iPhone up to his ear, expecting a telemarketer or a garbled Chinese robocall. Instead, he hears heavy breathing and the background whine of an engine.

"That you, y'fuckin' freak? Think you're real smart, huh?"

Elijah doesn't answer. The familiar wet suck of his cousin's mouth-breathing is clear on the phone. His arms prickle, all the fine hairs standing on end.

"You're not gonna get it that easy, just see, you can't make it a year, you little freak, that house should be ours." Lysander clears his throat. "You listening? Huh? You think you're better than us? We've got lawyers too, you know, that cow's will isn't worth shit."

Elijah holds his breath.

"You fuckin' freak," Lysander says again, but he's lost his momentum, there's a snorting grunt like he's working up a wad of phlegm, and then the call ends.

Elijah still has the phone pressed to his ear when Lachie passes by in the hall, giving him another wink and a half-smile. Elijah smiles back automatically. He waves as Lachie leaves, shutting the front door carefully behind himself. Elijah hurls his iPhone onto the lounge, where it disappears between the cushions.

His stomach aches. Elijah presses his hands flat over his belly and bends forward, trying to stretch it out. As his face comes level with his knees, there's a knock at the door, and he almost loses his balance, heart in his throat.

It could be Lachie. Maybe he forgot something. Maybe Elijah could invite him back inside and give him a *proper* thanks for his help. Or – maybe it's his cousins, graduating from stalking to a real confrontation. Elijah's hand itches, he opens and closes his fingers, trying to recall precisely where the fire poker ended up.

He shakes his head as there's another knock, and takes the few steps to open the door.

The man on the porch is tall, perhaps in his early forties, with auburn hair. He's wearing a neat black suit with a roman collar and his smile is restrained. "Good morning," he says, offering a hand to shake, "I'm Father Rowan."

"Oh, yes." Elijah shakes his hand and clears his throat. "I'm Elijah. You probably don't recognise me, but I came along to a service with Auntie Elle. A couple of years ago, now. I... uh, I look a bit different."

"No, I remember, your hair was shorter, and you seemed very unhappy. I came by to offer my condolences. You're looking very well, and I'm sorry we have to meet again under these circumstances. It's good to meet you again, Elijah." His solemn expression quirks into a faint smile. "The paddocks are pretty dry, Elijah. Could do with some rain."

Elijah laughs and steps out of the way. "Come in, do you want tea? Coffee? I had the kettle on, I think..."

As he leads Father Rowan into the sitting room, Mrs Fuller appears bearing a tray and a thunderous expression; tea pot, cups and saucers, and a coffee pot, milk, sugar and all the fixings.

"How are you, Mrs Fuller?" Father Rowan asks.

"Well I'm not dead yet," she says waspishly, and the tea things rattle as she arranges them on the coffee table.

"How optimistic," Father Rowan smiles again, catching Elijah's eye.

Mrs Fuller leaves, giving Elijah a dirty look on the way out, and he realises he's sweating, just enough to make his armpits sticky. He coughs, and wiping his face with one hand, he sits across from Father Rowan.

"I was sorry I couldn't go to Elle's funeral," Elijah says, watching Father Rowan pour himself tea. "I was still in the hospital. I talked to her, like, an hour before I went into surgery, and she wanted me to come stay with her while I recovered."

"It was very sudden," Father Rowan says. "She was very proud of you, you know. Have you deferred your degree for the year?"

"Oh, I finished my undergrad and honours. I had planned to start my PhD, but now I can use this year to get ahead on research and reading... get a head start on it all before I go back."

"And how's that going?"

Elijah rubs his palms over his knees, and shakes his head. "I just can't concentrate on anything. I have all the time in the world and it just… slips away."

"Don't be too hard on yourself," Father Rowan says. "Perhaps you just need some time to rest."

Elijah nods. He wants to make himself a coffee, but his stomach gnaws at him. He leans forward, one elbow on his knee, the other hand pressed into his gut.

Father Rowan smiles, and sets down his cup and saucer. "Would you like to hear my advice?"

"I mean… I'm not religious at all, but sure."

"Why don't you host a party?"

"Oh!" Elijah laughs.

★ ★ ★

The river is glassy black and the sky flawless blue. Elijah lies on his belly on a Turkish rug rolled out over the splintery wood of the jetty. A tray beside him holds a bowl of cut fruit and a mug of coffee. His laptop is open in front of him, and his iPhone is propped against a pot of sugar. Baby looks out at him from Facetime.

"It's great that you're getting this together." Baby is working on her laptop, and the rattle of the keyboard intersperses her words. "Work's killing me at the moment. I'm sorry I haven't been down, but y'know."

"It's fine." Elijah clicks 'create' on his event page, posts the link to several group pages, and then types up a short email to several more guys who aren't *online*. "It feels good just to be organising this, and the house is starting to look really good."

He stands up and stretches until his spine pops, then sits cross-legged. The iPhone's angle has to be adjusted so that Baby can see anything beyond his knee. For a moment he is quiet, looking over the to-do list that he's typed up. "It's under control."

"Oh, by the way, we have good news – Nala, c'mere, would you?"

"Hey Elijah!" Nala dips into view, her vividly rainbow hair bobbing in the top of the frame, her glasses catching the light in a way that makes the camera wobble and distort. Nala kneels on the bed beside Baby and snuggles up to her. "My dad's going to pay for us to visit him in Malaysia for a couple of months," she says, beaming, "as a graduation present."

"That's great," Elijah says. "Both of you?"

"Oh yeah!" Nala nods, and tucks her brightly dyed hair behind her ears. "He had a full-on argument with Nanna about it, and she hasn't said a word about it since. I mean it's not going to be perfect, but he likes Baby, and he knows we're happy."

"Well that's great, then, that'll be awesome." Elijah looks out at the water, holding his coffee mug between his palms. Somewhere in the garden, a magpie warbles. "I'll miss you guys."

"Don't be stupid, there's wifi in Malaysia," Baby says. "We'll chat, we'll keep you from going totally stir-crazy. You need more hobbies."

"Oh don't worry about that," Elijah taps his nose and winks at her. "I'm going to try and seduce the delivery boy. Or the local priest."

"It's good to have goals," Baby deadpans.

"Are you joking, or serious?" Nala says.

"Joking," Baby says.

"Serious," Elijah says at the same moment.

Nala laughs, then leans in to kiss Baby's cheek. In the background, there is a faint, shrill beeping. "Catch you later, Elijah, I gotta get that." She waves, and he waves back as she disappears from the screen.

For a while after he and Baby finish talking, Elijah lies on the jetty, enjoying the afternoon sun filtering through the casuarina trees. If he stands on the very end of the jetty he can look northward up the river and see the misty blue of the escarpment standing against the sky, and the hills marching down to the river valley. As the sun sinks behind the escarpment and the breeze turns frigid, he gathers his things, rolls up the carpet, and heads back to the house.

Mr Davies is on his knees by one of the garden beds, trowel in hand, and Elijah stops beside him. "It's looking better already, can I help you with it?"

Most of the weeds that infested the garden have been pulled, and the soil is black and broken up. Ready for new planting.

"Oh, no, no, no," Mr Davies says, shaking his head. "My son will help."

"Well. If you're sure." Elijah hikes up the rug under his arm and steadies the laden tray against his hip as he twists to look over his shoulder at the darkness under the mangroves, thicker at this time of day.

"Um-hm, he'll take me over one day."

"Alright, then." Elijah weaves through the garden back to the kitchen door. He sets his laptop on the counter and starts looking through the cupboards, but within minutes Mrs Fuller appears, scowling over his shoulder.

"Are you looking for something?" she says.

"Well, um." Elijah shuffles back to move out of her way, but she only looks at him. "I'm sorry for yelling at you the other day. That was uncalled for."

"Oh. Thank you." Mrs Fuller looks to the open laptop. "Planning a party?"

"Yeah, well. Yes. In, like, two weeks. Saturday." Elijah fiddles with his silk robe, tugging it tight around his middle and refastening the belt tie. "I guess you should have that day off."

Mrs Fuller tuts and shakes her head. "I don't think so. How many guests?"

"Uh, I'd guess thirty, but maybe fifty."

"That will be fine. I will call Alverson's and make arrangements for the evening." She leans over to squint at the laptop screen, producing a pair of glasses from a pocket of her cardigan and polishing them with her sleeve before she slips them on. They make her eyes look even more bulbous than usual.

"No, I think it's fine, I can handle it—"

"What do you think I'm here for? To look pretty?"

"Well… well," Elijah splutters, "Mrs… Mrs Fuller, it isn't a… I mean. This is… it's an orgy. It's going to be an orgy. I don't expect you to, uh, stick around for that."

She tuts again. "Is that all?"

"Y-yeah." Elijah shrugs and reaches past her to close the laptop. He clears his throat. "I was going to make some dinner, so—"

"I will bring your plate up to you in forty minutes," Mrs Fuller says, her chin tucked down to her chest like she's expecting a fight.

Elijah nods, clasps his laptop against his chest, and retreats upstairs to his study.

★ ★ ★

Car tyres crunch over the gravel drive and Elijah treads into the front yard barefoot to greet his first guests. Sean catches Elijah in a hug as soon as he climbs from the car, and Elijah must bend into it, leaning against Sean's round belly. Sean is greying, bald on top and with a bristly moustache-goatee combo that scratches Elijah's neck. He's tanned, and his teeth are square as tombstones.

"Watch out," Sean says sotto voce, "Jack's a little shy, so you might not hear much from him." Sean's hand slides from Elijah's shoulder blade down to the curve of his backside and gives it a squeeze.

Jack is short, with dark hair that sticks up in the front, and he has his hands tucked into his jean pockets and a slouch that makes his oversized cropped shirt hang *just so* around his waist. Freckles smatter his nose, and his eyes are a twinkling grey. He gives a flicker of a smile as he meets Elijah's eyes.

"Hey," Elijah says, "how's it going?"

Jack shrugs and glances toward the house, then back to Elijah. "Good, you?"

"Alright." Elijah runs a hand through his damp hair, chasing out tangles, then looks back to Sean. "There's a couple of hours 'til things start. Why don't you go round the back and have a swim? I've got a few things to get ready."

Sean nods and looks to Jack expectantly, but when he doesn't follow, Sean pouts and marches off around the side of the house. Elijah leads Jack inside. Sean described Jack as something of a nervous child, but Jack seems only calm, quiet, and he has a knowing look.

Elijah smiles and leads him up the stairs. From a landing window, he sees the river and the white flash of Sean's belly against the enigmatic darkness along the shore, where the casuarinas and the wattles cosy up to the mangroves. Under the foliage, something moves, rapid and ungainly, and a honeyeater bird startles and erupts from the canopy, wheeling away to the north.

Elijah tugs his T-shirt over his stomach and continues up the stairs. Jack slips a hand into his as he follows.

The light in the bedroom is golden and hazy. Jack flops on Elijah's bed, on his side, head propped on his hand, and watches him. Elijah looks Jack in the eyes, their shared gaze only broken when he lifts his T-shirt over his head. He runs his hand over his belly and his chest where his scars are still pink and tender. His nipples harden at the touch of cool air.

Jack wets his lips. "Are those real?"

"Yes," Elijah says.

Jack slides off the bed and reaches for Elijah. His hands are warm and his touches featherlight against Elijah's ribs. Jack traces the inverted Ts of Elijah's scars, one at a time, and then rubs the pad of his thumb over his nipples so that Elijah shivers.

"The nerves are still intact, full sensation," Elijah says.

"Who was your surgeon?"

"Dr Shepherd, at St Leonards."

"I went to Meyers, she's much cheaper," Jack says, and tugs his top off. His scars are straight and neat, already faded to a silvery pink. Where his nipples ought to be he only has a couple of dots of raised skin, with stitch scars fanned around them. "Once I get these coloured in, they'll be perfect; haute couture nipples."

Jack leans in, then, and flicks his tongue across Elijah's nipple so that he jumps and laughs. Elijah strokes the nape of Jack's neck and leans into his teasing mouth. "Sean told me you were a shy little baby."

"He told me you were a stuck-up cold fish." Jack's smile is wicked as he looks up at Elijah. He grazes his fingertips over Elijah's hips and tugs the hem of his shorts and then traces over his stomach to follow the outline of the minotaur tattooed on his ribs.

Elijah slips his shorts down and leaves them on the floor. Jack doesn't step back or help. His hands wander as Elijah leans by him to pick up the saffron silk robe he's decided to wear for the evening, and as he shrugs into it, Jack's fingers slip between Elijah's legs and skate over his ticklish inner thighs.

"There's a guest room across the landing, where you two are staying tonight," Elijah says, "but if you want, you can come into my room. Don't worry about disturbing me."

Jack doesn't respond but pinches at Elijah's nipples until they're red and standing hard against the silk of his robe.

★ ★ ★

The house fills with the low hum of conversation and the ring of laughter, and the air smells of cologne. Most of the guests are older, with greying hair and coarse hands, sparkling eyes and tanned, leathery hides. There are a few younger guys, of course, with spiked up hair and tattoos and piercings. Music plays, and in the sitting room one projector screen shows gay porn, and the other *Pink Narcissus*. The divans have been draped with soft fabric to protect them from stray bodily fluids.

A side-table is loaded with food, another with drinks and bowls of lubrication and condoms. Each guest greets Elijah with a kiss, and they bear bottles of sweet wine, or six-packs of beer, or boxes of chocolate. Sean finds him, at a lull, and stands at Elijah's elbow in the sitting room with the projections from the screens reflecting pink and gold on his face, speaking so closely that his goatee brushes Elijah's ear. "Well congratulations, I suppose. Despite everything, the evening seems to be a success."

"Mrs Fuller's done great with the food," Elijah says, expression neutral.

"I find her a bit creepy," Sean says, and he folds his arms and pouts. "This whole place is so dark and... and morbid. I don't know how you can stand it."

With the clutter gone, the light fixtures glow golden, the furnishings gleam with polish, all the velvet is smooth and well cared for, the carpets plush and richly coloured. Elijah raises his eyebrows and shrugs. "I don't know what you mean, it's a great house."

"It's *big*, you'll be able to sell it for a decent amount. But you don't need to pretend: it's *horrible*. The whole place makes my skin crawl." Sean's voice doesn't rise, but his plummy eastern suburbs accent lends that extra smidge of condescending bitchiness.

Elijah shrugs again. "You can leave if you want."

A knock at the door. Elijah breaks away, practicing his smile on the way. "Hey, come – huh?" Elijah stops, the door partway open, as his cousin Daniel smirks and stares him down for a second before a wall of blue blocks Elijah's view.

"Mate, we've had some complaints about a disturbance on this property?" The police officer looks uneasy, and her partner is behind her, at the bottom of the stairs with his hands on his belt. "A lotta cars in this yard, you having a party?"

"Yes," Elijah says. "I don't see how you could have a complaint, the nearest neighbour is at least a kilometre away."

"The issue is that–"

"It's not your place to have a party at, is it!" Lysander crows, cutting the police officer off before Daniel can restrain him. "You shouldn't even be here!"

"Bullshit," Elijah mutters, "go away, you pests."

"There's no need for that," the police officer at the bottom of the stairs says. "Let's keep it civil."

"Daniel, Lysander. If you've got a problem, you can contact my solicitor." Elijah's hand is clamped around the door so tightly that his knuckles ache. "And if you ask very nicely, he might even draw some pictures so you can understand it."

"Mate, if you're trespassing on the property, we can have you removed."

"*Trespassing!*" Elijah shakes his head, mouth agape. "You all need to leave and speak to my solicitor."

"You're gonna be removed!" Lysander crows as Daniel shushes. "Get the fuck out, you little freak!"

"Everyone needs to calm down…"

Elijah's mouth curls into a snarl, he leans into the doorway. "This is my house," he says, and when Daniel's mouth opens to argue, he straightens to his full height, and bellows it. *"This is my house!"* It echoes around the hills, across the grassy fields. In the paddock the horses startle, and in the darkness under the mangroves something turns over and over, and slithers across the muddy bank, and disappears into the water.

Daniel looks as though he's been slapped, and the police officer by the door rocks back on her heels. She reaches up, as though she might doff her hat, and then thinks better of it, and tucks her hands against her belt.

"This is my house," Elijah says again. "And you're not welcome here. No more calls, no more driving by in your shitty car. You're pathetic."

"Alright, come on," the police officer at the bottom of the stairs sticks an arm out and herds Daniel and Lysander away from the house, toward the gate.

"Right," the other one says, "sorry about the mix-up, mate. Enjoy your evening."

Elijah watches them off the property and then sees that a familiar white ute has pulled into the yard. Behind the wheel,

Lachie has been watching the whole time. He gives one of his slow, delicious smiles, and when he reaches the veranda, Elijah welcomes him with open arms and draws him into the house.

★ ★ ★

Under the fat silver moon, the river glimmers against the inky night. The moon's reflection rolls over the water, lapping with the river's gentle waves. A susurration of wind through the mangroves brings the salt from the sea, and the mist comes with it, hovering over the water and creeping up onto the shore, turning the night-time landscape hazy and indistinct.

Music spills from the door as Elijah emerges, walking barefoot into the night. His saffron silk robe trails behind him like a banner and eventually slips from his shoulders and flutters down to rest on the dewy grass. Lachie follows, gathering the fabric against his naked chest, and stops there, only watching as Elijah walks the length of the garden, right to the river's edge and stops, arms outstretched. He wriggles his toes into the black mangrove mud.

Everything is limned with silver. Elijah runs his hands over his chest, over his belly, he feels the fine hairs that curl below his navel. The breeze whispers to him, the mangroves' hushed voice tells him what he couldn't quite grasp before. It doesn't take much, just the pressure of his fingernails to split the fine skin over his sternum. His skin splits like a ripe peach, but without spilling juices. He opens himself to the moonlight, peeling back the layers of skin and muscle so that all of his insides are exposed, kissed by sea-salt air.

His liver gleams, glossy black, and the tips of his ribs shine white. The rhythmic, peristaltic squirming of his intestines makes it difficult to handle them as he digs down, searching past the silky smooth shapes of his kidneys, and down the ridges of his spine until he can trace the interior curve of his pelvis.

There, there it is. Like an invasive weed blooming where it oughtn't, the uterus squats amongst his beautiful organs, cluttering up the place, jangling his nerves. With some care, he holds his intestines and all their writhing enthusiasm aside, and reaches in to pinch it off at the root, an easy flick of the wrist to twist it off like a dead flower, and drop it onto the riverbank where it withers.

Elijah pushes his intestines back, and they wriggle into their customary place as he pulls his skin back together, seals himself up. He is whole now and complete, and entirely his own. He takes the time to bury the uterus in the black clinging mud, using his foot to dig it into the earth until it is only a disturbance in the bank that the river will wash smooth in time.

ABOUT THE CONTRIBUTORS

THE EDITOR

Celine Frohn

Celine Frohn is a publisher, editor, and PhD researcher with a passion for Gothic and LGBTQ+ literature. The *Unspeakable* and *Unthinkable* anthologies combine both her academic work on the nineteenth-century Gothic, as well as her love for contemporary speculative fiction. Celine runs Nyx Publishing, which has published queer SFF including S.T. Gibson's *A Dowry of Blood* and Holly J. Underhill's *The Bone Way*.

THE CONTRIBUTORS

Enmanuel Arjona

Enmanuel Arjona (Cancun, Mexico) is an art curator and amateur writer on his personal blog. He is a resident of the city of Seattle, where he operates his own gallery, and is currently working on his first publication. He has published in numerous magazines and anthologies in Latin America and served as media director for Seattle Escribe, the largest Hispanic writing group in the Northwest.

James Robin Burton

James is a University Graduate, Animator, Cosplayer and twin brother, who spends his free time creating art and written content. Fantasy and Gothic have always been part of his creative process in life thanks to the influence of works like *Howl's Moving Castle*, *Dracula*, *British Folklore*, *Blue Exorcist* and the *Ravenloft Modules*. His creative work reflects his exploration of personal identity, something he is still exploring. In fact, as a DnD enthusiast, he found a connection between the improvisation of playing a fictional character and how it could help him explore his own identity as a Bi man.

Ryann Fletcher

Ryann Fletcher writes queer science fiction and fantasy.

S.T. Gibson

S.T. Gibson is the author of *A Dowry of Blood* and other romantic fantasy books, and she works as a literary agent and subsidiary rights manager at the Speilburg Literary Agency. She holds a bachelor's in Creative Writing from the University of North Carolina at Asheville and a master's in Theological Studies from Princeton Theological Seminary. She currently lives in Boston with her partner and spoiled Persian cat.

Henry Glifort

Henry Glifort is a queer writer and editor living in New England.

Claire Hamilton Russell

Claire Hamilton Russell (they/them) is a bi, nonbinary, disabled and neurodivergent writer in their late thirties living in Glasgow, Scotland. They live with their beloved husband and equally beloved animal companions, a one-eyed rescue Staffie named Jasmine and a black cat named Alfie. A keen live action and tabletop roleplayer, they have just begun postgrad study in history at the Open University and are active in local queer and disability justice and green movements. They are an enthusiastic urban food grower and rewilder and enjoy textile art and decorative mending. They were the first winner of the Scottish Huntington's Association's International HD: Out of the Shadow flash fiction prize.

Mason Hawthorne

Mason Hawthorne studied creative writing at the University of Wollongong, and writes queer horror and weird fiction.

Sam Hirst

Sam Hirst is an author and academic whose work focuses on the Gothic.

Lindsay King-Miller

Lindsay King-Miller is the author of *Ask a Queer Chick: A Guide to Sex, Love, and Life for Girls who Dig Girls* (Plume, 2016). Her fiction has appeared in *The Fiends in the Furrows* (Nosetouch, 2018), *Tiny Nightmares* (Catapult, 2020), *The Jewish Book of Horror* (Denver Horror Collective, 2021), *Fireside Fiction, Grimdark Magazine,* and numerous other publications. She lives in Denver, CO with her partner and their two children.

Ally Kölzow

Ally Kölzow is a writer and lifelong daydreamer who lives in South West England. She is disabled, chronically ill and queer, and loves to write stories that are too. Her first published short story appears in *Unspeakable: A Queer Gothic Anthology.* You can find her on Twitter and Instagram @allykolzow.

Jenna MacDonald

Jenna MacDonald is a full-time science nerd and a full-time lover of words. Now working as an environmental consultant, she once dreamed of exploring the oceans as a marine biologist, a desire shared by the protagonist of her debut short story 'Lure of the Abyss'. She lives in Michigan with her dog (who may actually be Mothman in disguise), exploring the Great Lakes whenever she can.

Avery Kit Malone
Avery Kit Malone is a recovering academic and sometimes writer. His short fiction has appeared in *Dim Shores Presents*, *Planet Scumm*, and *Pseudopod*, among other venues. He favours cats, ginger sparkling water, and starry skies on cold nights.

Anna Moon
Anna Moon is a nebulous entity rarely directly perceived. She writes speculative fiction with a queer bent, and loves music, food, and befriending all the neighbourhood cats.

Jude Reid
Jude lives in Glasgow and writes dark stories in the gaps between full time work as a surgeon, wrangling her kids and trying to wear out a border collie. Her short fiction has been published in numerous anthologies and magazines, including *The Accursed and Sanction and Sin* (Black Library), *Places We Fear To Tread* and *Campfire Macabre* (Cemetery Gates Media) and *Spirit Machine* (Air and Nothingness Press). You can find out what she's up to on twitter @squintywitch.

E. Saxey
E.Saxey is a queer Londoner who works in universities and libraries. Their work has appeared in *Daily Science Fiction, Apex Magazine* and *Lightspeed* special issue *Queers Destroy Science Fiction*. Their first collection, *Lost in the Archives*, is chock full of speculative weirdness and historical oddities, and available from Lethe Press.

Eliza Temple

Eliza Temple is speculative fiction enthusiast and writer originally from the north east of England. She now lives in a creaky old Victorian house in Cambridge, where she works as a library assistant. When not writing, she spends most of her time watching horror films and wandering around the city to look at interesting buildings and think of other things to write about.

Heather Valentine

Heather Valentine is a queer speculative fiction writer based in Glasgow, Scotland, where she runs a fanfiction open mic night. She has worked as a proofreader, a receptionist, a student teacher and a tour guide, and her interests include knitting, fantasy roleplaying games and vintage horror films. Her original stories have been published in magazines and anthologies including *LampLight Magazine*, *We Were Always Here: A Queer Words Anthology*, and *Shoreline of Infinity*.

Katalina Watt

Katalina was longlisted for Penguin Write Now 2020, awarded a 2021 Ladies of Horror Fiction Writers Grant, and winner of the 2022 Ignyte Best Fiction Podcast Award for their work as founding Audio Director for khōréō magazine. They are published in various magazines and anthologies including *Haunted Voices*, *Unspeakable*, and *Reclamation* and appeared at Edinburgh International Book Festival, Cymera, and FIYAH-CON. Katalina is represented by Robbie Guillory at Underline Literary. She can be found at: katalinawatt.com and on Twitter @KatalinaWatt.

Katie Young

Katie Young is a writer of dark fiction and poetry. Her work appears in various anthologies including collections by Dark Dispatch, Scott J. Moses, Nyx Publishing, Ghost Orchid Press, and Fox Spirit Books. Her story, 'Lavender Tea', was selected by

Zoe Gilbert for inclusion in the Mechanic Institute Review's Summer Folk Festival 2019. She lives in west London with her partner and an angry cat.

THE DESIGNER

Ashley Hankins

Ashley Hankins is a fantasy and sci-fi illustrator. A native of Western New York, she spent several years in Humboldt County, California, where she became enamored with the mountains and mist-shrouded forests. She felt she had truly found someplace magical. Upon returning to New York, Ashley strives to inject her work with that same ethereal feeling she felt in those woods. Ashley is a primarily digital artist who loves palettes that feed into both a Gothic aesthetic and bright color pops, lots of mood, and experimenting with strong, graphic shapes. When Ashley is not working on her latest project, she can be found writing, hiking with her partner, and drinking excessive amounts of tea.

THE CREDITS

Creating a book takes a massive team effort. Haunt, the editor and the contributors would like to thank everyone who worked behind the scenes on *Unspeakable: A Queer Gothic Anthology*.

Managing Director
Rebecca Wojturska

Editor & Anthologist
Celine Frohn

Copy-editor
Ross Stewart

Cover Designer
Ashley Hankins
ashleydoesartstuff.com

Typesetter
Laura Jones
lauraflojo.com

We would also like to thank everyone who worked on the first edition of this book, published by Nyx Publishing in 2020. Thank you to the Editorial Assistants, Molly Llewellyn and Lucy Goodfellow; the Developmental Editor, Jasmine Gower; the Line Editor, Rowan Rook; the Copy Editor, Gwynevere Kipling; the Cover Illustrator, Jenni Coutts (whose amazing work was also used in the Kickstarter campaign); and the Cover Designer, Charlie Bramald.